galaxy man

OTHER BOOKS BY MWM

Galaxy Man

Mark Wayne McGinnis

Published by:
Avenstar Productions

ISBN: 978-0-9992147-3-2

To join Mark's mailing list, jump to
http://eepurl.com/bs7M9r

Visit Mark Wayne McGinnis at:
http://www.markwaynemcginnis.com

preface

March — 2117 — Alpha Centauri, Lorianne B. Commuter Station 9552.

John Gallic was the last one to hurry into the departing commuter shuttle before the outer doors quietly swooshed together. The old silver-haired steward irritably rammed the security latch into place.

He gave Gallic a wary look. "This is the last time I'll hold up departure for you, John. I don't care that you're a cop."

"Understood. Won't happen again . . ."

The steward had to crane his neck somewhat to look up at him. "You'll find an empty seat back in aisle Y4," he said, pointing aft.

"Thanks, Max." Gallic said still catching his breath and moving along the packed in rows of commuter passengers.

Midway down the aisle, Gallic wedged himself into the only seat still available—between a middle-aged woman, reading a chest-high projected novel; and a construction worker still wearing his hard hat and smelling of sawdust and sour body odor. Both the woman and the construction worker had to shift in their seats to make room for Gallic's not insubstantial frame.

He checked the time on his wrist. Midnight—he'd barely made the last shuttle heading back to the Sol System tonight. He relaxed into the seat, exhaustion beginning to engulf him.

Something has to change, he thought. His impossible schedule was screwing up every relationship in his life. The weekly five days on, two days off, bullshit had been going on for the better part of two years now. Gallic knew it wasn't only affecting him. Portsmouth, Southerland, Stone—all DI's—were on the same rigorous departmental merry-go-round. For Stone, it had led to a divorce—six months ago. Poor guy was still a soppy mess. Reeked of desperation—always lurking around the station—no life. Gallic didn't want that. He'd rather quit than face that wrecking-ball. His thoughts turned to Clair. Was she, too, ready to tell him to shove off? Had she had enough of this absentee-husband bullshit? One who, even when he *was* around, was so mentally and emotionally spent, he seemed simply to be going through the motions—acting the part of the normal devoted husband and attentive father—while in reality felt more akin to a jacked around robot on autopilot? *Christ!* Who, in their right mind, would want to marry a Detective Chief Inspector? Worse . . . one who worked three and a half light years away from Earth? But he knew the answer—Clair would. And she'd never complained . . . not once. The thought made him smile. And then there was Mandy—three-years-old, going on thirty. Hey . . . never experiencing a different type life-style, she probably figured all daddies were gone half the time. That was one plus, *right*?

Somewhere, behind and below him, the shuttle's big engines stuttered, then fully caught and then engaged. Already moving off into deep space, he knew well it would take about eight hours before they'd hit Sol system—get into Earth's upper orbit. He needed to grab a few hours of sleep first, before reviewing several case files. He purposely avoided thinking about his numerous *unsolves*: two murders; three missing persons that were undoubtedly murders; plus, some cold cases he also should be attending to but didn't have the resources for. For now, though—rest. He loosened his tie and unfastened the top button of his shirt; he closed his eyes and thought about Mandy . . . she wanted a puppy. Was she ready for that kind of responsibility? *Was he?* Before an answer could present itself, sleep washed over him.

* * *

Six hours and ten minutes later, his arm began to vibrate. Rousted from sleep, Gallic glanced down at his wrist—at his ComsBand. Blurry-eyed and groggy, it took him a moment to comprehend what was being projected—the repeating, flashing blue words there before him:

EMERGENCY ALERT – HOME BREACH!...
EMERGENCY ALERT – HOME BREACH!...
EMERGENCY ALERT – HOME BREACH!

Gallic sat up in his seat and tapped at the communications device. He said, "Call home," in a constricted voice that sounded like it belonged to someone else. Instantly, the ComsBand displayed the projected words, *Calling Home.*

He barely registered the startled, sideways glances, from both the construction worker and the book-reading lady, sitting alongside him. Gallic's full attention was focused on listening to Clair's unanswered ComsBand, which continued to ring.

"Come on, answer the damn thing!" he said, speaking loud enough for other commuters in the periphery around him to take notice.

He heard a decisive click, then Clair's voice—screaming something, but he could only catch the last part of it.

"...in the house...oh my god...oh my god...John!"

Gallic, up on his feet now, yelled back just as loudly, "Who's there, Clair? Who's in the house? Tell me what's happening? What's going on?"

All those in the shuttle compartment had turned toward him now, staring at him, fear mirrored across each face.

"...broken into the back of the house!" Clair said.

He heard her quick breaths and the soft echoes of socked feet running. He heard, too, the old grandfather clock chiming away in the background. They were in the downstairs hallway—probably coming out from the family room, going into the front foyer.

Clair said, "Shhhh . . . take my hand, sweetie! Hurry!" She was shushing Mandy.

He heard them padding up the stairs. Gallic's heart was in his throat. He looked around the confined shuttle, millions of miles away from where he needed to be.

"What's he doing here, Mommy?"

"I don't know, baby . . ."

The old steward, Max, was rushing down the aisle toward Gallic on spindly legs, motioning for those who had also risen to their feet to sit back down. He glanced at Gallic, with some trepidation. "You must take your seat while . . ."

"Clair . . . lock yourself in your bedroom. I'm calling the local police. Stay on the line. Do you hear me?"

"Yes," she whispered. He heard the desperation in her voice. "Hurry, John . . . oh god . . . I think he's coming . . ."

Gallic thought he heard distant, heavy footfalls coming up the stairs.

chapter 1

July 2120 — Frontier Planet, Muleshoe.
Three years and four months later...

G allic was in a particularly surly mood. Not about anything in particular, but then it never was. Another year
had come and gone. Another year spent without his wife and
child.

He squinted into the buffeting wind. Constant gusts that
were heavy with fine gritty particles—soil pulled up from
hundreds of miles of open planes. He pulled the collar of his
leather coat in closer around his neck. A gamey smell of livestock and manure, and also hay and other aromas he wasn't so
sure about, permeated his nostrils. Gazing off to his left, into
the Cimmerian veil of purples and pinks, he noted groupings
of cattle, mere blots on the landscape at this late hour and from
such a long distance away.

Muleshoe was a relatively small planet, colonized twenty-seven years earlier, for one intended purpose—producing beef; hundreds of thousands of pounds of beef annually. John Gallic appreciated the sight, even the odors. Familiar sights and smells that were, some twenty years in the past, now removed from Earth's slowly repairing eco-environ.

Gallic was running late. Being late adversely affected his earnings, something he couldn't let happen. Not with what was at stake. He mentally calculated how quickly he could grab the vehicle, load it into the *Hound*, and be back up in space. *It's going to be tight.* He thought about the irony. Here he was, about to repo a guy's high-end spacecraft for delinquency, when he was two months late making his own payments on the *Hound*.

Up ahead, partially obscured within the churning sand-cloud, he saw neon-colored lights: Muted reds, blues, and greens, plus multi-variations of those. The wind had picked up noticeably since he'd left his ship. Ignoring it, he fixed his attention on the suspended sign, hanging off angle thirty feet above the bar. The name on the sign, *Renegade's Haven*, blinked on and off; a staccato rhythm meant to attract visitors from miles away. For Gallic, it induced no reaction at all.

He approached the front of the bar, where he heard loud music escaping out through the rundown establishment's countless open gaps—between old and bowed timber planks and from three, small, ill-fitting, grease-smeared windows. The front door, though faded red with time, was a sturdy, stout affair—now wedged partially closed against the pounding wind by what looked to be an old, cast-iron anvil.

Seeing the parking lot completely full, the place must be hopping, he figured. Gallic surveyed the lot, more than a few of the closer-in vehicles were open-bed hovercrafts, holding long-handled tools strewn atop errant scatterings of dirt and straw. The vehicles, most likely owned by local field hands who worked hard doing whatever needed doing—perhaps helping to move herds from one location to another or delivering bales of hay; or escorting cattle to a sectioned-off area where they'd be put down, then readied for processing. Although Gallic didn't know much about either cattle or ranching, he did know a good deal about other things; such as determining the origins of physical, or trace evidence at a homicide scene. Or the best methods to use when interviewing a potential witness; or guess-timating the caliber of a bullet while studying an entry wound in the middle of a vic's forehead. But none of those capabilities would be needed for tonight's gig.

Gallic walked between various-sized spacecraft, the ones parked farther out in the lot. Though some were small, and some large, there were certain similarities between them, and even while some were older, looking ready to be replaced—others looked brand new and expensive—right off the dealer's lot. Here were the personal spacecrafts of wealthy businessmen, wealthy ranch owners, or their sons and daughters. Most of the vessels possessed approximately 800 to 1,200 cubic feet of inside volume capacity—perhaps about the size of an old school bus, during the turn of the twenty-first century on Earth. But any similarity stopped there. Here were sleek—precision-made—spacecraft. Most had exotic matter drives, capable of FTL, as well as being integrated with the latest highly complex AI brains. Undoubtedly, these designer rides were too smart for their own good and definitely far too smart for their current owners. At high, present-day costs, each individual ship, Gallic guessed, could be worth a cool half-billion dollars . . . *maybe more.* Gazing across the nearly full landing lot—in front of Renegade's Haven—he knew he was looking at, with the ever-increasing high rate of inflation, roughly fifty billion dollars' worth of fancy, high-priced, space transportation.

Hurrying up, it took Gallic another five minutes to pinpoint and find the specific craft he was searching for—one of the newer ships, a *Hausenbach L35T.* Built within the German manufacturing territories, close to a light-year's distance away, across a vast open space. A fine machine—very expensive—and the owner was three months' delinquent in making payments. Gallic, on site to repo the vehicle—mentally appraised the fine ship. *It would fetch a nice percentage.* Perhaps even enough to get him current with the *Hound.*

As he moved around the taxium-glass hull, a polished-chrome appearance craft, he slid his palm across the slick surface. Both the ingress and egress for a new *L35T* was completely AI-controlled. No seams—no hairline gaps—which would allow Gallic to use the tools of his trade to penetrate a hatchway. Of German-design origin, the AI, probably made by Spincher & Cowl, was a crazy smart artificial-intelligence unit. And, undoubtedly, it was watching him at that very moment—had already tapped into the CoreNet and knew who he was and what he did for a living. Also, what he'd been another life-time ago. Because this newer breed of AI was so thorough, so tenacious, it would have, by now, delved far deeper into his past—into every aspect of his life. But Gallic didn't really care what it had uncovered. It didn't change the fact that this very vehicle needed to be loaded onto the *Hound* then returned to the selling dealership, preferably tonight—tomorrow morning, at the latest.

He gave the craft an affectionate pat then headed off in the direction of the blinking blue, red, and green neon lights. *Time to do things the old-fashioned way*, he mused.

* * *

John Gallic entered the seedy watering hole through the faded-red door, knowing exactly what to expect inside. He'd been there before; had conducted business there. Had been there to drink and sometimes not to drink. The proprietor knew enough about him to know that disturbing him would be a bad idea.

John was well aware of the impact his presence made. He looked at the tightly packed-in patrons, those who usually came and went from Renegade's Haven, for the most part, unnoticed. But at six-foot-six, and close to two hundred forty pounds, he was an imposing figure. He pictured himself through their eyes—seeing the leather Stetson, worn low over his eyes; the dark-brown trousers and heavy black boots. Wearing a long, well-worn leather duster, supported by shoulders that just about spanned the open door's threshold, he watched as curious eyes moved in their sockets, seeing who, or *what*, had so obtrusively entered their space.

The music was loud and the smoky haze from cigarettes, cigars, and a few pipes, gave the place a far more mysterious ambiance than it deserved. The combined hum of chattering voices decreased several decibels as more heads turned around to face him. He continued to survey the room—taking in as much detail as he could. Good with details, he was trained to notice things the average person would disregard. Training that took place in another lifetime, when he was a different person—the DCI—the Chief Inspector for the Colonial Police, Space District 22.

But that life was ancient history, one that belonged in the past. For the last three years, Gallic was officially known as a Territory Abettor, more commonly referred to as a Frontier Marshal. Frontier Marshals were independent contractors that provided a handful of—and not always the most respected— services. Earth's distant spatial territories, lacking much in the way of institutional policing, engaged Frontier Marshals to fill in the gap. Covering everything, especially those that had high-end stakes, like investigating murders—of which there'd been a good number—Gallic was good at closing most cases on the Frontier Worlds. His previous years, spent as a DCI, had come in handy. He'd built a solid reputation in the Frontier Worlds for being relentless—a bulldog—said to always get his man. Or woman, if that was the case. Although not a hundred percent true, Gallic was fine with that general assumption. On the low end of marshaling, Gallic's duties included the errant breaking-up of bar brawls, petty crimes, even the repossessing of spacecraft; finding such side repo work paid surprisingly well. It also kept him busy—too busy to think; too busy to remember . . .

He made his way over to the bar and squeezed between two seated, conversing, elderly men. Forced off their bar stools, they grumbled something unintelligible. The pair leaned forward, peering around him, and resumed their conversation while drinking their house-brand whiskeys.

Gallic caught the proprietor's attention. He looked pretty much the same as the three other busy bartenders catering to needy patrons. Wearing a stained white apron, the medium-sized man with a receding hairline, wiped his hands on a dishtowel and made his way down the bar to where Gallic stood waiting. He asked, "Usual?"

"Not tonight, Randy." Leaning forward, Gallic spoke just loud enough for him to hear. "I'm looking for a guy . . . name's Larz Cugan."

The barkeep looked hesitant. "Don't bust up the place, Gallic. No trouble here tonight . . . okay?"

"Uh huh. Just point him out to me."

The proprietor gestured with his chin toward a large group, which had pulled three tables together. An eruption of laughter followed by arms raised high, the clinking of shot glasses; a rowdy, happy group.

"He's the one at the far head of the table. He's the one with that...thing...around his neck. Not sure what those things are called," Randy said.

"It's called an ascot."

"Looks pretty silly to me," Randy added.

Gallic said, "Anyway...thanks. Go ahead and ping my account for a double shot; either drink it yourself or give it away." He turned and made his way through the packed-sea of patrons, needing to shuffle between chairs and tables. Several times, he had to turn sideways, in order to maneuver his way toward the seated boisterous partygoers.

No less than twelve, they were mostly in their twenties, Gallic surmised. Dressed to the nines—designer clothes, meant to impress each other, and everyone else. The women were bare-shouldered, tanned, and wore an abundance of conflicting fragrant perfumes. The men, equal in number, wore suits with bolo ties and leather cowboy boots—etched with elaborate design work.

A lit cigarette hanging loosely from the corner of his mouth, Larz Cugan's eyes met Gallic's as he approached. Designer stubble on his face, he wore his highlighted, streaked hair parted far over on one side—his angled bangs strategically flopped over one eye. Sitting there, Gallic guessed he was about six-feet-tall. He'd soon find out.

A woman's thin tanned arm was casually draped over Larz' left shoulder; sitting close behind him, and just to the side, like she'd joined the party late and had to pull a chair up from an adjoining table. Her dangling, bobbling, earrings caught the light as her head turned this way and that. She wore faded snug jeans and some kind of halter-top that emphasized her breasts. All in all, though dressed more casually than the other women there, it all worked—she was stunning. As Gallic closed-in on the end of their table, a bemused smile crossed her lips.

Seated to Larz' immediate left and right sides were two big barrel-chested guys. Gallic knew the type. Sure, the bulk was there, but it was comprised more from pork than any real muscle. Looking weirdly similar, even down to their shiny grey suits and abundance of wet-looking product slicking back their hair—they were two matching, oversized, bookends.

Through narrowed eyes they assessed Gallic and smirked. His guess, they were more like a rich boy's protection than actual friends. As Gallic leaned down to say something to their boss, they tensed, straightening up in their chairs.

Larz took a pull from his cigarette and leaned forward. The girl with the bobbling earrings watched on with mild interest.

Gallic said, "Hey, man . . . you Larz?"

He exhaled a cloud of smoke, "What's it to you?"

"Looks like someone just backed into your ride. Hurry . . . and you can catch the son-of-a-bitch; probably still out there in the lot."

Larz stared up at him, then over to the bookends who Gallic had mentally assigned the names *Tweedle-dee* and *Tweedledum*.

Larz said, "Just know, that if it was you . . . you're a dead man."

chapter 2

Frontier Planet, Muleshoe — *Renegade's Haven.*

Gallic stood aside as Larz flew from his seat, shoved past him, and headed for the exit. Looking startled, the two bookends in their shiny suits clumsily extricated their legs from beneath the table and hauled their bulks quickly between chairs and tables, disrupting customers. After knocking over someone's drink and tipping over two chairs, they were hot on the heels of Larz.

They move pretty fast for porky guys, Gallic thought. The girl with the earrings rose to her feet, giving Gallic an appraising look. She stood there for several moments with that same bemused expression. She held out her hands, palms up, in a gesture that implied: *Are you going to move out of the way?*

* * *

Outside, the wind had settled down to a mild breeze— the sand cloud was moving away to the South. By the time

Gallic arrived at the *Hausenbach L35T*, Larz had apparently completed his circling of the ship's hull, giving her a quick look-over. Undoubtedly making sure there were no new dents or scratches on the vehicle's pristine finish.

Seeing him approach, Larz studied Gallic from head to toe, an expression of distaste crossing his face; like he was looking at a bug, or maybe a wayward turd lying on the ground.

"What the fuck's your problem, dude? There's absolutely nothing wrong with my *5T*," he said, moving into Gallic's personal space. Placing his hands on his hips, cigarette still dangling there in his lips—his angry face glared up at Gallic.

And there they were, Tweedle-dee and Tweedledum. They hovered a close step behind him—one on each side trying to act menacing.

Gallic hadn't known the proper abbreviated vernacular for Larz's ship was simply *5T*. It had a nice ring to it. *5T*. "Hey, it's your ride, man," Gallic said. "It's no skin off my nose if you think she's fine."

"So why don't you tell us what you *think* you saw?"

Gallic shrugged. "Looked like an old Buick Starflight. Green . . . I think. It bumped your *5T* down low . . . over there in the front . . . jostling her pretty good; but hey, she's probably fine." Gallic turned, as if he were going to leave, then spun back around. "Um . . . you did fire her up, didn't you? See that she's still operational after being slammed into like that. I'm sure I don't need to tell you—that's a fine-tuned precision craft."

Larz seemed to contemplate on his suggestion for a moment. Then, turning his attention to the girl with the dangling earrings who'd just arrived, now standing closer to Gallic than to Larz himself, he raised his brows, questioningly. "Maybe he's right. Maybe I should at least check her out to be on the safe side."

"Certainly, couldn't hurt," Gallic said.

Larz, patting his breast suit jacket pocket, brought out a *start-cube* and walked around the *5T* to where, Gallic figured, the vessel's hidden access hatch was located. Holding the cube between two fingers, he positioned it at waist-level height against her pristine fuselage. The cube flew—disappeared into the ship, as though it had melded in there. *Curz* technology. Gallic had heard about this latest application of the alien science and wondered how much extra Larz paid for such a useless option: *A million? Two million?*

Then, almost magically, the *5T*'s hatch began to lift up and outward—like a graceful gullwing in mid-flight.

Gallic let out a breath. *So, so easy!* Having the start-cube in place was exactly what he needed. The vehicle, now accessible, was also drivable—either by him or anyone else. He said, "Hey, hold up there a moment."

Frowning, Larz halted, one leg poised on the first step leading into the ship. Gallic reached him in three strides— already unfolding an electronic *vid-sheet*. Handing it to him, he said. "This authorizes me to take possession of this vehicle. I'm repossessing it. Step away from the craft. Do so, now!"

Larz' cigarette flipped end over end from his lips and bounced off his knee. "Like hell you are!" he spat. He grabbed ahold of both sides of the hatchway. "No one's taking my 5T . . . there has to be a mistake . . . I pay my fucking bills."

Gallic shrugged, "Either that, or your daddy does. Unfortunately, one of you has missed a few payments . . . three, to be exact. You can either take care of the default at your bank or at the dealership. She'll be waiting there for you in the morning. Now move aside."

Larz, hunkering down, wasn't going to make this easy. "Johnnie . . . Donnie, don't just stand there! Take care of this guy!"

He sensed the two of them had moved in closer behind. He could smell their foul breath. Gallic felt a heavy palm on his right shoulder. A surprisingly high voice then said, "You're going to give Mr. Logan a bit more time to take care of this business. If you don't . . . we'll hurt you. Hurt you bad. Leave you here bleeding in the dirt and gravel. You understand me? Now, why don't you put that little vid-sheet back in your pocket . . . you know . . . before we get angry . . . and do something we'll laugh about later."

Gallic, not turning around, glanced at the meaty hand still resting on his shoulder. "Which one are you? Johnnie or Donnie?"

"I'm Donnie."

Gallic said over his opposite shoulder, "Johnnie, best you head back into the bar. Ask for Randy."

"Yeah? What for?"

"Ask to borrow a bucket. You know, one of those big steel jobs . . . with a metal handle."

He snorted and made an irritated expression. "What would I need with a damn bucket?"

Gallic sensed the beefy twosome were exchanging perplexed looks.

"Because, if your friend here doesn't take his hand off my shoulder, you'll be taking what's left of him home in it . . .'"

Gallic felt Donnie's hand come off his shoulder and he sensed Larz' bodyguard was in the process of turning his upper torso—that he was winding-up to deliver a punch. Gallic didn't need to look at him to know precisely what he was going to do. The mistake most people make in this situation is to try to duck away. Avoid being hit. But Gallic did the opposite. You never do what your opponent expects you to do—in this case, what Donnie would expect. Instead, he stepped back—right into him—up close and personal. When Donnie's punch came, there was no room for him to extend his arm. No way for him to put any of his porky weight in behind it. Directed at the vicinity of his kidneys—it arrived more of a love tap than a real punch. Without hesitation, Gallic—half-turning and faking a half-step forward—quickly rocked back on his heels while at the same time, he ratcheted his right elbow back hard. The height differential between Gallic and Donnie couldn't have worked out any better. The familiar knob protrusion, located at the end of the elbow, is actually a part of the humerus bone. Gallic's arms were large and muscular, and the round knob at the end of his humerus was poised to act more like the business end of a sledgehammer than that inconsequential bone most people took for granted. Gallic's fast-moving elbow made contact with Donnie's nose and, in the process, totally annihilated it. In that fraction of a second, Donnie's nasal bone—the supporting septal cartilage, as well as both sides of the maxillary bones—either splintered outright or instantly turned into something akin to toothpaste.

The sudden impact was enough to bounce Donnie's brain, hard forward first, then just as hard backward, within the confined space of his oversized cranium. Suddenly unconscious, Donnie dropped like a sack of rice. Gallic next turned his attention to Johnnie—holding a semi-automatic handgun in his left hand—whose attention was still focused on the bloodied heap lying at his feet. Gallic stepped forward and grabbed the gun out of his hand. Fully intending to do the same thing to Johnny that he'd just done to Donnie, the girl said, "Stop! Just leave him alone."

Gallic hesitated.

Looking over to Larz, she said, "You can get the *T5* back tomorrow. Let the creep take her. Larz . . . it's not worth it."

Larz glared at Gallic, whose expression remained impassive.

Eventually, Larz stepped down from the open hatchway. "Do you know who I am? Who my family is?"

"Nope. Can't say that I do," Gallic replied.

"You're done! I hope you've enjoyed this lowlife job of yours because you're finished. You'll be fired by morning."

Gallic, after pushing past him and stepping into the open hatchway, turned around to face the still seething Larz Logan. "Good luck with that, I work for myself. An arbiter. Best take care of your friend there . . . I'd turn him over onto his side for a while, if I were you."

Stepping inside the craft, he caught the girl's eye as the gull-wing hatch began to close. Not quite reading her questioning expression, she said, "You're a piece of work . . . you know that?"

"Yeah . . . well, I've been called worse, sweetheart."

The *5T*'s cockpit, with its myriad of glowing dials and indicators, was just as impressive inside as it was outside—a sweet high-end spacecraft. And Larz certainly hadn't foregone adding the more luxurious options. Gallic sat down in the pilot's seat, feeling it automatically adjust to his girth.

He'd never sat in anything so comfortable. Certainly, a far cry from the rock-hard cushions found in the *Hound*. Spinning the seat around, he studied the craft's warm and inviting cabin. Padded leather was everywhere—cushy, wrap-around leather chairs and sectional couches. Inset strips of decorative wood—perhaps walnut—accented the padded interior sides and overhead bulkheads.

Gallic swiveled his chair back around, ready to face the business at hand. Firing up the *5T*'s propulsion system, he took the controls in his hands. He activated the underbelly thrusters and lifted off. Thirty feet above the landing lot, he cranked the controls hard left. Accelerating fast, he left behind Renegade's Haven, the sprawling pastureland, and the sporadic clustering of cattle.

At a quarter-mile out, Gallic reached into his inside coat pocket and fingered the small opener device. The rear hatch on the *Hound* began opening up. Light instantly peeked through the quickly expanding gap around it. He slowed the *5T*'s progression and waited for the hatch—doing double-duty as hatch and gangway—to descend all the way to a reverse downward angle. Goosing the *5T*, he piloted her directly into the *Hound*'s hold—a hold large enough to transport several old jetliners, if the need for such a thing ever arose.

It took him another five minutes to carefully strap down and secure the *5T* onto the inside deck. Any damage incurring to the craft now would come right off the top of his repo fees. Once satisfied, he initiated the closing of the hold's rear hatch—he glanced around to ensure the handful of other vehicles in there were also strapped into place. Everything looked to be in order.

By the time he crossed the hold into the entranceway of the rear airlock, he heard the familiar pressurized *thunk* sound as the *Hound*'s massive back hatch seated into the cowling surrounding it. Exiting the airlock, Gallic headed up the ship's internal stairway, which led to the second level.

* * *

The top level of the *Hound* looked more like an open, New York City loft *build-out* than the top deck of a working hauler-type spacecraft. Fifty-five-feet wide by fifty-nine-feet long, it seemed like one huge square. Even though the large compartment looked industrial, there was something strangely inviting about the space, nevertheless. Due, perhaps, to its wide-planked timber decking and the soft, indirect lighting, generated from large canned lights, fifteen feet overhead. Also, there was a decorative intermixing of home furnishings—colorful Navaho throw rugs draped over stuffed, worn, leather couches, and a set of multi-prism Tiffany lamps set on craftsman style side tables. Long observation windows, installed on opposing bulkheads, provided scenic, high-up views to the now-darkening landscape below.

Gallic moved swiftly across the sectionalized space to a bank of extending out forward-facing windows—where two rotating seats, and a waist-level-high, semicircle-shaped, console were positioned—the paint both dinged and scratched. Not fully a ship's bridge—nothing that elaborate—or a cockpit. More purposeful, it was the *Hound*'s command center. As he approached, a projected holographic display came alive on his right. Nearly as high as himself in height, the display was in the process of updating his weekly job log. He noticed the latest repo job:

Vehicle: *Hausenbach L35T*; **Owner: Mr. Larz Logan; Current Standing: impounded/transferring, Final Destination: Dealer @ Bantum Exotic Starcrafts.**

As Gallic traced with his index finger other open work repo orders, he noticed another three, which would also require his attention over the next day or two.

A reminder window popped into view: *You have two vid-messages! Both messages are tagged high-priority.*

Gallic, after taking a seat, addressed the *Hound*'s AI, voicing out loud, "Go ahead, play first one."

A blue-tinted, life-sized holographic image came to life. A short, bald-headed man, in a wrinkled Hawaiian shirt, stared at Gallic. One of Gallic's past associates—Polly Gant—a less than scrupulous provider of both repo and bail bondsman services, that he tended to avoid, unless there was absolutely no other work at hand. Polly smiled, "Hey, Galaxy Man, call me. You pick up that *Hausenbach* craft yet? Listen . . . I've a special project for you. It's perfect for someone with your . . . unique capabilities. Time-sensitive, so don't—"

Gallic said, "Skip message . . . go to the next."

On the projected display, an older black man appeared—dressed in a smart-fitting, navy-blue uniform. His heavily lined face seemed more covered with age spots than Gallic remembered. And his hair, although still mostly black, looked peppered now with more white, as did his immaculately trimmed goatee. The man was Chief Superintendent Bernard Danbury, who—three-and-a-half years prior—was his boss, friend, and mentor. Gallic resisted the oncoming flood of memories—like snakes—trying to twist and wiggle their way into his consciousness.

Danbury said, "Hello, John. I hope this message finds you in good health."

"Pause message," Gallic commanded the AI. He stared at the frozen-in-time holographic image. He'd worked for the superintendent for close to a decade, rising quickly within the Territorial Police Department, Spatial District 22. On becoming DCI Chief Inspector, he reported directly to him. He left the position soon after the murders—murders never solved—which he had not been allowed to have any involvement with.

John closed his eyes, fighting to keep the ever-intruding vermin at bay. Nothing held more importance for him than finding the person responsible for the murders of the young and beautiful thirty-one-year-old woman and her equally beautiful three-year-old daughter—John Gallic's wife and little girl. His old life, as he knew it, ended the day the two were taken from him. Now, he merely *survived*, though he continued to follow-up on what he wasn't permitted to do as DCI for the Territorial Police Department, Spatial District 22. Since he was both the husband and father of the homicide victims, he wasn't allowed to have direct involvement in the case. Deemed a serious conflict of interest. Something the lead Investigator, Freddy MacDonald, was all too happy to enforce. There had already been bad blood between the two for years; Gallic, younger and newer to the department, had quickly moved up in the ranks to the coveted Detective Chief Inspector, DCI, position, above MacDonald. He hadn't taken it well. As the lead investigator of the case, MacDonald stonewalled him—restricting any further access to the case files. Gallic and MacDonald fought continuously. Blows were exchanged.

The grisly crime was front-page news for weeks as the investigation proceeded in earnest. His disputes with MacDonald aside, Gallic knew everyone involved in the case had good intentions: Three, full-time investigators were assigned, each working hard and piling on the OT. But encouraging leads eventually hit a dead end. As the promising prospects dried up, official personnel, plus other resources, were assigned to new active cases. Other crimes now captured the media's headlines.

But that didn't halt Gallic's off-time pursuit. For months, his friend—Chief Superintendent Bernard Danbury—turned a blind eye to Gallic's growing number of sick-days off; days spent in his private crusade to find the killer, or killers, of Clair and Mandy.

Ultimately, he was forced to resign, which was for the best. Now, some three-plus years later, Gallic—during his off time—continued the pursuit. Seeking to find the one who'd ruined everything; who had stolen away his life.

The life insurance policy hadn't provided much, but he had some savings. Financing a high-interest loan, he purchased a wrecked *Hewley-Jawbone* carrier, for pennies on the dollar—the *Hound*. It took him over a year to make the craft space-worthy.

With the snakes now held somewhat at bay, Gallic said, "Continue the message."

"John . . . I wanted to be the first one to tell you. There's been a . . . development in your wife and daughter's case. We may have a strong lead."

chapter 3

Frontier Planet, Gorman — Heritage Plains Township.

H is actions were unhurried, almost methodical in nature—well practiced. He moved within the home's darkness silently, like a whisper or a slight breeze; a breath. He stopped and listened to the sounds, louder now, emanating from the family room. The killer tilted his head, not wanting to miss a thing. *How he'd missed this.* There was a short giggle—really more of a snort—from the young girl, *Tami.* He smiled. *What a lovely sound that was.* He needed to remember it; mentally catalogue it away for later—for forever. The sound of playing cards being shuffled echoed into the hallway where he stood.

"Oh no, you don't! You little cheater," the mother exclaimed, laughing.

Ah . . . that would be Catherine. The killer took a step, then another. He wasn't concerned about being discovered within the home. They were alone here. Only the three of them now—he'd made certain of that. He took another step—this one quicker, more deliberate. A rustling sound was suddenly more audible, his hard leather belt rubbing against the fabric of his disposable overalls. Also, a jingly sound as small nails collided within his oversized pouch. His eyes fell to the tool belt, secured around his narrow hips. Glaring down at it, he listened, hearing only silence. But then came their soft whispering:

"Did you hear that?"

"Did I hear what?" the mother replied, her voice playful.

"I'm serious!" came the young girl's excited whisper.

"Your turn to deal; I'm getting up to pee. Want anything from the fridge?" the mother asked, continuing the whisper game as she moved into the kitchen.

Right then the killer shot forward into the kitchen—a mere blur of motion and wild kinetic energy. He spun, reached out for Catherine's long hair and felt its softness, its slippery nature, in his palm—trapped now within his fingers. Tightening his grip, he tugged hard. Jerked backwards, Catherine's scream was cut short by an uncontrolled inhalation of breath. As she toppled over, the killer dragged her, caveman-style, as she kicked and flailed about. Together, they moved out from the kitchen into the family room.

Rising to her feet, Tami's mouth gaped open: her eyes wide, not understanding.

"You!" Catherine yelled, kicking out and connecting a solid, painful, blow to his upper thigh. The killer released his hold on the woman's hair and spun, punching out with fury to the side of her head—a punch that contained sufficient force to crack concrete. More than enough force to crack the side of her skull. He glanced up, noting the pretty daughter's horrified face. *She wants to run.* Instead, though, Tami lost control of her bladder. The killer fondled the handle of the ten-inch knife at his hip, next to the head of the ballpeen hammer. "Please don't hurt..." Tami's eyes followed the motion of his fast-moving hand—the knife's sideways trajectory—and moved to cover her throat. But she was too slow...

chapter 4

Frontier Planet, Muleshoe.

Gallic didn't move—simply stared at the blank display and the hovering *End of vid-message* prompt.

"AI, request a real-time channel to Superintendent Bernard Danbury, at D-22. Let me know when you have a connection." Gallic knew the request for an encoded synchronous coms channel could take anywhere from ten minutes to several hours: sometimes longer.

He headed toward the loft's portside, while removing his outer coat. Draping it over the back of one of the leather couches, he entered into the cooking, mess area—located at the rear far-side of the compartment.

Pulling out three separate frying pans from the low-placed cupboards, he set them on the cooktop while willing his mind into submission. One-by-one, mentally closing all inner doors and windows and locking them shut; he then rechecked each one again, battening down the hatches. He'd practiced this same mental exercise a thousand times—maybe ten thousand times. For the most part, it worked. He managed to stay in control, keeping the wiggly things from slithering in—infiltrating his thoughts. He opened the refrigerator and retrieved a nearly full carton of large brown chicken eggs and placed them on the steel-top counter. Using his shoulder to prop open the door, he next grabbed a glass pitcher filled with fresh milk, a stick of butter, and a generous slab of uncut bacon—setting each down by the carton of eggs.

Next, Gallic opened the top cupboard, where he retrieved a loaf of unsliced sourdough bread. Firing up three burners, he adjusted the flames before adding ample pats of butter to two of the pans. The butter quickly sizzled down, its oily liquid coating the bottom of the pans. As he jostled the pans around, the clang of metal clanging into metal was both a familiar, and welcome, sound—grounding him—keeping him present. Pulling a long knife from a drawer, he quickly sliced through the slab of bacon. Hungry, he cut the slabs thick and placed them into the ungreased heated pan, which began to sizzle. Making four wide cuts in the loaf of sourdough, he situated the slices, one at a time, in the larger buttered pan. One by one, he cracked open seven eggshells, letting their contents slurp into a large red bowl. Pouring in seven generous drips of milk, he rapidly beat the mixture with a fork to ensure enough air was swirled into the eggy-mixture. Sufficiently beaten, he poured the contents into the other buttered pan. Using a fork to turn the bacon and flip over the slices of bread, he suddenly had to squeeze shut his eyelids.

Without warning, a mental door had cracked open, standing ajar. Gallic caught movement there in the semi-blackness, lying just beyond his closed-tight lids. The paralysis came first. He heard them approaching—a muffled, awful sound—like a stampede of oversized vermin. As the bacon began to burn— the eggs thickening, then scorching—greasy smoke rose into the compartment's air and swirled around him. Gallic continued viewing the ever-widening inner door, where, in the near-darkness and obscured by the billowing smoke, he saw the small, reptilian, non-human faces. Clamoring to get out— fighting one another—each wanting to be the first to come forth. But suddenly, in an instant, he was no longer peering inward into an open doorway, or concerned with crawly snakes, or even aware a fire had started on the stovetop. His entire attention was transported to another time, where, centered on his scratched, weathered, D-22 desk, was an open-case-file— more precisely, a crime-scene case file. He reached for the stack of 8x10 vid-sheets. Hot bile crept into his throat, his heart rate jumped, becoming almost tachycardic, as their distorted, bloated faces—blurry at first—came into view.

"Fire! Mr. Gallic! Fire! Fire! Mr. Gallic! Fire!"

Gallic's focus returned from the past—from three years, four months, and thirteen days ago. He turned off the burners and stacked the three, blisteringly hot, pans into the sink. Flames erupted momentarily when bacon grease sloshed onto what remained of the ruined toast. "AI, increase mess area ventilation until this damn smoke clears."

"Yes, sir. Your requested coms channel has been re-established and Chief Superintendent Bernard Danbury is waiting for you."

Gallic walked from the cooking mess area toward the control center, his heart rate still accelerated, not yet a normal beat. Cursing under his breath, he was irritated with himself. He'd obviously forgotten to properly latch and lock up an inner door inside his screwed-up mind. He had to be much more careful in the future.

* * *

The holographic image of Superintendent Bernard Danbury was waiting for Gallic. With concern furrowing his brow, Danbury asked, "Did I hear something about a fire?"

"Nah ... everything's fine. The *Hound*'s AI can be a bit dramatic."

"How are you, John?"

"Fine ... right as rain."

"You're still working?" the older man asked.

"What else am I going to do? Plant tulips back on Earth?"

Gallic quickly let their small talk come to an end; his blank stare was all the coaxing Danbury needed to get down to business. "As I mentioned in the ... um ... message, there are a few new developments."

"How is that even possible, since there have been zero resources allocated to the case since I left D-22?"

"You know that's far from the truth, John. But I'll let that go . . . because we're friends. Do you want to hear what I've got or not?"

Gallic asked, "Credible?"

"I don't know. Hell, I hesitate even bringing it up to you before things can be followed up at D-22. But John, there's strong similarities; no, more than just similarities. I'm talking about a near-identical crime scene to . . . Clair and Mandy's."

"You getting this from a D-22 inspector?"

"No, John . . . I'm getting this from another arbiter, one who resides in the Agricultural belt within the Territories."

"I'm in the Territories."

"I know that."

Gallic asked, "Where then, exactly? Give me the details: Who's the Frontier Marshal, where'd it happen, and when?"

"All in good time, John. I've dispatched Tori. You remember her, don't you?"

Gallic did indeed remember Tori—Silvia Tori. Three-and-a-half years ago she was new to the department—a walking-talking cluster-fuck. "Really, Constable! Tori? That's the best you can do?"

"She's Sergeant Tori now. And when, might I ask, did you last hear of D-22 sending someone out to that God-forsaken section of space? Don't be such an ungrateful ass."

The Colonial Police Department-District 22 was under Earth's British purview—the same section of agricultural territories that Gallic now inhabited. Many of the same geo-political boundaries found on Earth also extended into the vastness of space. Whether large or small, the same superpowers dominating Earth had rushed to stake their claims in space over the last hundred years.

Danbury continued, "She'll be there tomorrow morning. Stay where you are ... she's got your coordinates."

Gallic thought about the *5T*, now sitting in the *Hound*'s hold. He needed to get her into Polly Gant's meaty palms within the next twelve hours or take a hit on the commission. Without that fee, he could lose the *Hound*.

"I'll be here," Gallic said.

"And let me be perfectly clear, John. This is Tori's case. You are tagging along as an observer only. No direct intervention. Do you hear me?"

Gallic nodded.

"I'm serious. That order goes all the way up to the Deputy Assistant Commissioner. Keep a low profile. Give her your thoughts and opinions, but more than that, she's been instructed to kick you to the curb. Screw this up, I'll have your arbiter's license pulled ... that's how serious I am."

"Understood," Gallic said back.

Danbury's face turned less serious. "I'm staying in the loop on this, John. We should talk in a couple of days."

"Thank you, sir. And I'll play by the rules ... best I can."

Clearly, that was not what the superintendent wanted to hear, and Gallic knew it. But ribbing his old boss came naturally.

The coms connection faded to black. Gallic checked the time on his ComsBand, wondering if he could do it—make it all the way to Rawlins City, drop off the bratty kid's luxury ride, then make it back here in time. It would be close, but he was fairly sure he could manage it. If not, Tori could cool her heels for a few hours at Renegade's Haven. He hesitated, briefly considered why he would even think about leaving. What could be more important than this apparent new lead, one possibly connected to his wife and child's murders? The answer presented itself immediately—*stay objective*. Carry on with your life. *You know what happens when you get too consumed, too fixated.* He'd come close before, almost crossing the thin line that separated sanity from insanity; was on the verge of being locked away, put in a padded room and medicated—sedated 24/7. No, he needed to stay focused, maintain some semblance of his former lifestyle that he'd worked so hard to rebuild. Treat this new murder case, which may or may not be related to his, like any other murder case. Mentally stay detached from seeing some personal connection. As of now, his focus must strictly remain objective. He needed to stay sane.

chapter 5

Frontier Planet, Muleshoe.

A thunderous roar rumbled across the prairie as the *Hound* lifted off. There was nothing subtle about her two powerful *gravitorque* drives, even inside the vessel's thick fuselage the noise level was substantial. But Gallic hardly noticed after three years of frequent takeoffs and landings. And, just like him, wherever the Hound came and went, it was always noticed.

Still pitch-black outside, Gallic stared out the control center's forward window and into the nothingness beyond. He felt the *clunk, clunk, clunk* beneath his boots as the landing struts folded up, becoming seated inside the *Hound's* underbelly. He then leveled off on the upward thrust as gravity began to release its hold on the ship. Within a moment, as the outer atmosphere began to thin, stars could be seen—dancing and sparkling in the far distance. He rechecked that the AI had inputted the correct heading—Rawlins City. That would place him three light years distance out from the territories. Rawlins City, back in the general direction toward Earth, was closer to Alpha Centauri—4.22 light years from Earth and the Sol system. Alpha Centauri had three stars and 600 known planets—forty of which were colonized.

"Transitioning to FTL, Mr. Gallic . . . on your command."

"Proceed," Gallic said. The trip would take hours and he needed to get his mind off Danbury's comments. Old memories stirred up that he didn't want to think about. Not now. "AI . . . resume the Earth news broadcast I was last watching . . ."

Gallic, glancing at the display, viewed the projected face of Professor Harkins, with his Albert Einstein-like hair, which was red and gray, not white. Standing amongst several teens, he was recognizing the great hall addition to the National Air and Space Museum, in Washington, D.C. Gallic had met the professor several times and genuinely liked the older man. An Asian boy pointed toward the high, suspended fuselage of a spear-tip-shaped vessel.

Professor Harkins said, "Well . . . everything changed with that amazing, singular discovery on Mars."

"When was that, Professor?"

"The year was 2029. Almost a hundred years ago, on the second manned mission. *Explorer Zheng He*—a cooperative U.S. / Chinese space exploration venture . . . was decreed to reach the red planet and establish a far larger, far more elaborate base than their first installation on Mars. The new site—*Musk-Horizon*—lay adjacent to the area known as *The Hidden Valley*. Where, in thick mudstone strata from an ancient evaporated lake bed, rich with river and stream-related deposits, and a mere seventeen feet below the Martian surface, that incredible alien spacecraft was discovered.

Another teen, a girl with long blonde hair, asked, "Why's that? It doesn't look so incredible to me."

"What you're looking up at . . . that alien vessel . . . is estimated to be close to five thousand years old. What do you think you'll look like in five thousand years, Brianne?"

The others in the group laughed. One of the boys said, "Bet she'll look better than she does now," and they laughed even harder.

The professor continued, "In history, there have been other such monumental discoveries: Discoveries that not only changed, but bettered, existing life conditions. The discovery of fire; and the use of weapons, either hunted with, or to ward-off predators; and the wheel, which single-handedly and inexplicably, transformed ancient societies. Prompting early man to stray from what had become familiar and safe, and venture forth—and explore! The wheel was just such a discovery." The professor's excitement was contagious. Gallic could see it on the lit-up faces of the teenagers.

An Asian boy asked, "Did the ship still fly? Did they fly it back to Earth?"

"No, since it crash-landed on the surface of Mars. It took them three-and-a-half years to bring key components of the ship back to Earth. As more aeronautic scientists from around the world came to evaluate the highly advanced technology—especially the vessel's unique, exotic-matter propulsion system—it quickly became evident that space transportation, henceforth on, would forever be altered. The discovery, designated *Curz*, the name bestowed on the ship's originating alien race, catapulted science and technology hundreds of years forward. Soon, distant twinkling stars, with their accompanying planetary systems, would be within man's reach. As with the advent of the prehistoric wheel, nothing again would be the same."

"Turn it off," Gallic ordered the AI.

* * *

The *Hound* came out of FTL five hours and fifteen minutes later. Of the three stars within Alfa Centauri, the closest to Earth was Proxima; the farthest away were Centauri A and Centauri B. Since Gallic was approaching them from their opposite direction, he'd be reaching Centauri A's planetary system first, where Rawlins City was situated—on an Earth-size, yet far more desolate planet, called Grimes252.

Named, undoubtedly, after some scientist with a big telescope—the first to spot the shithole of a planet decades earlier. No one called the planet Grimes252. Everyone just called it Rawlins City, since there was nothing worth mentioning about the rest of the planet. The only exception, at first, was what seemed to be some promising rare mineral deposits. Although the mineral deposits failed to live up to their initial hype, Rawlins City flourished nevertheless. Although considered a United States territory township, the city was actually highly international and where the majority of galactic business took place. Large banking and insurance institutions built their high-rise mega-buildings there. And where buying and selling, whatever came out of the territories, usually took place: for the agricultural quadrant, the mining quadrant, the manufacturing quadrant, and for the newest quadrant, Oceanic—where ten, recently terra-formed worlds, were breeding a variety of aquatic life forms within massive, submerged, fish farms.

Like bees swarming around a hive, hundreds of space-crafts—freighters, haulers, space liners, mining vessels, you name it—were steadily ascending and descending the planet below. Navigation was handled via AI's, communicating with other AI's. The *Hound*, in a holding pattern of first-come, first-served cue, was eventually cleared. Gallic was given specific heading instructions—a designated lane to follow to the planet's surface below.

* * *

Along the seedy outskirts of Rawlins City, proper, vested establishments—such as spacecraft repair and body shops, nudie-dance halls, tattoo parlors, and the like—could be found, as well as Polly Gant's *Imperial Bail Bonds & Repos*. Gallic, who'd done some work for Polly five or six times in the past, had sworn to himself each time that it would be the last. It wasn't that Gant was obtusely dishonest. He simply had a tendency to withhold pertinent information. Yet, here Gallic was again. Taking in the congested city below, he let out a tired breath and shook his head.

At a thousand feet above the surface, he assumed manual control of the *Hound* and looked for a suitable place to land.

Imperial Bail Bonds & Repos was a sprawling, fifteen-mile-square compound; although some was allocated to office space, the majority of acreage was dedicated to numerous landing slots for various repo-spacecraft. Finding an adequate-sized open patch of concrete for landing, Gallic maneuvered the ship's substantial bulk, engaging the landing thrusters.

* * *

Gallic descended down the gangway at a half-run, since he was running behind schedule. He needed to get over to the office and find Polly. Then get paid and get the kid's *5T* hover carted off the *Hound*. He was already having second thoughts about taking the repo job. Nothing was more important than meeting Tori; being there on time. She easily could blow him off if he was late—work the case without him.

"You motherfucker!"

Gallic turned around, seeing two men hurrying in his direction.

"I've been waiting twenty minutes for that landing spot!"

Gallic didn't slow as the two men approached him on his right side. Both, also repo guys, were Native Americans, wearing dark ponytails and leather vests. Gallic knew them both. The elder one had a pockmarked face—like he'd suffered a bad bout of smallpox as a child. The other man, shorter and younger, had a narrow, chiseled-like face, with two beady, close-set, eyes. Gallic remembered the pockmarked guy's name—Sargento. Not sure, though, if that was his first or last name since he only went by Sargento. He couldn't recall the other man's name.

But Sargento was a bad egg. Had tried several times to get his arbiter's license to become a Frontier Marshal, but he had a police record. The *Hound*'s AI had proven to be a good resource—providing all kinds of information, even when the file was supposedly closed. In Sargento's case, it was mostly minor infractions—misdemeanors. Known to have a bad temper—one he'd supposedly taken out on his common-law wife when back on Earth. In New Mexico, Gallic remembered the case. Her last hospital visit was just that . . . her *last* anything. He'd broken her jaw—and her neck. Sargento claimed it was a fluke accident—a nasty fall down an embankment. But her autopsy report showed multiple past injuries, most never properly treated. An ulna, broken in two places; a messed-up metacarpus that made using that hand virtually impossible; and a mouth filled with either missing or broken teeth. At twenty-four, she looked like she'd gone through a war. Needless to say, Gallic had nothing but negative feelings toward the guy. It'd be best for all concerned if he and his little friend keep their distance.

They caught up to Gallic twenty paces from the front entrance of the one-story, glorified mobile-home-type, office structure.

"Hey, asshole!"

Gallic glanced in their direction but didn't slow. "I'm in a hurry, boys."

"We're all in a hurry. You took our spot. Been circling around like a fucking vulture . . . then you swoop in and grab it. Had to land clear on the other side of the lot."

Gallic stopped and faced them. "Yeah, well, as you can see . . . I'm already here. What do you want me to do about it now? Call your mommy for you?"

"For a starter, you can move that big rust bucket of yours and we'll swap places. We've got five repo crafts to bring out, and we're not about to hover them here from way out there."

"I'll be done in here in a few minutes. You can take my spot then," Gallic said, moving up the ramp toward the office doors.

"No man . . . you're going to move it right now! I'm the last person you want to make an enemy of."

Gallic shrugged then turned away. "Uh huh . . . I'm shaking in my boots," he retorted back, as he pulled open both swinging glass doors, leaving them behind on the sidewalk. Entering the office, he glanced left and right, seeing the familiar stifling—claustrophobic—space, where stacks of papers and vid-sheets were strewn everywhere. Gallic's head nearly touched the low-hanging, yellowed ceiling. The place was as bad as he remembered.

A woman, seated at a nearby desk, looked up as he stepped forward. Not there the last time he visited, she must have been pushing sixty. A lit cigarette dangled from one corner of her mouth, bobbing up and down, when she asked, "You Gallic?"

He nodded.

"You're late."

"Not by much. Where's Polly?"

She gestured toward a closed door. "He's on a vid-call. Shouldn't be long."

"Can't you handle the business?" he asked.

She shook her head. "No, dear. Polly wants to talk to you."

The swinging-glass doors opened behind him and the two Native American repo guys entered. Glaring at Gallic, the cramped office space put them less than a foot apart. Gallic stared back at them with a blank expression.

The inside office door opened and Polly Gant emerged, wearing a bright-red Hawaiian shirt that was decorated with a repeating pattern of palm trees and coconuts. He brightened when he saw Gallic. His baldhead glistened under the overhead lights—like he'd just polished it—as he waddled over with an outstretched hand. "There he is . . . Galaxy man! Good to see you . . . though you're a bit late."

Gallic wasn't sure when the nickname first took hold, probably a couple of years back. He briefly wondered if Polly had coined it first and if it spread out from there. People could call him whatever they liked, just as long as he got paid and things stayed on the up and up. Gallic said, "The *5T*'s in the *Hound*. Pay my commission, and I'll be out of your hair."

Polly ran a hand over his shiny dome. "Come into my office . . . I have a job for you."

"I'm in a hurry, Polly. Need to get right back to the territories."

"Oh, come on. Five minutes won't kill you big guy." He didn't wait for an answer, hurrying back into his office as Gallic followed him. Quickly seated, Polly's head was barely visible above his cluttered desk, with mountains of file folders and stacks of vid-sheets. He entered something on his terminal.

"I've pinged your account. Gave you a small bonus, too. Hold on." Bringing a radio close to his mouth, he said, "Bart . . . that *Hausenbach L35T* is here. She's in the hold of the old *Hewley-Jawbone* carrier." Polly looked up at Gallic: "Is it open?"

Gallic nodded. "Yeah . . . it's open. And you'll get the *5T* over to the dealer for me?"

"Of course." Polly tossed the radio onto the desk, then looked up at Gallic. "Sit . . . you're going to like what I have for you."

Gallic checked the time on his ComsBand. Even if he left now he'd still be an hour late getting back to the territories. Taking a seat in the only other available chair, he said, "Five minutes. No more. What's up . . . another repo?"

"Yeah, well . . . kind of. But on a totally different scale." Polly rifled through several file folders on his desk until he found what he was looking for, then pulled out a vid-sheet. Gallic saw movement—probably an active video—on the flimsy, paper-like sheet. "Here we go: Her name is Tillman, Allison Tillman . . . a business owner in the manufacturing territories. She reported it missing from her storage facility a couple of days ago."

Gallic raised his brow, questioningly. "What's she lost?"

"Stolen, not lost. This is grand theft, but on a whole new scale. Some sort of high-tech marvel: a technological proto-type of some sort. Something called a *Hayai* spacecraft, worth a hundred . . . a thousand times what that *5T* you just brought in goes for."

Gallic stared. "Glad somebody's got discretionary funds these days . . ."

"You have no idea. Anyway, the owner wants you. Says she wants the Galaxy Man."

Gallic thought about that; it was a lot of money. Life-changing money. He could pay off of a good portion of the *Hound* from that bounty reward; quit the repo side of the business; dedicate himself full-time to only Frontier Marshaling duties. He thought about the new revelation Danbury had mentioned, that Silvia Tori was heading out to the Frontier worlds this very moment. *Stay objective . . . don't fixate . . .* "What's the bounty?"

"It's five million dollars."

Gallic whistled.

"You're the perfect man for this, Gallic. Your experience alone; previously the DCI, and all . . ."

"Who else have you sent out on this? I don't want to be tripping over ten other guys."

"Well . . . this is *big*! And that's a lot of money. As you know, police don't venture much into these territories, but there's a few Frontier Marshal's, other than you, who may jump on this too. All I can promise is you'll have a head start."

"Fine, I'll do it. Send me everything you have on this Tillman lady, along with the vessel's last known whereabouts. I should be able to move on it fairly quickly."

Polly looked excited—practically salivating. His take would probably be as much as Gallic's. "I'll send you everything I have on the spacecraft, as well as Tillman's contact information. But you can't wait on this, Gallic—you need to get on it right away. And one more thing: She wants you to nab the ones responsible; wants them brought to justice. That's why she particularly picked you. This is more than just a repo job . . ."

"I get it. It shouldn't be a problem," Gallic said, with far more confidence than he actually felt.

chapter 6

Deep Space — On board the *Hound.*

The return trip back to the settlements was uneventful. He'd grabbed a few hours of sleep and successfully reattempted making breakfast. A half hour before reaching Muleshoe, the case file on Allison Tillman's theft arrived, via a CoreNet mail-beam.

Gallic had just enough time to print the vid-sheets and skim their contents. Polly had done an adequate job collecting the information, and it did seem, at least for the most part, fairly complete. He checked to see if the background info on the *Hayai* was there, and it was. He skimmed down to the section that talked about Allison Tillman. Younger than he expected, she had a respectable resume. Highly accomplished, for a thirty-five-year-old. Gallic viewed the replaying, five-second vid-image of the somewhat distracted-looking woman. She certainly was attractive. There was something about her expression too—the way she looked back into the camera lens—showing humor, even some annoyance at being photographed mixed with something else—vulnerability perhaps. The moving vid-image spoke volumes: She wasn't there for herself, and she didn't have time for such trivial activities. Gallic looked forward to reading the rest of the bio information—when he had time.

Seated within his book-shelved-lined study, situated on the opposite side of the loft from the kitchen, Gallic closed the file, placing it down on his desk. He stared up at the large projected murder board that his life had revolved around for over three years. Seven-feet-wide by five-feet-high—the 3D construct hovered unobtrusively; it had become part of the environment, like a chair or a couch. Everything that had to do with his wife and daughter's murder case was on the board and organized into sections: Suspects, Victims, Evidence, and Leads. There was much still missing—but there was information he'd pieced together through his own unofficial, unauthorized, investigation. Not having access to the original lead investigator's case file had put Gallic at a big disadvantage. Still, there were new developments on that front. Inspector Frederick "*Freddy*" MacDonald had recently retired, due to health issues, Gallic heard. Restraining order or not, Gallic soon would be paying the old D-22 investigator a visit. Faces of the remaining suspects looked back at him on the board construct—as if taunting him to get off his ass and solve the case. Solve it so he could get on with living whatever years remained of his life. *But would that ever be possible?*

He felt the subtle cadence of the drives increase, as the ship neared the planet Muleshoe. He stood and said, "AI . . . close down the murder board." The projected murder scene images and various suspect faces faded from view. He crossed the open space to the ship's command center, taking in the view out the forward window. The *Hound* was now entering high orbit. He checked the various console hover displays, verifying everything was as it should be. The ship was due for a serious maintenance overhaul within the next few weeks. He'd have to save a portion of his *5T* commission for that expense, for it wouldn't come cheap.

* * *

It was midday when the *Hound* touched down—landing on the exact spot it took off from on the day before. Grabbing his coat and hat, he rode down the rickety, noisy, internal lift from the loft to the sub-level airlock below, just forward of the hold area. He usually took the stairs, but since he was running late getting back, he hoped to shave off a few minutes getting to Renegade's Haven. Exiting the outside airlock hatch, he paused, waiting for the ship's underbelly metal stairway to fully extend downward.

The wind had again kicked up, bringing along with it a dozen, distant, spinning dirt-devils. Like miniature tornadoes, they were near Gallic's height and the color of sand.

* * *

Reaching the dilapidated bar, Gallic took in the landing lot. It was nearly empty. Close to the entrance, nestled between two, open-bed, hovercrafts, he saw the unmistakable green and black, beat-to-shit, government-issued police star-cruiser. About the same size as Larz Cugan's *Hausenbach L35T*, it lacked his ship's sporty clean lines, luxury accoutrements, and her powerful propulsion system. Entering the establishment, Gallic scanned the patrons through the hazy, smoke-filled air. He almost didn't recognize Sergeant Tori. Sitting at the bar and facing outward—her elbows propped up behind her—she was staring back at him. She'd changed very little; still had the same plain Jane appearance. Wearing no makeup, her unkempt, mousey-brown hair was worn blunt-cut to her shoulders. Like before, she wore an ill-fitting, D-22 issued uniform that seemed somewhat oversized, giving her a unisex appearance. But something extra showed on her face—a more confident expression? Also, there was that deep-seated weariness in her eyes from witnessing, all too often, the terrible things human beings can do to one another.

Gallic reached her in four long strides.

Tori gave him a half smile. Gesturing with a waving finger, she said, "The whole macho cowboy garb suits you, Gallic. Christ . . . I'd forgotten how big you are."

"Been waiting long?" he asked.

"Few hours," she replied back.

He noted an empty bottle of beer on the bar and an ashtray half-filled with smashed- down cigarette butts.

"You ready to go?"

"I've been ready for hours," she answered.

Gallic caught Randy's eye behind the counter: "Put it on my tab."

"Can't. She's already paid up."

Tori, giving Randy a nod, hefted her body off the stool. Together, they headed for the door. Holding the door open for him, she said, "We'll take my ride."

"Where are we going?"

"Township called Heritage Plains... a planet called Gorman. Do you know where that is?"

Gallic said, "Gorman? Sure ... it's here, amongst the other agricultural planets within the settlements ... two over from this one. All were given old-western-style names: Muleshoe, Rio Bravo, Rawhide, Alamosa, and Gorman."

She hesitated at the front of the vehicle. "I want to be perfectly clear here, Gallic, right from the get-go. You're here at the discretion of Constable Danbury. I didn't want you in on this. Even with your investigative experience, it's still a conflict of interest. So, you'll be joining me as an observer only. You'll keep your mouth shut and stay the fuck out of my way. That clear?"

"Crystal."

"Good ... get in."

* * *

Tori glanced over at Gallic, who was miserable with his large body folded into the confined cockpit space. "You like it out here? Away from people?" she asked.

"There are people here."

"You know what I mean. The remoteness of life around these parts?"

He shrugged. "It's fine. I keep busy."

She snickered at that.

"What?" he said.

"You know, you've sort of become a larger-than-life cartoon character back at Colonial Police HQ. You do know that, right? People call you Galaxy Man."

He inwardly groaned but didn't outwardly respond to the taunt. "Tell me about what we're going to see."

"On Gorman?"

Gallic nodded.

Reaching back, Tori grabbed a folder off the rear seat. Inside was a stack of vid-sheets. "I'm reluctant to even show it to you. On account of what . . . well, you know—"

Taking it from her, he opened the folder, immediately feeling his chest constrict. Noting three repeating vid-images on the sheet, he tapped on the top one. Now playing, it showed a fresh crime scene video. One that, he suspected, had neither been moved, nor altered, in any way.

"Who took this?"

"A Frontier Marshal, named Phil Hough. Know him?" she asked.

"Yeah . . . I know him. Knew him back on Earth. He's all right; certainly not the worst of the lot."

"Hey . . . that's the same lot you're a part of," Tori added.

"Who called him to the scene?" Gallic asked.

"Another rancher's wife. The woman vic's best friend. She found them."

He continued to watch the top video as the Frontier Marshal, Phil Hough, walked the crime scene's inside location. It was an expansive, one-level, log cabin-style home. So far, Phil hadn't viewed the actual room where the crime took place. The video ended just as he entered the home's family room. He tapped on the second video, feeling Tori's eyes on him.

Two undefined bodies lay on the floor, although the camera quickly moved past them. Perspiration formed on Gallic's brow, and he felt the small cockpit start to close in around him. In his inner consciousness, he heard the soft rumbling of vermin on the move.

"Was Phil able to approximate TOD?"

"Not from a scientific . . . pathological . . . perspective. He doesn't have the right equipment for that sort of thing. Plus, we don't want the crime scene messed-up by anyone else— amateurs. Anyway, the mother and daughter were last seen two days ago. They'd been horseback riding and were later spotted in a field . . . a quarter mile away from the cabin."

Now the panning camera was documenting the blood splatter on the light, fawn-colored, timber walls. There was a lot of it—most likely arterial spray, Gallic surmised. Phil had been thorough, chronicling the actual murder scene. The progressive panning movement suddenly halted then zoomed in. Gallic found he was unable to swallow. He stopped breathing, staring at the scene that came next. It was the woman—attractive, in her mid-thirties. Full frame now, her face stared upward, her eyes shut. On her eyelids could be seen the heads of nails. Her eyelids had been nailed closed. One hand covered her mouth, which was tightly secured to her cheek by another nail. Her other hand had reached across the hardwood floor to another, smaller, hand—her daughter's. Grasped tightly together, they held hands. The girl, Gallic guessed, looked to be about twelve. Her eyes were open. Nailed open. The hand her mother wasn't holding was covering her mouth. Both faces had been cleaned of any residual blood from all the nailing.

"Has the ME looked at this?"

"Of course."

"The hammered-in nails . . . post mortem?"

"Yes. Every indication is they were already deceased."

Gallic's pulse rate momentarily spiked. After so many years had the murderer struck again? Although he tried to feel empathy for the victims, his only concern was catching the son of a bitch.

A new crime scene meant new evidence . . . new leads. This time he wasn't going to be locked out. Captivated by what he was viewing, he was equally aware of his personal, self-centered, reaction to it all. Yet something was wrong. Sure, things seemed to pretty much match the crime scene of his wife and daughter—but . . .

Gallic said, "I seriously doubt it's him, probably not the same guy."

Tori leveled her gaze on him. "How can you say that? It's . . . identical, or incredibly similar to . . ." letting her words drop away.

She didn't know what he knew. "The one who did this . . . atrocity . . . was certainly a sick fuck. But until I see the actual crime scene, I can't rule out a copycat." Gallic tapped on the last video, which showed deep lacerations on both vics' ankles and necks. The source of all the blood. Yes—it seemed close; everything perfectly staged. But there was one important aspect that had never made it into the official file. He needed to get to the crime scene. Only then would he know if this was the work of the *hammer-and-nails murderer*: Clair and Mandy's killer.

chapter 7

Deep Space — D-22 Star-cruiser Cockpit.

W arm, morning breezes inwardly billowed the sheer bedroom curtains. Clair wore a snug-fitting, baby-blue T-shirt and nothing else. His eyes roved down the taut soft cotton material—revealing small, erect nipples underneath it. Straddling him, her long straw-colored hair hung forward, touching his face. It was Sunday morning. This was their time. No work demands and Mandy was either asleep or watching cartoons downstairs. He gazed up at her, her bottom lip seductively captured between upper and lower front teeth. She leaned down to kiss him, when suddenly a commotion came from downstairs. Someone was knocking on the door. A dog, three houses down, began to bark. Mandy yelled something from the bottom of the stairs, and the intimate moment was gone. Clair gave up and laughed out loud. He rolled her over onto her side and tickled her, which made her softly scream.

She hated to be tickled. Trying to sound angry, she chided him to knock it off, but losing control, she laughed hysterically. He tried his best to keep ahold of her flailing arms as she wiggled to free herself. Gyrating her legs, she kicked him hard in the stomach, but upon noting his pained reaction, she regained her position atop him. "You're in so much trouble, Mister . . ."

A rapid jostling motion awakened him.

The ship was coming out of FTL. All too quickly, those treasured, heartfelt images began to fade away, returning once again to wherever one's lost hopes and dreams resided. Where they would wait—somewhere in the stillness of time and space—until again returning to torture a man's soul; to someone like Gallic, who had lost everything that mattered.

He rubbed his face in his hands and looked out the forward window.

Tori glanced his way. "Anything you can tell me about this planet before we get there?"

Gallic yawned and sat straighter in his seat. "Gorman's not a hell of a lot different from Muleshoe, at least from a geographical perspective. It has a far larger population, and there's a bit more water on this planet. A milder climate too; it's where the hoity-toity ranchers prefer to live."

"I need to ask you one more time . . . you going to be okay? The crime scene being so similar, and all?"

"You need to stop worrying about me. I'm a big boy. Look . . . I was a homicide investigator when your biggest problem was deciding what shoes best matched your dress for your high school senior prom."

"I didn't go to my senior prom," she said flatly.

Gallic wasn't surprised to hear that. "I'm actually more worried about you," he said. "The crime scene's sure to be ripe by now, with the house closed up. What's it been? Thirty hours? It'll be ghastly."

Gallic watched her face, the effort she made not to show any concern. No matter what Danbury had conveyed to him, about Tori being one of his best, was pure bullshit. You don't send out your best investigator to remote territories. Gallic pictured a handful of Danbury's inspectors standing around in the D-22 break room, kibitzing and laughing about Tori's big assignment to the remote territories. He suspected that she, although somewhat more seasoned now, was still a walking-talking cluster-fuck.

He asked, "Can you tell me more about the woman vic . . . Catherine?"

"It was in the file I showed you. Instead of sleeping, maybe you should have been reading."

"I read the entire file. I'm talking about her personal life. Who were her friends and what did she do with her time? Where did she typically go during the day? What's the situation with her husband? Were they solid . . . or having marital problems?"

Annoyance crossed her face. "The husband's not a suspect. Was away on business. He's on his way back from Earth, as we speak."

"Come on! The husband is always a concern. Unless he's dead . . . you investigate that angle first. Eight times out of ten, the killer has a personal relationship with the vic. You do know that . . . right?" Gallic asked.

"Of course, I know that. But he wasn't anywhere near here . . . and we're fairly certain this is the work of that same hammer-and-nails killer."

Gallic gave a half smile. "That's a pretty strong assumption, since you haven't visited the crime scene yet. Let's hold off speculating on that until we know more."

Tori's cheeks flushed, her mouth narrowing to a thin mean line.

"Who will be there . . . to open the house?" he asked.

"Phil Hough and Linda Cugan. She's one of the neighbor's and was the vic's best friend. She found the bodies."

Cugan? He'd read her name in the file. He wondered if having the same last name as Larz Cugan was a coincidence. "What do you know about Linda?"

"I know enough that she's not a suspect!"

"Is she married?"

Tori, bringing the star-cruiser into high orbit around the mud-colored planet, answered, "Yes, she has a daughter, Juaquin. Twelve, she's the same age as the dead girl, Tami. Also, an older son—Larz—who's in his mid-twenties."

Quite a wide age-spread between the siblings, Gallic thought.

* * *

Quickly descending out from blue skies several thousand feet up, Gallic took in the landscape below. The word *picturesque* came to mind. Green pastureland, like velvet, reached out to the far horizon. Occasional shimmering ponds, and several sprawling, timber ranch-style homes—each with an adjoining stable—shared white, split-rail fences and large, red, white, or timber-colored, barns. A cluster of white moved below and then another—a herd of several hundred sheep. Three hovering drones herded them toward a group of men on horseback. Ranch hands, Gallic figured.

As Tori maneuvered the cruiser toward one of the further-off ranches, she said, "So here live Gorman's super-rich."

Gallic saw the unmistakable profile of Phil Hough's ship: A U.S. made *Gallivanter-Series 3* transport truck. Fairly large, about half the size of the *Hound*, his vessel was also a decade newer. Four smaller vehicles were parked in front of the home. Two were spacecraft, while the other two looked to be personal hovercrafts—*expensive*—and probably from neighboring ranches. He saw a handful of people milling around the front of the house.

Tori engaged the landing thrusters and brought the cruiser down near Phil's *Gallivanter*. She queried Gallic, "Help me with the equipment?"

"Sure."

Reaching across him, Tori put an open palm on Gallic's chest—pressing him backwards into his seat. "And remember . . . you're an observer here. Don't even think about fouling up my crime scene. Got it?"

"Got it," Gallic said, keeping his outer demeanor neutral. Within he felt anything but, needing to remind himself that it wasn't Clair and Mandy inside the house. Feeling intense uneasiness, which could easily turn to paralysis, it took all his willpower to clear his mind. *You need to detach . . . disconnect.*

Tori slapped a button on the dash and both hatch doors released, opening at the same time. Gallic, after climbing out, stood and stretched and rolled his shoulders. He joined Tori at the back of the cruiser, where she'd opened a cargo hold. She handed Gallic a satchel—marked Processing Kit—then handed him a toaster-sized metal box, which had a cone-shaped *sniffer* on one end. Gallic had used similar FDS units—*Field DNA Samplers*—more times than he could count. Gone were the days of taking fingerprints; of swabbing and scraping and collecting. The FDS unit did all that, and with far more accuracy, along with specific, real-time 3D relational crime scene correlation down to the micron-level. The data collected by the FDS unit would enable the forensic geeks, back at D-22, to recreate a simulated—virtual—crime scene. From the amounts and locations of organic matter, DNA would be determined. With such sophisticated equipment, getting away with murder in the twenty-second-century was highly unlikely. But not impossible. Especially out here—almost ten light years distance from Earth.

Straps over both shoulders, Tori carried three satchels as the two headed for the house. The first one to greet them was Phil Hough. Gallic remembered Phil, who had about ten years on him and looked it. Wearing a paisley, snap-down western shirt, dappled with an assortment of food stains, along with scuffed cowboy boots, he wore his graying hair long and slicked back.

Two, or three, days' growth of a grisly beard completed his unkempt demeanor. Someone, *obviously*, who didn't give *two bits* what others thought of his appearance. Gallic instinctively liked the man and accepted his outstretched hand. His firm handshake, along with steady eye contact, reminded Gallic that here was a man he knew he could trust.

"Hey, Phil . . . how's it hanging these days?"

"A bit to the left . . . mostly," Phil answered with a smile. "Been a while, huh? You doing good?"

"I'm all right," Gallic said.

Phil went to shake Tori's hand, but they were still full. "I'm Phil Hough . . . and don't believe a word this guy's told you about me. Unless it was something good."

Tori returned a perfunctory smile, moving toward the house.

Gallic's attention was then drawn elsewhere. He could see one of the pristine vehicles parked on the property's front driveway was a brand new *Hausenbach L35T*. If he wasn't mistaken, the ship was the same *5T* he'd recently dropped off with Polly Gant, at Imperial Bail Bonds & Repos.

"What the hell's he doing here?" Larz Cugan asked, stepping out of the harsh, mid-day shadows, running along the side of the house. Minus the white jacket and ascot, he was wearing the same clothes he'd worn yesterday. The young man must have gotten a ride—hightailed it to Rawlins City, paid his delinquent billings, then returned on the *5T* to Gorman, arriving ahead of them. Gallic knew the *5T* was one fast vehicle . . . but that was impressive! Johnnie, minus Donnie, was with him, wearing a tucked-in, red flannel shirt. His blue jeans, worn ridiculously high, covered his protruding belly.

Larz took a final drag on a cigarette butt then flicked it away. With Johnnie in tow, he quickly approached Gallic—his eyes narrow and full of malice.

Phil said, "Well, I see you two know each other. Let me make some introductions. This is Linda Cugan, the vic's ... um ... sorry ... Mrs. Bower's neighbor and close friend. She was the one who discovered the bodies."

Linda Cugan looked to be in her early forties, though possibly older. She was nicely put together, wearing both designer jeans and hairstyle, and with makeup done just so. Her exposed tanned arms were wrapped about her, and she looked like she'd rather be anywhere than here. She glanced toward the house and shuddered.

"You the one who took my boy's *5T*?" she asked.

"That, I did, Ma'am," Gallic said.

She didn't comment to that. Head down, she maintained the same sour expression then asked, "Can we just get this over with? I need to get back home."

Tori came over to them after dropping her bags at the front porch. "Mrs. Cugan ... I'm Sergeant Tori. An Inspector for the Colonial Police—Space District 22. I'll be the one speaking with you today." Tori gave Gallic a dismissive glance. "First of all, I'd like to say how sorry I am for your loss."

Linda widened her eyes and exhaled, conveying she didn't want to hear it.

Tori made a series of taps on her ComsBand, then asked, "I'll be recording both questions and answers, so there's an official record. Is that all right?"

Linda Cugan shrugged her thin shoulders. "There's not much to tell. I walked in . . . I found them dead. I screamed . . . and got the hell out of there."

"Which door did you enter through?"

"The front. It was unlocked."

Gallic asked, "Is that common . . . for you to enter without knocking?" He ignored Tori's annoyed expression.

"We never knock. Catherine and I . . . and the kids . . . are like family. Closer than family."

Larz and Johnnie were now at Linda's side. Once close together, it was easy to see they were mother and son. Gallic looked off to the horizon and asked, "Where's your home in relation to this property?"

Larz answered for her: "It's right over there, butt-wipe. We're next-door neighbors."

"Don't be rude, Larz . . . I won't stand for it," Linda scolded.

Gallic suspected the distant ranch was hers—twice, maybe thrice, the size of this one. He then suggested, "What do you say we talk to you later, Mrs. Cugan. Being here must be uncomfortable for you. Would it be all right if we drop by, say in an hour or two?"

Tori looked as if she were about to blow a gasket. Giving a *be patient* expression at her, he turned back to Linda.

"Yes ... that would be much better." For the first time, she looked up at him and held his gaze for a second—thanking him with her eyes.

As she turned and walked away, she said over her shoulder, "Larz ... take me home."

Larz flipped Gallic the bird before hurrying after his mother. Johnnie, staying still, said, "I'm not going to forget what you did to Donnie. You and I have unfinished business."

"Whatever. But you first might want to ask Donnie how that worked out for him," Gallic said.

Like Larz, Johnnie too flipped him the bird then waddled off after them.

Phil looked confused. "I see you still have a good way with people, Gallic."

Tori, waiting for the other three to be out of earshot, exclaimed, "Damn it! That was exactly what I told you not to do. I wanted to question her here ... at the scene."

"No, you don't! You saw her. All hunched over ... wound up tighter than a spring. She'd be useless here. No ... let her go home. Have a Manhattan ... maybe two. Talking to her at her home, she'll be far less guarded ... far more revealing. And one other thing...."

Annoyed, she shook her head. "And what's that?"

"We need to take a good look inside her house. Can you think of a better way to do that?"

Tori pursed her lips for a second then said, "No, I guess not."

"Good. What say we go work the crime scene now?"

chapter 8

Frontier Planet, Gorman — Heritage Plains Township.

Just keep it together... a mantra Gallic kept on constant replay.

He felt the surrounding chill. "You cranked up the AC in here?" Gallic asked.

"Oh yeah ... all the way up," Phil said.

"Good." Gallic helped Tori move the crime scene satchels in from the outside porch. He put down the equipment and closed the doors. Gallic began setting his own ComsBand to record video and sound. The record feature on a ComsBand was nothing like a typical camera. Full-spectrum micro sensors reached out to gather an immense amount of three-dimensional—relational—information. Later, playing back the recording would allow him to hear and view the events that transpired from a variety of viewing perspectives.

"We don't both need to do that," Tori said as she did the same thing on her own ComsBand.

Gallic ignored her. He didn't like relying on someone else—hoping they'd be as thorough as he would be.

Phil reached down for the FDS unit and Tori slapped his hand away, as if he was a petulant child. Tori said, "Hands off things you don't understand. And stay behind me. This is a crime scene ... one that has already been unduly compromised." She glanced at Phil with annoyance before she reached down for her FDS unit. She powered it on and—with the *sniffer* pointed forward—she headed off deeper into the house. Five paces down the hallway the smell hit them hard—hit them like a city bus. Tori reached for her mask and covered it with an open palm. Phil looked back over his shoulder and Gallic realized, behind his mask, he was smiling.

Decomposing human remains have a unique smell. Probably from a combination of things—like the human diet, which plays a big part. Humans consume processed foods that metabolize quickly into noxious gasses—and humans ingest all kinds of stinky spices that only exacerbate the issue. Not a smell one really gets used to, it was a smell one learns to deal with. More like compartmentalizing. One needs to stash away, not think about the implications of what was smelled. Tori's head was lowering—as if she was trying to dodge the waft of stale air ahead of her. *She hasn't learned to compartmentalize—not yet anyway*, Gallic thought. Up ahead, he heard her reflexively gag several times in succession.

They followed the same route through the expansive house that Gallic had viewed earlier on Phil's video. The hallway was wide, lined on opposite walls with a mishmash of framed family photos. He took in all the smiling faces. Some were posed—stiff backed school-age children of another time, having their yearly portraits taken. And there were portraits of an elderly husband and wife couple. Nestled between his two arms, she was wearing a dress: he, a suit and tie. The photograph looked weathered—most of the color gone now. Most of the photos were of Tami: Tami as an infant, wearing a pink onesie. Tami riding on the shoulders of her father. Tami wearing shorts and a bright-orange shirt, playing some kind of sport—maybe soccer. Tami, arm in arm, with another, less attractive, girl of about the same age. And there were plenty of pictures of the mother, Catherine and the father, Donald. But none of them together in the same photograph. Gallic slowed when he noticed there was an open space between photographs. The paint was a shade lighter here within a frame-sized rectangular shape—that of the surrounding wall.

They passed by open hallway doors. Peering in each, he noted a powder room, guest room, and a cluttered-looking office. Gallic figured the girl's room and the master bedroom must be on the other wing of the house. Each would have to be swept.

Eventually they reached the main room—the great room. Where much of the house was a combination of drywall walls and timber walls, this room was all stacked timber logs. Above, giant roughly hewn beams crisscrossed and supported an angled

A-frame ceiling some forty feet high. They'd entered from the hallway at the middle of the room. To the left was a large chef's kitchen with an island you could land the *Hound* on, and to the right was a big family room with overstuffed couches and matching chairs. A broad river rock fireplace that reached up to the ceiling filled the wall to the right.

Gallic stood and took it all in. Mentally categorizing his impressions, taking in dozens of details at once—details that he'd typically stack up against the hundreds of other crime scenes he'd processed over the years. But right now, he was only comparing this crime scene to one other.

The timber walls directly in front of him looked to be splashed with tar. It looked as if someone had used a bucket and sloshed copious amounts of blood—making a mountain rage effect with high peaks and low valleys. Flies were everywhere. The buzzing was constant.

He let his eyes lower to the furniture before him. It had been rearranged to make room for the vics in the middle of the floor. Playing cards were strewn about, some on the floor, some abandoned atop the sofa. Splatters of blood dotted the two of spades.

Tori was already using her FDS unit. Making broad sweeping motions with the sniffer end. She'd started in the kitchen and was methodically cataloging, high and low, every square inch of the room. The unit's internal software was smart enough to reconstruct the surroundings. Building an internal, virtual model, of everything. Watching her, she was being overly careful—like over-steering when learning to ride a bike or a hovercraft—but Gallic wasn't here to teach her how to use the damn thing.

Phil was standing off to the right and was leaning against the wall with his hands crossed over his chest. Smirking, he watched her slow progression. Gallic figured Phil was thinking the same thing he was ... she was avoiding moving into the main room.

Gallic lowered down to his haunches and observed the scene from that level. Six feet in front of him, the mother and child's feet were facing toward him. Both were bare foot. The two bodies were fully clothed—*just as Clair and Mandy's had been*. Blood was everywhere, had saturated their jeans and T-shirts. But not their faces, which had been meticulously cleaned. The same had been done to his wife and daughter's faces. Gallic wondered what the killer had used to do that. He scanned the floor and didn't see anything like a towel or rag. *He must have taken it with him.*

Tori had finished up in the kitchen and was now heading into the family room. She saw the bodies lying in front of Gallic. Startled, she dropped the FDS unit and it landed with a loud clunk—she pulled her mask up with one hand, retched once, twice, and—uncontrollably—threw up onto the crime scene. Specifically, onto the side of the young girl. The FDS unit continued to roll around on the hardwood floor. Eyes wide, Tori looked at what she had done. A whimpering sound emanated from her gaping mouth. She ran back to the kitchen and leaned over the sink. She continued to blow chunks. She turned on the faucet—which helped camouflage some of the retching sounds.

Phil said, "She's obviously in way-the-fuck-over-her head here, dollars to donuts; the kid's never processed a violent murder scene before."

"I don't know. But she's definitely compromised the scene. Vomit on the bodies . . . vomit mist in the air . . . like a circling cloud . . . it's already spreading her DNA all over the place. Phil . . . get her outside. She needs fresh air. I'll finish up in here."

He waited while Phil ushered her out the way they had come in. No protest. No arguing that this was her crime scene. Both hands over her mouth, she ran out of there as if her pants were on fire.

Gallic got to his feet and moved to the other side of the bodies. He picked up the

FDS unit, checked to make sure it was still operational, and resumed the broad sweeping motions.

It took him twenty minutes to completely catalogue both rooms with the FDS unit. Next, he began sweeping the furniture—couches and chairs. Backs, sides, tops. Then the- pushed-out-of-the-way, oversized coffee table. Then the hardwood flooring all around the bodies. Hundreds of disturbed—angry—flies swarmed upward as Gallic waived the air around his face. Fortunately, the FDS unit was proficient at discriminating between insectile and human DNA.

He'd avoided looking at the faces of the two victims. Gazing now down at Catherine's and Tami's bloated and discolored faces, he waited. Waited for the tumble and rumble of fast approaching vermin. For the slithering snakes to come crashing into his consciousness like a hurricane blasting through a grass hut—like a freight train crashing through a house. But all was quiet. All was calm.

Still holding the FDS unit, he waived the sniffer over both of them—starting at the top of their heads and progressing over their bodies and ending up at the soles of their feet.

He moved back to their upper torsos and leaned in close. He leaned over—within inches of Catherine Bower's face. This close, he now could see the postmortem frothing that occurs from a body's natural orifices—both nostrils and mouth exhibited this. He looked at the nail head protruding up a quarter of an inch above her right eyelid. Driven through the lid and into the pupil behind. He tilted his head and squinted his eyes. The nail head was the right size: definitely a two-penny nail. Since the murder of his wife and child, Gallic had become an expert on nails. The manufacturing—the various types and sizes. The various kinds of metal used. From his research, the whole *strange* measuring of nails seemed to have started as early as the fifteenth century. The 'd' measurement symbol came from Latin *denarius*. That evolved to the French *denier* and is also the symbol for the monetary penny today. A 2d nail is one-inch long. Each 1d increase is one-fourth inch increase in length up to 10d followed by a 12d, which is three and one-fourth inches long.

The nail used here was what is considered a 2d *box nail*. Not used as often as a common nail. A common nail is slightly tapered just below on the underside of the nail head. This nail was thinner and not tapered at all—and it was made of steel. This was definitely a *box nail*. Gallic sat up and considered the implications. It was the exact size, type, and material of nail as the ones used by the murderer of his wife and daughter. *It could be a coincidence.*

Flies were becoming too friendly, and he swatted them away from his own face. Phil reentered the room.

"What are we looking at, here?" he asked.

Gallic looked at the two bodies. He wasn't sure how much Phil knew about crime scene forensics. "As you may or may not know, there's basically five stages of decomposition. Fresh, bloat, active and advanced decay; and finally, dry remains. Coupled with that . . . there are two stages of chemical decomposition . . . autolysis and putrefaction."

Gallic repositioned himself lower on the woman's body. He took her left foot in his hand and manipulated the ankle in a circular motion. He repeated with the right foot. Holding the leg higher up, at the thigh, he raised the leg and watched how easily the knee bent. He let go of the leg and moved back up to her upper torso. Gently, he moved the head from side to side. It moved easily.

"Yeah . . . we're way past the rigor-stage . . . and well into bloat. Normally I'd want to get a temperature of the liver. But I'm already pushing things . . . an observer here. In reality, based on what I see, the state of decom of the corpse is consistent with the eye-witness last seeing them riding horses in the pasture on Thursday afternoon. The timetable works that they were killed a few hours later . . . that night . . . it coincides with what I'm seeing. There again . . . I'm no ME.

Phil, the lines on his forehead bunched together, said, "This tied to what happened to . . . you . . . your family?"

"Could be. Help me turn her over?"

He didn't answer but moved closer and, being careful to avoid the surrounding pools of blood and vomit, Phil lowered down to his haunches.

"Let's bring her right shoulder up and over—away from her daughter, Gallic said. He gave Phil a nod, and together they carefully lifted her over onto her stomach. Her back was relatively free of blood. He stood and used the FDS unit— again waving the sniffer up and down from head to toe. Setting it aside, and with one hand, he lifted the woman's hair away from the back of her neck. Steadying himself, Gallic held his breath—not sure if he wanted to see what might be hidden there. What might be carved into the flesh—there at the napes of both their necks. It was something that had purposely never been made public—and never entered into the official case file. Here, the hair was matted with blood, and he needed to use his thumb to wipe away the gooey residue. And there it was. The killer had most likely used the sharp point of a nail.

TCW

The speculation had been that the initials were most likely that of the murderer himself. That this was some kind of branding of his victims. Three and a half years earlier, criminal databases had been scoured for perps with the first, middle, and last names beginning with the letters T, C, and W. But Gallic suspected they wouldn't lead them anywhere. He also suspected the letters were not the initials of a person. He thought they stood for something else. Just as RM stood for the Royal Marines—the three initials perhaps designated an organization. Gallic had served in the Royal Marines for four years. He leaned back up straight. The implications were tremendous. This was, in fact, the work of the same killer. Adrenaline was coursing through his veins. He felt a building sense of both trepidation and excitement.

chapter 9

Frontier Planet, Gorman — Heritage
Plains Township.

They'd used the FDS unit in all of the other rooms in the
house. In total, another forty minutes had passed by the time
Gallic and Phil emerged from the front of the house. They were
carrying the shorter of the two chryo, temperature-controlled
body bags between them. Gallic saw Tori sitting half-in and
half-out of the passenger seat of her cruiser. Elbows on knees,
her head was supported in her hands. Evidently, by the wet
stain on the concrete at her feet, she hadn't fully recovered—
she'd been sick again.

Gallic yelled over, "Let's get the back hatch of that cruiser
opened up."

She reached inside and a moment later the back of the craft
lifted up, revealing a large, empty cargo hold.

Gallic and Phil hefted the remains inside and together returned into the house. When they returned again, they had the larger chryo body bag with Catherine's remains inside. They placed it right next to the smaller one within the hold. He secured them both down with available straps.

"I'll grab the equipment," Phil said and headed for the front door, one more time.

Gallic approached Tori from around the side of the cruiser. He lowered down to her level but didn't say anything.

She stared at the mess on the ground. "I'm so fucked," she said.

"And why is that?"

She turned her head just enough that one eye peeked out through a tangle of hair. "A novice investigator that can't stand the sight of blood ... not to mention that god-awful smell ..." she cut her words short, looking like she might be sick again. "I'm going to be fired."

"I don't see it that way, Tori. In fact, I imagine you'll get a commendation."

She lifted herself up and let out a stale breath. "What are you talking about?"

"Come on ... no one needs to know about the puking. Happens to everyone in the beginning," he lied. "What I can tell you is the perp was no copycat."

"Oh really ... you're that sure of yourself."

Gallic nodded and proceeded to tell her about the carved letters on the napes of the vic's necks and how that information had not been made public, or even provided in the official case file. Only a handful of people at D-22 knew about it—including Chief Superintendent Bernard Danbury. There'd been too many department leaks, so holding back that kind of information was not uncommon. "So, it's him ... it's the same one who killed Clair and Mandy." But even as Gallic spoke those words, he was trying to figure out how that could be possible after all this time.

"I'm sorry I've been such a bitch to you," she said. "I'm surprised you're holding it together. This is a big revelation ... that the murderer is still out there ... somewhere. How do you process something like that?" she asked.

Gallic shrugged. "I mentally shelve it. I keep busy."

"That doesn't sound healthy."

"It's how I survive."

She nodded then suddenly was distracted by the approach of something gargantuan heading in their direction. "Isn't that your ship ... the infamous *Hound*?"

"Yeah ... AI's at the controls. I called for her soon after we arrived."

"You mean when I started hurling my breakfast ... right?"

Gallic said, "Look, I want you to head back to D-22. You have the bodies ... all the evidence picked up by the FDS unit, plus I'm sending you the data from my own ComsBand. Additionally, you'll see a full audio report I made inside ... all of my initial findings. I want all of that being worked on as soon as possible," Gallic said.

"I still haven't gone through all the rooms ... collected physical evidence ... grabbed their personal AI devices. And what about the neighbor? You wanted to interview her. It should be me that does that."

"Not necessary. I'll speak to her and forward the recording on to you."

"It's not your job . . . I feel terrible."

"Just assure me, that as far as Superintendent Danbury will know, I was simply an observer here."

"Deal. I'll be quiet as a church mouse."

"I better get going . . . give that monstrosity of yours a place to land." She stood and walked to the back of the cruiser. She stared at the two matte-black body bags. "It's so sad. It makes me want to cry . . ." She reached in and tapped something within the hold, and the hatch began to close. "I'll be back here tomorrow to finish." She motioned toward the house. "Obviously, this is where the trail begins . . . again. I'm thinking . . . maybe we can work together? Unofficially . . . of course. I promise not to be . . . you know, like how I was."

"Sure. I'd like that," he said. "Oh . . . one more thing, can you push for them to start cutting on the two vics right away? And cue me in on the ME's autopsy findings?"

"I can try," she said.

Gallic was aware she wanted to say something else. He waited.

"Do you think . . ." she hesitated.

"What?"

"That this is the start of more murders? I mean, it's strange the guy would commit a copycat murder after so long . . . what has it been . . . three and a half years? *Why would he stop now?*"

The same questions had been nagging at Gallic as well. Officially, this was now a serial murder case. And she was right to ask, why would he stop now? Perhaps the more important question would be, *when* will he strike again?

chapter 10

Frontier Planet, Gorman — Heritage Plains Township.

Gallic watched as Silvia Tori piloted her beat-to-shit D-22 star-cruiser off the concrete drive—hesitate there twenty feet in the air for a few moments—and then gunned the propulsion system. He watched her until she gently banked and gained altitude as she went. Soon she was a mere dot on the distant horizon—and then she was gone.

Phil joined Gallic at his side. Both were watching the *Hound* descend a hundred yards away, out in the pasture where there was enough room for her. Landing struts locked into place just prior to the massive *Hewley-Jawbone* carrier being eased down onto solid ground.

"That's quite a ship."

Gallic glanced over to Phil.

Phil said, "I must say . . . I'm a bit envious."

"Can you hang out here for a while?" Gallic gestured toward the distant ranch.

"Interview the woman? Sure . . . wouldn't miss it."

* * *

The neighbor's ranch was about a half a mile walk. On the way, Phil spoke about his life living here in the territories. He didn't live here on Gorman, beyond his pay grade. Nor did he live back on Muleshoe. He lived on Rawhide, the farthest in the chain of agricultural-based worlds within the territories. Gallic thought about that. About having a house . . . a home. What the implications were of that. Perhaps a feeling of belonging somewhere, or to someone. Gallic wasn't sure if Phil was married or had someone special in his life. He didn't really care enough to ask. He thought about his own situation. That after so many years now of living on the *Hound*—having the freedom to pick up stakes and leave any place at any time—he had no desire for a different kind of life. Not without the people that had made that kind of life possible.

They'd reached the neighbor's barn. Like the house in the distance, it was freshly painted white. The contrast between all the white and the surrounding emerald green pastures was dazzling.

"Quite a barn . . . you could put my damn house in there five times over," Phil said.

Not mine, Gallic thought, reflecting on the size of the *Hound*.

They were making their way around the back of the barn. Phil stepped around the corner first. There was a *thump* sound and Phil's body flew by in front of him. He hit the ground with arms and legs askew. Gallic had just enough time to hold back and step sideways. A man holding a shovel appeared. He was gripping the end of a four-foot-long wood handle—batter-up, style. The business end of the metal spade was up in the air above his right shoulder. He was ready to swing again. Two more men appeared behind him. Ranch hands. They were dressed in jeans and T-shirts. Two had beards. One was clean-shaven. All wore cowboy hats. And all of them were young and big and most likely in the best shapes of their lives. But there was a difference between being in good shape from activities such as lifting hay bales or pile driving fence posts, or whatever ranch hands do. They had a different kind of muscle memory than Gallic had. A muscle memory that was ineffective when going up against someone that had spent years as a Royal Marine—the years prior to becoming a policeman and the eventual rise to become DCI for the Colonial Police—Space District 22. As a marine, he'd learned how to stay alive. And how to end the lives of those trying to take his away from him.

Gallic glanced at Phil's inert body. There was a crimson colored welt in the middle of his forehead. Phil wasn't moving.

"We're the welcoming party," the ranch hand with the shovel said.

The two others fanned out making a semicircle around him. Gallic stood with his arms loosely held at his sides. The three of them were smiling and looked pleased with themselves. Gallic, looking bored, continued to stare at the man with the shovel.

"You know ... when planning something like this. You really need to think things all the way through."

The one with the shovel adjusted his grip and raised the shovel higher. "Don't worry ... not a lot of thinking will be necessary for what's planned for you."

"Well, maybe if you're a group of ten-year-old bullies on a school yard. Sure, that's fine ... you just go for it ... go for the new kid or the awkward kid without any friends ... it's a free for all. But you're not ten-year-old's ... are you? You have somewhat, although minimally, matured brains. The planning becomes more of an issue. Like what precautions should be made before going up against an unknown quantity."

"Precautions?" He laughed. "That's not how we roll, jerkoff. That's not how this is going to go down."

Gallic continued, "Well, let me give you an example. A hypothetical one ... Okay? ... one you, as the apparent leader here, should have considered. What happens when I take that shovel away from you? Use it on you in a way that will haunt you for the rest of your worthless life. Will cause you embarrassment ... and humiliation ... because you'll know what others will be thinking about when they see you gimping along at the side of the street. They'll be picturing how you had endured having the long end of a spade handle shoved so far up your ass. Farther than anyone would have ever imagined possible. And you need to consider what your friends here will do. Will they stay and fight with you? Or will they cut their losses—run and thank their lucky stars above that they didn't have to experience the same unpleasant effects of that hardwood, probably hickory or maybe ash.

The confident smiles wavered. Eyes were shifting in their sockets.

"You have a big fucking mouth. You like to talk too much—"

Caught mid-sentence, it wasn't the shovel baring guy that Gallic came for first. It was the closest one who was mouthing off—directly to his left. Gallic lead with a left jab that caught him with a stinging blow to the chin, immediately followed by a straight on punch to the face. He went down fast—like he fell through an open trap door.

Gallic spun away, but not quick enough to avoid the already swinging spade coming from behind. It missed his head, but caught him, a slicing blow, on the upper back. The pain was immediate and intense—as the sharp edge of the tool ripped through his shirt and the flesh beneath. He wind milled his straight arm around and captured the handle before it could be pulled away. Gallic grasped it and jerked it out of the hands of the attacker. Out of the corner of his eye, he saw one of the other ranch hands take off. Gallic twirled the handle around and readied himself to take down the lone standing ranch hand. The lone man took a hesitant step backward. He eyed the shovel. He looked at the long handle. Gallic was fairly certain he was dreading what was coming next.

A nearby shotgun blast stopped everyone in his tracks.

"Knock it off . . . all of you!" It was the girl with the bob-bling earrings. Only now she was on horseback and pointing a bolt-action Winchester rifle at Gallic's head. "Jordan . . . get your idiot friends and pray you still have a job tomorrow."

Jordan did as he was told. The other handyman, lying on the ground, was a little slow to get up, but eventually he rose to his feet. They headed off and disappeared around the side of the barn. Gallic heard the sound of two nearby hovercrafts start up then speed away.

Gallic went down to Phil's side. He hadn't moved since he'd been hit. He put two fingers to his neck and waited to feel a pulse. It was there. Strong and steady. Phil's eyes fluttered open.

"What the hell . . . happened . . . I was hit . . ."

"With a shovel," Gallic said, finishing his sentence.

Phil came up on his elbows and winced. Gallic helped him sit all the way up. Phil touched his forehead. "Christ! Does it look as bad as it feels?"

"Fraid so," Gallic said. Careful . . . undoubtedly you have one hell of a concussion." He took one of Phil's arms and helped him stand. Phil waivered there. They both looked at the girl sitting atop the horse. Gallic watched as she lowered the barrel and dropped the weapon into a leather scabbard at the side of the saddle—which ran parallel to her lower leg.

Gallic said, "I'm going to need your help . . . get Phil here over to my ship where he can lay down."

She seemed to mull that over for a few moments before she dismounted, loosely tied the reins around a nearby fence rail, and hurried over. She took one of Phil's arms and placed it over her shoulder while Gallic, wincing, repositioned the other arm.

* * *

Climbing up the *Hounds'* extended underbelly stairs, while holding a nearly comatose body—even with there being two people—was challenging. At the top of the stairs, the girl said. "You've lost a lot of blood."

"I'm fine." They moved into the *Hound's* airlock and right through to the hatch on the other side. "In here . . . we'll take the lift."

She eyed the cramped space. "We won't all fit in there."

"Sure we will . . . just huddle in."

She had to press her body in closer to both Phil and Gallic for the open metal cage door to slide down and latch. So close to her, he could smell her shampoo. Like strawberries. Gallic reached over and hit the Level 2 button. The motor squealed to life—the lift began to rise—cables and pulleys and other mechanisms strained under the added weight.

She glanced up at Gallic. "Am I going to die in your old elevator?"

"Probably not."

"So . . . my name's Lane . . . by the way."

Gallic nodded. "Did you have anything to do with that?"

"With what?"

"That ambush by the three ranch hands."

"God, no. That, most likely, was the work of Larz or Johnnie . . . or maybe both of them, for repossessing his *5T*. The ranches around here often share the help. I'll deal with it."

"They could have killed Phil . . . hitting him like that."

The lift slowed then grinded to a stop. Gallic slid up the gate and with Lane's help half-carried, half-dragged Phil out into the loft area.

"Over here. We can put him on the couch."

They got Phil situated, lying flat on his back. His eyes were open but unfocused. Gallic reached over, pulled the Navaho blanket from the back of the couch, and spread it over Phil. "Try to stay awake if you can, Phil. For a while anyway."

Phil mumbled something unintelligible.

Lane glanced around the *Hound's* large, open loft-like space. Her eyes settled on a long bookcase, set up against a far bulkhead within the study section. Gallic watched as she approached the deck-to-ceiling shelves, packed tight with his hardback books. Running long tapered fingers across the book spines, she walked from one end of the bookcase to the other. "Boy . . . someone's really into American history . . . late nineteenth century. I'd say . . . the old west." Taking a half-step back, she studied a lower shelf. "Most of these books deal with criminals of certain eras," she said.

For some unknown reason, Gallic felt a little embarrassed. Not used to anyone staring so closely at his things. Certainly, no one before had ever taken anything more than a passing interest in his books. Books blatantly exposing—to anyone who took the time to look—his hidden passion for the American crime figures.

"So, who's this Boles character? Quite a few books are dedicated to him."

Actually, four books are dedicated to him, Gallic silently mused, saying nothing.

Lane pulled one of the books free from the shelf and then held it up. "Mind?"

Gallic shrugged, as if her request was inconsequential to him, though it was anything but.

Flipping through the pages, Lane paused every so often to examine a photograph or read some arbitrary passage of text. She looked up and smiled—almost conspiratorially. "You admire this . . . what is he, a thief?"

"Not so sure *admire* is the best way to put it," he said.

"Who was he?"

Gallic, joining her at the bookcase, said, "Well . . . if you really want to know, he was a gentleman criminal. Born in England, his real name was Charles Earl Boles. Better known later as Black Bart."

"So, what makes him so interesting?" Lane asked, as she flipped to an illustrated page depicting a stagecoach being held up by a lone robber. She turned the book around toward him, raising a brow.

"Got financially screwed-over in some financial dealings in Northern California . . . around the gold-rush time period, late 1840's. He had a particular hard-on for Wells Fargo Bank."

"I've heard of them."

"What made Boles, or Black Bart, so interesting was the simple fact he was a gentleman robber. Although he carried a rifle, he never used it. He was courteous and humorous. Likeable. Also known to leave poems behind in the stage-coaches' emptied-out strongboxes."

"Really? Hey, I like this guy. And was there a girlfriend in the picture?"

"Had a wife and a couple of kids. Didn't see them much, though. As a young man, he joined the army—was a Union soldier in the Civil War. After he was injured in the Battle of Vicksburg, he returned home to Illinois. But soon thereafter, he got the itch to head west . . . follow the gold rush craze sweeping the country. Unfortunately, he never saw his wife or sons again."

"Typical male . . . so what happened to him? Wait . . . don't tell me . . . it'll only depress me. Like what happened to Butch Cassidy and the Sundance kid . . ." Closing the book, she slid it back into the empty waiting gap on the shelf.

"He got caught . . . eventually . . . did a few years in jail, but he got out. Some say he then picked up where he left off . . ."

Lane's fingers rested on the book's spine a moment, seeming to appreciate Gallic's further explanation. "Black Bart . . . gentleman robber, poet, and survivor. I can see why you've taken an interest in him." She looked at the rows and rows of books then at Gallic. "Well . . . you should, um . . . take a hot shower. Cleanse out that open wound on your back. I can help bandage, dress it when you get out . . . if you want."

chapter 11

Frontier Planet, Gorman — Heritage Plains Township.

Escaping steam swirled as Gallic, a towel wrapped around his waist, emerged from the shower. He was surprised to see Lane, sitting on the edge of his bed.

Smiling, she held up a zippered red plastic case. "Found your med kit in the kitchen, or should I say in the *mess*, since this is a ship?" Patting the spot next to her on the bed, she said, "Sit. Let's get your wound sutured and dressed."

"Phil?"

"Asleep."

Gallic sat on the bed then turned so that his broad back was facing her.

"Wow! That's even worse than I thought. Maybe I'm not the best person to do this . . . you probably need a real doctor."

"You'll do just fine. Everything you need is in that kit." Gallic felt the tip of a cool finger outline the wounded area, then move on to touch several other, older wounds. "You're either ridiculously accident-prone, or you've seen your fair share of combat . . . action."

Gallic didn't respond to that, saying, "There should be suture gel in there."

"I see it. I'm going to disinfect the area first. This might sting."

It did. A lot! He drew in a quick breath through tightly clenched teeth.

"Told you so," she said. Next came the suture gel. Using one of the special application sponges, which came with the gel, she dabbed it on. Almost immediately, the skin surrounding the open wound began to constrict—closing in on itself. He gave it a minute to let the stuff do what it was designed to do. As he prepared to stand up, she said,

"Hold on! The wound needs a bandage . . . suture gel only goes so far."

Gallic sat back down and waited as she placed a self-adhering bandage over the injured area. Then, giving his back a pat, she said, "That should do it."

Gallic re-shifted his position around so he could better see her. "Thanks."

"Don't mention it."

He was taken aback by how lovely she was—sitting there on his bed putting the various items back into the med kit. An awkward silence prevailed until he said, "So you live here . . . on Gorman?"

"Among other places. But yeah, this is where I grew up . . . where my family is."

"You live with your parents?" Gallic asked.

"Come on, I'm twenty-six, Gallic. Went four years to college . . . Yale . . . lived a spell in France, *mon ami*, and spent some time knocking around the Frontier worlds."

Gallic slowly nodded, taking in the information.

"As for my mother . . . she died when I was young. My dad's usually away on business. Truth is, we don't speak much. Other than the obligatory hi and goodbye. The house here is usually empty."

"Siblings?"

"I have a brother, Scott. He prefers to live on Earth."

"So, he's not a rancher?"

Lane shrugged a tan shoulder. "I heard you were once a cop . . . you interrogating me?"

"Sorry. Old habits."

"My brother has . . . issues. As much as I don't get along with my dad, he and Scott can't be in the same room together without an all-out-war happening. Maybe someday they'll grow out of it. Wasn't always like that. As kids, we were just an average family. Grew up with the Cogan's. You met Larz."

"And you, you're visiting?"

"No, I just told you, I live here now. I manage the ranch. All three thousand acres of it."

"I'm impressed," Gallic said, and meant it.

"Don't be . . . it practically runs itself. We hire a lot of folks who know what to do and when to do it."

"You mean like those ranch hands, the ones who waited for Phil and me?"

"There was no excuse for that . . . I'm truly sorry. Like I said, I grew up with Larz. Those three idiots, I suppose, were simply being protective of him. They'll be fired. Like you said, they could have killed Phil . . . and you."

"Not so much me. If you hadn't come along when you did, you'd probably be notifying that boy's next of kin."

Lane studied him for several beats. "You're one dangerous Frontier Marshal. Truth is, I think you scare me."

"No need to be scared. We 'Frontier Marshals', like everyone else, have a job to do. We're as close to law enforcement as these parts are going to get. With that said, we are given enough leeway to protect ourselves . . . and others, too, within our purview," Gallic told her. "Speaking of that . . . I should get back to doing it." As he stood, his towel stayed behind him on the bed. Unfazed, he reached for it.

Lane let out a reflexive laugh. She grabbed his wrist and held on. "Can I tell you something?"

"Shoot."

She laughed again—her face flushed. "Back at Renegade's Haven, we watched you when you came in—me, and every other person in the place—women and men. You draw a lot of attention."

"I'm a big guy . . . tend to get noticed."

That evoked a crooked smile. "Yeah, but it's more than that. More than mere confidence."

Gallic continued to stand before her—buck-naked.

"It's just so obvious you don't give a shit. About anything or anyone. That's a *whole lot* of dangerous." Keeping a firm grip on his wrist, she leaned back on the bed, pulling him down with her—atop her. She kissed him, and he kissed her back.

She said, "Just know this is only going to happen once. I'm not looking for a boyfriend or—

Cutting Lane off, he kissed her again—harder this time.

Turning her head aside, she said, "Hey . . . I was talking to you."

"Is that what you want to do . . . talk?"

Panting, she shook her head. "No! Help me take these boots off."

chapter 12

Frontier Planet, Gorman — Heritage Plains Township.

Lane was asleep—her head lying softly upon Gallic's chest. Beneath the sheet, his left hand cupped one of her compact, surprisingly firm, butt cheeks. Lane wasn't the first woman he'd slept with since the death of his wife. But there hadn't been many.

He needed to move. His back throbbed, and the gears in his head were again spinning. Working the crime scene reminded him of old times, back when he was DCI for the Colonial Police—in Space District 22. He'd fallen back into a familiar routine—the process of searching for evidence, clues, to identify a potential suspect, or suspects, in a death caused by either violence or some other unnatural cause. In this case, a young mother and her child. Superintendent Bernard Danbury was right. The similarities to Clair and Mandy's murders were, of course, far too similar to be a coincidence. But Gallic needed to be careful. Bringing baggage from one murder scene to another murder scene, even unintentionally, was a rookie mistake. Each investigation had to be run by the book. All progression going forward solely determined by whatever trace evidence and clues were gathered. *Can I really be objective, or am I only kidding myself?*

The truth was, this wasn't Gallic's case. Not really. He was no longer DCI. Right now, he couldn't *big foot* himself into the ongoing proceedings. Any mishandling could back-fire badly—getting him kicked to the curb. That could not be allowed to happen. He'd waited years for just this opportunity and nothing was going to stand in his way—finding the mur-derer of Clair and Mandy. He always knew he wasn't looking for justice. Seeking something far more primal than that. He was out for revenge—pure and simple.

Carefully, he managed to extricate himself from the bed without waking Lane. He stood, watching her breathe evenly in and out. She'd told him *this* would only happen once. He needed to ensure that would hold true. She was one hell of a distraction—one he didn't need in his life right now.

Hearing a groan, Gallic padded his way into his closet and quickly dressed. On entering the *Hound*'s main compartment, he quietly moved over to where Phil lay, sprawled out on the couch. The Navaho blanket lay on the deck in a heap. Phil's eyes were closed, and the gash—along with a good-sized purple knot on his forehead—made Gallic grimace. He softly said,

"That's going to hurt like a son-of-a-bitch when you wake up, buddy." He figured it best to just let him sleep.

Gallic wondered if there was anything on the news about the murders. Heading for the *Hound's* control center, he said, "AI ... bring up the local news broadcast." Taking a seat, he swiveled the chair around toward the 3D display. A story was being reported about a rancher's hybrid bull. Some kind of genetic concoction, it resembled water buffaloes more than cattle. The ginormous beast was in the process of mounting a far smaller, struggling, common cow as a circle of rancher businessmen watched the scene in rapt silence. Gallic, using a hand-motion, changed the channel, and the trailer to a new movie appeared in its place. An action flick, it starred Zip Furlong. Gallic, huffed and shook his head. He remembered Zip, whose real name was Teddy Walters. He and Clair met the action star when they lived in London. His Oxshott mansion burned down while he was filming an out-of-town feature film. Someone in bed fell asleep with a lit cigarette. The exotic, primarily hardwood structure went up like dried kindling. People were killed and Gallic was called in to be the DCI in charge. He thought back to his interview with Teddy, upon his arrival back in town. The actor felt awful about the situation—felt responsible. Gallic always liked the actor's 'tough guy' movies and found him to be genuine and unpretentious. They got along instantly, and he still considered the movie star a good friend.

The preview was nearing its end when Lane, now dressed, wandered over to the control center. Her hair was brushed and she still had the afterglow of a woman who'd spent an after-noon in bed, having sex with a near-stranger. Noticing the holographic movie clip winding down, she froze, her expression a kaleidoscope of emotion—changing from shock, to fear, to something akin to anger.

"Hey there . . . What is it?" Gallic asked.

"Nothing." Shaking it off, she only smiled. "I really have to go. Gabby is still tied to a post . . . I have a lot of work to do . . ."

"Gabby?"

"My horse, silly." Leaning in, she gave him a kiss. "Um . . . will I be able to find my way out of here?"

"Probably best if I walk you out. The *Hound* isn't a place you'd want to wander around unattended."

"You serious? Why, do you have the thing booby-trapped?"

He shrugged. "Lots of unsavory types can come a-knocking in my business."

* * *

By the time Gallic returned to the *Hound*'s upper level, it was dark outside. He checked in on Phil, who was still asleep. Picking up the fallen blanket, he draped it over the older Frontier Marshal since it had turned chilly.

Feeling tired he made his way back to his bed to lie down. Sleep came quickly. But much too soon the dream vermin arrived—arrived in mass. He'd forgotten, mentally, to batten down the hatches. A torrent of twisting slithering forms moved like an alive, churning ocean. Approaching closer, sharp teeth nipping and snapping, hundreds—maybe thousands—of creatures proceeded to enter unhindered into his consciousness. And then they were upon him. *No, not upon him, but someone else*—it was Lane. Wrapping their slimy, snake-like bodies around her. Then, in an instant, the snakes and vermin were gone, and Gallic found himself walking into a house. He had his equipment with him. He was on the job. Something about the house was disconcerting—the silence went well beyond quiet. And it was stifling—warm turning to hot—a bad smell pervaded the space. Proceeding down a wood-paneled hallway, where shag carpeting, the color of tangerines ran beneath his disposable booties, he entered the main room. And it was like he'd stepped back in time, with sectional couches upholstered in paisley patterns, and a television console that doubled as a Hi-Fi turntable. Beyond was a kitchen, with avocado-colored appliances and the kind of Formica countertops popular 150 years earlier on Earth. Coming around the end of the couch he saw a body, positioned on the carpet, then remembered this was a hammer-and-nails murder. Why he was there. Something about the woman's figure, lying there on the floor, seemed familiar. Kneeling down, he sees her face for the first time. It is Lane. Her eyes are closed, nailed shut. Why, he wonders, didn't he immediately notice the other, smaller form lying beside her? They were holding hands. Oh god . . . Mandy was holding her hand, and suddenly the woman was no longer Lane. It was Clair. Eyelid nails no longer present, she opened her eyes, turning her head toward him. She opened her mouth to speak, but no words came out. Only vermin, rushing up from the darkness—to escape from her gaping open mouth.

Gasping, Gallic awoke. Drenched in sweat, he struggled to catch his breath.

chapter 13

Frontier Planet, Gorman — Heritage Plains Township.

The early dawn sun was now cresting a distant rise. The surrounding pastureland had taken on a pinkish-gray cast that soon would warm to amber, then to an emerald green by mid-day. Gazing out the window, Gallic noticed a handful of cows had gathered close to the *Hound*.

He finished adding grounds into the antique coffee maker, knowing too that if he used the replicator the coffee might come out tasting just as good. But Gallic liked his morning routine. The aroma emitted from freshly ground coffee beans was one of the few small pleasures he allowed himself.

"Have I died and gone to heaven? Smells wonderful."

Gallic, surprised, hadn't heard Phil get up. Wrapped up in the Native American blanket, eyes bloodshot, pasty-white pallor, he looked terrible.

"Why don't you take a seat before you keel over," Gallic said.

Phil, doing as told, pulled out a chair then plopped down at the small kitchenette table. "I feel like I got hit by a space trawler."

"Not a trawler . . . a shovel."

"I think I remember seeing it coming . . . didn't have time to duck." Probing his forehead with two fingers, he queried, "Please tell me you mercilessly made the one responsible pay . . . and pay dearly."

"Three of them. They were lying in wait, all armed with garden tools. You got it in the head . . . me in the back. And yes, they all paid."

"Garden tools? What the hell was their beef with us?"

"It was with me . . . you just happened to be along."

"Lucky me. What did you do to rile them up so badly?" Phil asked, accepting the steaming mug of coffee from Gallic.

"Repo'ed their boss's ride. A brand new *L35T*."

"Oh yeah . . . you mentioned something about that before. Not easy to gain access into one of those."

"Not unless you have the owner around to do it for you."

Phil nodded. "So, you not only repo'ed the *5T* but humiliated the owner as well?"

"Yep, in front of his friends to boot," Gallic added.

"Well, I hope you got paid, that it was worth it."

"At least it'll keep me current with the *Hound*. Sorry it cost you that lump on your head."

Phil, his brows tightly knitted, looked up from his coffee, "Hey ... did I see a beautiful blonde moving around in here earlier this morning, or did I just dream that?"

"You weren't dreaming," Gallic said, leaning back against the counter.

"So, you're telling me you got paid enough to bring the *Hound* current and ... you got laid, too?"

Gallic simply shrugged his shoulders in response.

"I had a strange dream," Phil said.

"Oh yeah?" Gallic said, not thrilled of being reminded of his own personal nightmare. Noting that Phil looked a bit shook up, he added, "Probably the bonk on the head ... you'll be okay."

"My father was in it. Weird, he died when I was a kid ... a teenager." Phil's eyes looked tired. As he sat there, mentally reliving his dream, Gallic saw him chewing on the inside of his lip.

Gallic, pulling out the other chair, sat down next to him. After taking a sip of his coffee, he reluctantly asked, "What was the dream about?"

Phil didn't seem to hear him. "You know," he said instead, "everything we are, and everywhere we've been, is due to that discovery on Mars nearly one hundred years ago. Where would we be now if that never happened? I remember my daddy being obsessed with Mars; talked about it all the time. Only it wasn't in a positive way. Folks in our small town in Montana thought he was delusional. My father thought there was something evil going on up there. He was pretty much pushed aside, considered a crazy loon. I was told by others not to listen to him. By the time I was old enough to really ask him about Mars and what he was talking about, he'd gone off the deep end." Phil glanced up, pain in his eyes. "When I was seventeen, he shot himself in the head."

Gallic didn't quite know how to respond. *What could he say?* He said nothing.

Phil looked away then out the window, as if searching for *something* out there. Gallic thought he saw him tremble.

"In the dream, my father told me about one particular Mars conspiracy. That it was all true... the truth was right before me." Phil sat up and drank his coffee down, regaining his composure. He then smiled and said, "Damn, dreams sometimes seem so real, eh?"

Gallic, not one for talking much about his feelings, or his dreams, said, "How 'bout I fry us some eggs and bacon?" Rising, he topped off his own, then Phil's, coffee mug. "Then later, if you feel up to it, we'll head over to Linda's ... try to get that interview."

* * *

They caught Linda on the way out her front door, wearing knee-high black leather boots and tan, formfitting riding pants—the skintight kind, worn when one rode English. Securing a leather crop under one arm, she closed and locked the front door.

"Mrs. Cugan?"

She jumped, hearing Gallic's voice come from behind her and spun around startled. "For God's sake, don't sneak up on a person like that! Not with . . . what's happened." Annoyed, she looked first at Gallic then at Phil. "What happened to you, Phil?"

Before he could answer, Gallic said, "You may want to ask your son about that . . . and several of his ranch-hand buddies."

Exasperated, she huffed in disbelief. "Look, I'm on my way out. We'll have to do this another time." She started walking toward the barn—the same barn Gallic and Phil met the business-end of a metal spade.

"No problem," Gallic said. "I suppose we can make this a more official interview by conducting it later. Once the court subpoena gets issued, you can appear at the Distrct-22 station." As a contract Frontier Marshal, Gallic had no such authority to even request a subpoena, but he knew Linda wouldn't know that.

Her back to them, she hesitated, standing mute on the driveway, as if rallying the necessary energy, and/or patience, to deal with the added trouble. When she turned around to face them, she'd composed herself, wearing a phony smile. "I would be happy to give you ten minutes. Will that suffice, Mr. Gallic?"

* * *

Gallic sat across from Linda Cugan in what was clearly the mansion's study. Phil stood, leaning against a distant wall jamb, well within earshot. "This shouldn't take long, Mrs. Cugan."

"Just call me Linda. And good—the sooner it's over, the better."

"I'll need to speak with your daughter, as well."

"I don't want to bring her into this. She's very upset."

"I'll be as easy on her as possible," Gallic said, making a few taps on his ComsBand. "I'll be recording this interview."

"Whatever . . ." she said.

"Um . . . you mentioned you entered the Bower's residence without knocking."

Linda nodded.

"About what time was that?"

"I don't know . . . late morning, I guess."

"What was your reason for entering the house unannounced?"

"I hadn't seen them . . . Catherine or Tami, in a while. It was strange. Not like them. As I told you . . . we were close. Like family."

"And when was the last time you saw her husband?" Gallic tapped on his ComsBand then added, "Trent Bower."

Linda shifted in her seat, looking like she'd rather be anywhere but there with him. "I haven't seen Trent in weeks. He travels a lot . . . on business."

"Just like your own husband," Gallic said.

"Your point?"

"Just an observation, Ma'am."

"Don't *ma'am* me . . . makes me feel ancient. Linda will do just fine."

"Can you tell me a bit more about your relationship with Catherine?"

"We were next-door neighbors and best friends."

"And you hung out socially, together with your husbands?"

Linda nodded, suddenly unable to speak. She dabbed at her eyes with a balled-up tissue Gallic didn't notice earlier. Swallowing hard, she said, "Catherine was the social one. Loved get-togethers ... barbeques ... all holidays. The life of the party, that one, and always the center of attention."

For the first time, Gallic detected a touch of resentment in her voice. "She was pretty ... beautiful, even," Gallic said, recalling the vic's body, lying dead on the floor just next door.

"She most definitely was the prettiest one. The local joke was that it wasn't the dogs in the neighborhood you needed to keep a leash on ... it was the husbands."

"So, Catherine was ... unfaithful?"

Linda narrowed her eyes at Gallic. "I didn't say that! She would never ..."

"Mom?"

Gallic turned, seeing a teenaged girl enter the study. She looked about the same age as Tami. *This must be Juaquin.* The girl sat next to her mother's chair on the ottoman. Her hair hung down straight, covering most of her face. Gallic could see her cheeks were quite pink—it was obvious she'd been crying.

"Who are these people?"

"You know Phil ... he's the Frontier Marshal ..."

The young teen shyly glanced over her shoulder, finding Phil still standing there. Her eyes next flashed to Gallic.

"This is Mr. Gallic. He's investigating . . . what happened next door. He'd like to ask you only a few questions. Would that be okay, dear?"

"I don't know anything," her daughter replied, her head lowered, her voice barely audible.

"Then just tell him what you do know," Linda said. She looked at Gallic with a stare that instructed *be kind to my daughter or you're gone*.

"Hi Juaquin, that's a great name you have."

"Thanks."

"Your mom tells me the last time you saw Tami and her mother was when they were out for a ride. Can you tell me a little about that?"

Scowling, Juaquin's head spun around. She stared at her mother. A typical teenage gesture that said—*that is not the last time I saw them*.

Linda waved her hand dismissively and rolled her eyes. "She wouldn't remember what she had for breakfast. Remember, Juaquin, they were out in the pasture. Tami was walking her horse . . ." Linda stared at her daughter—her eyes laser beams.

"Oh yeah, that's right," the girl replied softly, her gaze back to staring at the carpet.

"Do you remember what Tami and her mother were wearing that day?" Gallic asked.

Juaquin glanced at her mother before answering then simply shook her head. Studying the teen, Gallic took in the way she was dressed. White designer jeans, patterned with large black symbols—Asian letters haphazardly positioned up and down her legs. Pink high-tops, looking as if they'd just popped out from a new shoebox, and a snap-down plaid shirt that not only matched her pink shoes, but also the dyed patch of pink hair in her long bangs. The girl was a young *fashionista*. No way she hadn't noticed what Tami was wearing, as well as her mother's outfit too. The real question was why was she lying? The better question—why was her mother forcing her to do so?

"Let me ask you this, Juaquin. Did Tami mention anything that seemed out of the ordinary to you lately? Anything at all?"

Almost imperceptibly, her eyes momentarily widened— some inner thought unconsciously expressing itself. She looked to her mother then replied, "I don't really want to talk anymore. Can I go to my room now?"

"Of course, dear. Say goodbye to Mr. Gallic and Phil."

Waiting for her first to leave the room, Linda stood then said, "I'm sorry, but I'm going to have to ask you both to leave. This is all too upsetting."

"Fine. Let me ask you one more thing. What does your husband do for a living?"

"Rick? He's an attorney though primarily works as an agent."

"What kind of agent?"

"For the entertainment business. High-profile actors and directors . . . that sort of thing."

* * *

Gallic, finished questioning both Linda and her daughter, thought little new had been revealed. It was obvious certain information had been withheld. More than once, Juaquin looked to her mother before answering.

"That's why you don't interview potential suspects together," Phil said, standing outside on the driveway.

"There was no way I was going to be granted that option, Phil. I was lucky to get even those few minutes with her. Look, I don't think anyone around here had anything to do with the murders. With that said, still something's going on," Gallic said.

"We need to talk to the husbands. I know them both. How about I work that end . . . get interviews set up over the next few days."

"I'd appreciate that. I still have a few other loose ends to tie up. Maybe take advantage of the lull in the case."

"Repo work?" Phil asked, and Gallic nodded back.

"I'll catch you later then. Thanks for . . ." pointing to his head, "keeping me alive."

"Don't mention it."

Gallic watched Phil head off toward the distant *Gallivanter*. It took the older Frontier Marshal time to amble across the pasture and disappear into the ship. A minute or two later, the craft's under-wing thrusters engaged, and the vessel began to rise.

chapter 14

Frontier Planet, Gorman — Heritage
Plains Township.

B ack in the *Hound*, Gallic, with reluctance, went to work
reviewing the earlier information sent over by Polly Gant
concerning the missing *Hayai* spacecraft. His heart wasn't in
it. He was a Frontier Marshal first and foremost, and he had
a murderer to catch. Still, the last time he checked repo side
work paid the bills.

Sitting at his desk within the study, he replaced the projected murder board with the Imperial Bail Bonds & Repos'
missing *Hayai* case files. With a hand motion, a past holographic interview of Allison Tillman began to play. Attractive,
mid-thirties, the businesswoman spoke with an air of confidence. Gallic wondered if it derived from personal successes
over her short career, or if it came from her astounding family
wealth. He wondered if she had never been denied anything.

Her on-screen presence was impressive to watch. Her glossy lipstick the same shade as her ruby-red silk blouse and her platinum blonde hair feathered and teased to appear naturally wind-tousled; a look that probably took hours to achieve at the salon. Allison Tillman was certainly beautiful, but there was something a tad too perfect about her looks. Almost like the young executive had been pre-packaged in a design factory.

Gallic listened as she described her family's exquisite, personal, spacecraft collection. Some were antiques, while some possessed state-of-the-art technology. A few were military vessels—kept on display, at their invitation-only pseudo museum, on the top floor of their corporate offices. She spoke about the collection, ships varying in size and shape, as if they were dear family members. Ships that, at one time or other, belonged to the ultra-famous—either from the entertainment or political sector. Or ships that were in some unique way most remarkable, like the early prototype vessels utilizing alien *Curz* propulsion technology. These were the Model T's of the twenty-second century. The more Polly Gant spoke about the collection, the more Gallic thought he'd enjoy seeing the eclectic mishmash in person.

She spoke as though all others should relate to having a multi-billion dollar collection, such as theirs. And as if what had taken place was more akin to a kidnapping than to elaborate grand-scale theft.

Gallic checked the time on his ComsBand. Polly had set up a pre-arranged, interactive interview for him with Allison. Now, having gained sufficient background on both the company and Polly, he felt somewhat more comfortable doing a one-on-one.

The *Hound*'s AI softly announced: "Your requested CoreNet channel has been established. Allison Tillman is awaiting your activation."

"Fine, I'm ready . . . go ahead," Gallic said.

The holographic display instantly filled with Allison Tillman's slim upper body. In the background, slightly out-of-focus, were a number of personal, high-end spacecraft. She'd positioned herself within the museum proper. *Was that more for his benefit or for hers?* Gallic wondered, briefly catching the distinctive outline of a *Hausenbach L35T*.

"Ah . . . there you are! The Galaxy Man, himself, I've heard so much about," Allison said with good humor.

Gallic fought the urge to roll his eyes at the mere mention of his ridiculous moniker. "Ms. Tillman. It's good to meet you."

"Well, Polly tells me if anyone can find our stolen baby, it's you. You come highly regarded, Mr. Gallic."

"You can just call me Gallic . . . everyone does."

"And you can call me Allison. Shall we get down to it? I still have a wicked amount of work to get to today."

Her lipstick no longer colorfully matched a red silk blouse. In fact, there was no blouse. Instead, she now wore a crisp white button-down shirt under a gender-neutral business suit. Although one of the stripes in her peach-colored necktie did in fact match her lipstick.

"By all means," he said. "First, I'd like to discuss your security—"

Allison, interrupting him, began to speak: "Look . . . our security measures are the very best money can buy. Military-grade, of course. You are aware of our government contracts division . . . I'm sure."

"I am."

"Well, whoever took the craft somehow disabled our five-time redundancy security protocols. Virtually the same measures presently used to protect the new U.S. Pentagon. And before you speak about the theft being an inside job, rest assured, we've internally investigated that prospect ad nauseam."

"You're telling me you want me to . . . what? Ignore any internal company investigation? To concentrate primarily on—"

Again, she stepped all over his words. "That's right! There will be no internal personnel investigation. Period."

Gallic let out a breath, already hating this gig. But she was the client. If she didn't want him poking around her company, her people, then so be it. The big problem—he wouldn't get paid if he didn't find the *Hayai* before someone else did. "I can certainly concentrate my efforts on pursuing known spacecraft thieves. Make the rounds to *chop shops* in relatively- near space."

"Well, that sounds like a good start," Allison said. "You're the expert, not me."

"Still . . ." he replied, "I'd like to review your security vids. Bring in a fresh pair of eyes and all."

Allison studied him, as if she wanted to admonish him for returning to an already closed subject.

"I won't release that sort of thing over the CoreNet. It's completely unsecure." She pursed her lips, appraising him. "You'll need to come to Spector . . . view the security feeds in person. But that's as far as it will go. No internal investigation."

Gallic inwardly groaned. He didn't like Spector—a city and planet that shared the same name. Spector was a frantic-paced metropolis, with too many people in a too-confining space. For a man his size, it was like forcing a size twelve foot into a size ten shoe. Also, it would take him an entire day's jaunt just to get there.

"Let me ask you another question? How many Frontier Marshals have asked for museum access?"

"You are only the second."

"I see. Um . . . okay, getting back to the *Hayai*. Before I get there . . . can you give me a bit more background on the ship itself? Perhaps provide me some perspective on why that one craft was appropriated when all those behind you were not."

Allison stared at him blankly then fluttered her eyelids in such a way she resembled an android accessing data. "The *Hayai* is a third-generation prototype. The relatively sporty-sized spaceship, like all other crafts created over the last century, utilizes the same alien *Curz* propulsion technology, to some degree. But the *Hayai* is a vast improvement over that tech. An artificial, minuscule in size black hole is projected near, actually well past, its event horizon. Now, due to quantum physics limitations that we—and all others—have no control over, there was only so much our engineers could do to improve performance. Namely, breaching higher end FTL limitations. Still, some ingenious *cheats* were implemented by our own people. The *Hayai* propulsion system is like none other . . . I assure you." Nodding to herself, she took a deep breath. "Without delving into top secret waters, I can tell you we now use a different propellant. Fissure Nine radiation, which creates a steadier electromagnetic effect. One million tons of negative mass is used. And finally, we've incorporated a brand-new gamma laser. But I cannot go into further detail on that subject."

Gallic understood very little of what she'd just discussed with him. His astonishment wasn't so much about the technical information he'd been bombarded with but that Alison—obviously brilliant—did know what she was talking about.

As if reading his mind, she said, "This job wasn't handed over to me by chance or perhaps nepotism gone awry, as you've probably surmised, Mr. Gallic. In addition to being an engineer—five years spent at MIT—I'm a physicist in my own right. As company president, and CEO of Tillman Enterprises, it helps when one understands what we're manufacturing." She then went silent, waiting for Gallic's response.

"I'll be underway, within the hour," he affirmed.

chapter 15

Deep Space — On board the *Hound* — en route to Spector

With Muleshoe 700 million miles behind him, Gallic— standing at the control center—waited for another CoreNet channel connection, to one channel over—D-22.

"I have established your requested channel, Mr. Gallic."

"Go ahead and put the superintendent through, AI."

The virtual image of Superintendent Bernard Danbury now stood before him within the projected vertical display. "Glad I caught you, Superintendent. Must be close to what . . . 7:30 there?"

"Yeah . . . it'll be another late night," Danbury replied, sounding resigned to the fact. "There's still no shortage of felonious behavior in District 22, John. Today is no exception, with eighteen murders, twenty-two rapes, and nine abductions. Those numbers don't include frontier space either . . . out in your neck of the woods. That could double those numbers . . . easily."

Gallic's old boss looked tired and beaten, showing signs of hopelessness not evident days before. Perhaps he'd just caught him at a particularly bad moment.

"So, what can I do for you, John?"

"As requested, I just wanted to update you. I'm sure this will be a repeat of what Sergeant Tori's given you. Tori worked the crime scene . . . did a fine job. A lot of evidence was collected. Be interesting to hear back what Forensics has to say. We also spoke with the neighbors, Linda Cugan and her daughter. In my opinion, they are hiding something. To what extent, I'm not sure yet. It needs to be followed up on."

Danbury said, "You need to nix all further contact with Mrs. Cugan, also with her daughter."

"Nix? Why? Look . . . there's something there; something's off."

"Do I need to remind you, John, this is not your case—that you are no longer a D-22 DCI? This is becoming a much higher-profile case than I'd like. In the future, all interviews relating to it will be conducted solely by Sergeant Tori."

"What's changed? Why all the stonewalling?"

Irritation flashed in Danbury's eyes. "There's been a registered complaint."

"By Mrs. Cugan?"

Wearily, Danbury shook his head. "By her husband. She must have sounded off to him, and he put an official complaint into D-22."

"Since when do we cater to a suspect's needs when investigating a murder?"

"Mrs. Cugan, and certainly not her daughter, isn't a suspect. So, drop it. Tori will be arriving back at Gorman tomorrow. Take a step back, and let her perform her job."

Gallic shrugged, holding back what he wanted to say.

"It's probably a copycat murder. We've both seen them before... with other cases. It's not the hammer-and-nails killer," Danbury said.

"You're probably right," Gallic said.

Giving an exhausted half-smile, Danbury said, "Let's talk in a few days. Try to stay out of trouble, John." The feed then went black.

Hours later, the *Hound* returned to the worlds of Alpha Centauri. Gallic stared at the approaching cluster of twinkling lights. This time he'd traveled close to 5.6 light years distance, and his body felt it. Space-lag was an issue Interstellar travelers had to learn to deal with. An effect that really kicked in once one entered a given world's atmosphere, with its own unique time continuum properties. Bypassing Rawlings City, Grimes252, Gallic navigated in closer to the red dwarf star, Proxima Centauri, where the planet Spector was situated. Like Rawlings City, Spector was a planet where big business took place. The only difference, Spector was privately owned by a consortium of prominent U.S. and European families; families like the Tillman's. A beautiful world—modern technology and architecture melded together perfectly—within an undisturbed, desert-like ecosystem.

Slowing, the *Hound*'s two gravitorque drives changed their vibrational cadence.

"Entering Spector high orbit, Mr. Gallic," the AI said.

Gallic fought back a yawn. "Take us in, AI. Submit the necessary flight plans into *Harriot*,"

Harriot, the name of the actual city on this small world, was where Tillman Enterprises resided. Somewhere in the past, Gallic learned that it was the namesake of a sick Tillman child, who'd died a century earlier. Gallic never had the opportunity to visit the city before. By invitation only, the unique world maintained its own small military faction—one that took protection of its inhabitants very seriously.

"We have been granted permission to enter Sirius, specifically Harriot airspace, Mr. Gallic."

But Gallic's attention was already drawn toward two sleek *Strife 5* attack ships, which suddenly appeared on the *Hound*'s port and starboard wingtips. *Some genuine firepower there*, he observed

An unfamiliar male voice, breaching the *Hound*'s internal coms channel, spoke with deliberate, if not hostile, intent. "Vessel, with designation *Hound*, will change course on vector 53.934, reduce velocity by one-third, and drop down to a matching altitude."

Gallic said, "You got that, AI?"

"Yes, Mr. Gallic," the AI replied.

Below, the surface of Spector came into view. A striking planet, the rocky—mostly scrub and rock—landscape was in varying shades of blue. It was like viewing a world through blue-tinted sunglasses. Bright reflections glimmered off high-rise buildings; up ahead, Tillman city.

Again, the same male voice filled the compartment: "Proceed to the provided set-down coordinates on building 6AA. Do not veer from your current approach vector." And with that the two *Strife 5* attack ships were gone.

There were about sixty buildings in all, of varying heights. Cylindrical in shape, they were glass-paneled and beautiful. What differentiated this little city from others Gallic encountered was that all the buildings—in fact, the entire city—were contained within a great circle of water. Each building sat within the huge artificial lake or reservoir. The water was the only visual aspect not a shade of blue. It was violet.

One building in particular stood tall above the others. Clearly, that was where the *Hound* was now being directed. Glancing to the nav-panel on the console board before him, Gallic noted the Tillman Enterprises headquarters meta-tag designation.

The *Hound* slowed, descending to within several hundred feet of the building's rooftop. The 3D display showed their downward descent. *The building's massive*, Gallic thought, *perhaps three-quarters of a mile across*. Batches of parked space vehicles covered the roof of the building.

"Mr. Gallic … there is a problem. The provided set-down location, 1328, is not entirely vacant." Gallic, now looking closer at the display, noticed there were clearly designated pad locations.

He had to smile. Sargento's smaller and much newer repo ship was taking up pad 1327, as well as a portion—just a tad—of pad 1328. Normally, this wouldn't have been a problem. Not for most vessels, anyway. An arriving ship would simply squeeze into the space remaining, as the pads were pretty large. But the *Hound* was immense; would barely fit into pad 1328 even without an obstruction present.

"I'm taking the controls," Gallic said. The AI remained silent as the underbelly thrusters came alive.

Gallic brought the *Hound* down but didn't extend the landing struts. Whereas the *Hound* was nearly indestructible—a beast of a ship with heavy-metal hull plating—its landing struts were somewhat more delicate. It was possible to bend retract arms or reaction links; a trunnion leg could be tweaked or misaligned. Landings needed to be controlled but what Gallic was planning was not a landing at all. Instead, a little brute force was all that would be required.

Lower and lower the *Hound* descended. A dense cloud from the thrusters made visibility difficult. Now, using only his fingertips, he manipulated the controls, altering the ship's angle to a nose-down orientation. The slightest mistake, or misjudgment, could drive the nose of the *Hound* into the top floors of the building.

A proximity alarm began to wail, and the AI announced dangerous conditions. Gallic continued to lower the behemoth vessel downward, until it was ten feet above the landing pad and five feet out from Sargento's ship—a *King First Carryall*. A transport like the *Hound*, only a much smaller and far more sophisticated ship. *Sargento's business must be doing very well*, Gallic mused. The ship was clean and unblemished. *He really takes good care of the thing.* Then, out of the blue, he thought of something more. Recalled viewing an autopsy photograph of a once-pretty, young Native American woman, Sargento's woman—her name had been Nascha.

Now, with only the slightest pressure on the controls, Gallic goosed the throttle. The sturdy, reinforced nose of the *Hound* came into contact with the portside of the *King First Carryall*. Sounds of metal crunching metal reverberated all around the compartment. A glance toward the display showed the Carryall's hull was not holding up so well after the repeated ship-against-ship nudging taking place. Gallic tried to be as delicate as possible—a somewhat tedious back and forth process. By the time the ship, *King First Carryall*, was sufficiently shoved back fully into its own 1327 pad location, the once-pristine ship looked somewhat crumpled.

With well-practiced hands, and much quicker movements now, Gallic engaged the ship's high-thrusters to raise the *Hound* 200 feet up. Then, lowering the landing struts, he said, "Go ahead and set us down, AI."

chapter 16

Frontier Planet, Muleshoe — Stanford Pride.

The killer lay on his back, staring up at the ceiling. He hummed a sweet melody. The same one the child had been humming quietly to herself not so long ago. His eyes followed the almost imperceptible deviation beneath layers and layers of paint—where taped drywall joints hadn't been adequately sanded before the texturing process was started. So much work was done half-assed of late. What happened to the days when workers took pride in their skill? When being a true craftsman was a badge of honor one wore?

He adjusted the pillow beneath his head. Turning his face to the side, he breathed in the mother's—Melissa Johnson's— fresh scent. *Hmm, what is that? Lavender,* he thought. He flipped back over onto his stomach, so he could see over the side of the bed. He stared down at his handiwork—at ten-year-old Blair, younger than the others, who looked at peace. He'd tried to tidy up, both her and her mother's appearance, their faces. He reached down and using the back of his gloved fingers, stroked the girl's cheek.

Rising up on his elbows, he contemplated changing the wording on the nearby wall. *Good luck with that*, he mused. Blood was not exactly erasable. Then again, it got the message across. He tried to picture John's reaction; the contours of his face as he pondered its true meaning. The killer smiled then became serious. He wanted John to know he missed her too; that it wasn't all about him. *At what point*, he wondered, *would John realize that?* Probably not for a while—not until more were silenced.

chapter 17

Planet Spector — Harriot — Tillman Building.

Coming down the *Hound's* ramp, Gallic spotted the competition. Sargento and his partner approaching at a full out run from the far side of the rooftop. He then remembered that Sargento's partner's name was Hok'ee, which meant something like high-backed wolf. Dressed similarly to what they had on the other day, both wore identical leather vests. Today Hok'ee's hair was tied back into a long hanging braid. Sargento, the bigger of the two, was two strides ahead of Hok'ee. His pockmarked face was set tight—defined by an angry sneer. Gallic could hear his angry voice, though not what he was saying.

Gallic casually turned his back on the approaching duo to tap in the code that retracted the *Hound's* ramp. From this vantage point, he could see the side of Sargento's ship. The damage looked even worse up close.

The angry repo man came to a stop two paces behind Gallic. Turning around, Gallic found the guy's chest still heaving, murder in his eyes.

"Hey, Sargento . . . what's up?" Gallic noticed Hok'ee was no longer with him.

"You son of a bitch!" Coming close to Gallic, he raised a fist. "First, I'm going to kill you, then I'm going to cut you up and feed you to my dogs."

"Where's your boyfriend?" Gallic asked, looking around.

The implied question momentarily took Sargento off-guard. "Boyfriend? What the fuck . . ."

"I just assumed. You know . . . with the matching vests and all. Hey, it's the twenty-second century. I'm certainly not here to judge anyone's preference . . . who they cohabitate with . . ."

"Cohabitate? What . . . you think . . . we're like . . ."

"Easy there, boss," Gallic said, his palms raised up. "Looks like you've got bigger problems on your hands. Have you taken a look at the side of your ship lately?"

"Yeah. You did that! I saw you . . . you shoved my ship. You and that monstrosity of a ship. You know what a *King First Carryall* costs these days? You're going to pay for that damage. Every penny."

"Come on . . . all I did is land within my designated set-down space. The one I was instructed to use. Let me ask you a question. Were you designated one or two set-down spaces?" Gallic didn't wait for an answer, instead walking over to the damaged section of the *King First Carryall*, then over to the nose of the *Hound*. "Do you see any damage on my ship?"

Sargento, who'd followed behind him, stared up at the bow of the larger vessel. No damage was evident. "Don't turn this around . . . you did that to my ship."

Gallic shrugged. "Prove it." Prepared for Hok'ee when he jumped out from behind the *Hound's* front landing strut, he had time to move his head aside. Even so, he took a glancing blow to his ear—an old-fashioned roundhouse punch that the smaller man put all his weight behind. It hurt like a son-of-a-bitch. Enough to cause Gallic's eyes to water and shut down all hearing in that ear for the time being.

Sargento's arm was drawn back for his own punch to Gallic's face. It came at him in the form of a jab. Gallic slapped it away with little effort. "You should probably stop now while you're still ahead," Gallic said, suddenly conscious he didn't have time for this. He was expected to meet up with Allison Tillman soon.

Then Hok'ee was again on the move—circling around and coming in low on Gallic's right side. Timing his move, Gallic waited another second and then, not taking his eyes off Sargento standing right before him, he used a step-back kick to plant the sole of his boot hard in the middle of Hok'ee's chest. Like a mule kick—no, more like a Clydesdale kick—the kind that snaps someone's sternum and a handful of ribs. Suddenly airborne, Hok'ee landed with a painful sounding thud some eight feet away. Gallic caught the glint of something metallic in Sargento's right hand. His pocked face sneered as he rushed forward, swiping the six-inch blade fast sideways, and coming within an inch of Gallic's neck—his carotid artery. Gallic

MARK WAYNE MCGINNIS

caught the now off-balanced Native American's ponytail, wrapping it in his fist, first once then twice. Yanking down hard, he flipped him onto his back. Sargento gasped, the air knocked from his lungs.

Looming above him, Gallic placed the heel of his boot on Sargento's exposed neck.

"Life isn't always fair, Sargento. Hell, ask Nascha. See what she has to say about fair. Oh yeah . . . you can't do that, can you? Not since *someone* pushed the young woman down a flight of stairs. Someone who claimed she was clumsy . . . that she'd simply tripped."

Sargento didn't respond to his comment.

"I'm going to wait right here while you collect that pile of trash lying behind me. Wait for you to climb into your little spaceship and fly far away. Deviate from that, even in the slightest, and I'll break every bone in your body. Now move!"

* * *

Already running five minutes late, Gallic walking fast entered the lift. Arriving one floor down, he entered into the Tillman Penthouse Museum. While exiting the elevator, he glanced down at his perpetually vibrating ComsBand. The *Hound*'s AI was all excited about something. About to make the connection he heard—

"Stop where you are!"

Gallic did as told and looked up—looked up into five ominous black holes. Each was trained, he was certain, at a precise point right between his eyes. He was looking into the muzzles of five automatic rifles. The men holding those rifles were dressed in matching gray uniforms that were topped off with matching little caps upon their heads. They each wore military issue assault vests and had alternate side arms strapped to their thighs. They were loaded for bear.

Gallic closed his eyes. Of course, there would have been security feeds all around the rooftop and taking in every possible angle. His altercation with Sargento, and his hopefully still unconscious partner, surely captured into digital media for all time. *Crap!*

A sixth man, short and dressed exactly like the others, with one exception—a silver star mounted on the crown of his cap just above the bill. "Raise your hands over your head. Mr. Gallic. I am Security Chief Pepper. You are under arrest. Your vessel is in the process of being impounded."

Two men from the firing squad quickly shouldered their weapons and hurried over to where Gallic stood. Four hands began patting him down. His coat was thrown open and various items were methodically removed—his wallet, his arbiter's license, with an attached badge, and his Emanuel Dual 5. A rare, dual-barreled, over-under, .45 handgun, which had been secured into a custom-made holster inside his coat. The gun was tooled within the outer Frontier regions and given to him by a friend. Actually, he was more of an associate than a friend. Gallic had fired the weapon in the course of his arbiter duties six times. Of the six men who had drawn down on him—six were now taking a forever dirt nap. Two of those had been on Muleshoe.

Chief Pepper glanced at his license then spent more time looking at his weapon. He paid extra attention to the trigger mechanism.

"Not often you see that ... huh?"

Chief Pepper's eyes looked up at him.

"Two barrels, two firing mechanisms, one trigger and one hammer. Both lethal and compact ... don't you think?"

"What I think is the carrying of this weapon on Spector is illegal. Will only add to the minimum incarceration times for your other highly egregious offenses."

His arms were being pulled backwards, behind his back. Gallic felt his wrists being secured together with some kind of security bindings. Then Security Chief Pepper was holding two fingers up to one ear. His face went taut and he said, "Yes. Of course, Ms. Tillman ... but ... no ma'am. I work for you ... yes, but ... right away."

Chief Pepper took in a frustrated breath and then said, "Release him."

The two security guys, on each side of Gallic hesitated.

"Now!" Chief Pepper's face had reddened and a vein throbbed on his left temple. He stepped in close to Gallic and spoke just above a whisper. "I will be watching you. You won't be able to crap without me knowing about it."

"You want to know when I take a crap? Is that the important kind of work you guys do here?"

By the look in Chief Pepper's eyes, he didn't appreciate Gallic's humor.

"Give him back his things."

They did as told, then all six of the security detail hurried off leaving him standing there alone.

Gallic looked about the Tillman Penthouse Museum. The first thing he noticed was the penthouse's ceiling, easily looming seventy-five to one hundred feet above him. A breathtaking panorama, too, was the view out the floor-to-ceiling encircling windows—just spectacular. But nothing compared to what was featured within the building—exotic personal spacecraft. Even more ships than Gallic expected to see, yet from his present vantage point, he was viewing only some of them due to the curvature of the massive building. Some suspended from above—others not—each space vehicle was presented in a showroom-like condition.

"Welcome. They are presented in chronological order . . . the date they were first launched or flown into space."

Gallic heard the voice but didn't see the man connected with it.

"Up here, mate."

Gallic tracked the Aussie-accented voice upward to the closest spacecraft, one easily recognizable as a *Kipling Toring Una*. Thirty feet up, standing on the nearest wing, a man stood—hands on hips—in a "king of the mountain" pose. His royal-blue suit jacket fit snugly around his clearly muscular chest and upper arms. Nearly indiscernible, a faint bulge protruded just under his left armpit—a concealed weapon.

"What do you think of her?"

It was obvious to Gallic that great pains had been taken to bring the ninety-something-year-old craft back to its original grandeur. "I think I'd like to take it out for a test drive."

"You and everyone else. Hold on, be right down," he said, then turned and disappeared from sight.

Craning his neck upward, Gallic circling, eyed the antique spacecraft. The *Kipling Toring Una* was a medium-sized ship, little attention given to either style or aesthetics. Even the color, an Army olive-green, gave the vessel a more brass tack—utilitarian—appearance. The bow was rounded and bulbous—bug-like—while the remainder of the ship was mostly cylindrical. Two sets of stubby, angled-back wings were on each side. The last quarter of the ship, all the way back to its stern, flared out like the barrel of a Blunderbuss war musket.

"Ridgy-didge," the blue-suited man said, exiting from a power lift at the ship's midpoint.

Gallic looked at the man questioningly.

"Sorry . . . silly slang. All are its original parts. The *Una* was one of the first Tillman acquisitions. One of only three that exist . . . anywhere." Putting his hand out, he said, "Stannis Kay, at your service . . ."

The flamboyant Australian had stubby arms and legs on an oil drum of a body. His wheat-colored hair was slicked back, looking like he'd spent a lot of time on it. Gallic took the man's outstretched hand and shook it. Fleshy and moist, after shaking it, Gallic wanted to wipe his hand on something but thought better of it.

"John Gallic here... I have an appointment to see Ms. Tillman."

"Yes... I am the curator of the museum. All that you see here is under my charge. As I mentioned to the others, Ms. Tillman is running late. I'm here to assist you... answer any of your questions. Security of the building is also within my purview."

The others? Stannis undoubtedly was referring to his competition—Sargento and Hok'ee. Gallic briefly wondered if the curator had posed high up on the *Una*'s wingtip for them, too.

"Can I see where the *Hayai* was parked?" Gallic asked, starting to walk underneath the next ship in line.

"Best we go the other way around... the *Hayai* was one of our later additions. No need to walk past one hundred years of history. Come, we'll go this way, sir."

chapter 18

Planet Spector, Harriot — Tillman Building.

Passing in front of the same bank of elevators Gallic had emerged from only minutes before, they came around near the end of the circular exhibit. They passed under three vessels, billionaires' toys, each nearly reaching the penthouse ceiling. Shiny, new, and ultra-modern, one was dark red, one a neon-blue, and one polished metal. Gallic could spend all day viewing the luxurious, *oh-so-sleek-looking* vessels inside and out, but with Sargento and Hok'ee already on the hunt, that wouldn't be smart.

Stannis came to a halt in front of an open space where the fourth spacecraft should have been on display. He shook his head, looking genuinely sad. "Do you know what the name *Hayai* means, Mr. Gallic?"

"It's a Japanese word, isn't it?"

Stannis nodded. "It means fast, and this ship," he gestured to the open space, "is very, very fast. But more than that, it is the quintessential pinnacle of luxury and high-tech."

"Wish I could have seen it," Gallic said.

"These days ... most of Earth's finest designs come from Fukuoka, Japan ... on the island of Kyushu ... from furniture to fashion to industrial and mechanical design. The *Hayai* was designed there. Of course, nothing is built on Earth ... not anymore."

Gallic's thoughts flashed back to the Cugan's den and to Juaquin, in her designer jeans. It wasn't news to him that the fashion design capital of Earth, and eventually to the frontier of space, was Fukuoka.

"Can you talk to me about security. How was it possible to move a vessel out of here without tripping an alarm?"

"It wouldn't be possible. It would be impossible, Mr. Gallic."

"I imagine your insurance premiums will skyrocket now."

Stannis looked as if he'd swallowed a bug. "When activated, this building has it all ... infrared sweeps, pressure plates, atmosphere analyzers ... which can detect when CO_2 levels change after hours. Temperature triggers, vibration triggers, auditory triggers, continual diametric laser comparison technology, not to mention all the rooftop alarms and security up there, which is the only way a vehicle could have been removed." Stannis pointed to a large, nearly imperceptible access panel on the ceiling. "There's a long list of security measures that, combined, are simply impossible to avoid."

"Yeah, and the Titanic was unsinkable," Gallic said flatly. "Standing now, in front of this empty space... someone's figured it out. Either that, or—"

Stannis stopped him. "No... not an inside job."

Glancing about the space, the strut indentations still visible in the low-pile carpeting, then at the big ships both left and right, Gallic wondered if this wasn't an insider job. How could someone defeat all those safeguard systems, otherwise? And how many would it take to do so? "I'll need all the specifics. Brands... the model numbers of your security equipment, specifications. There are a finite number of people with the technical background... the wherewithal—to pull off a job like this. I still have connections within D-22. I should be able to database, cross-match potential criminal elements. Those who could possess the capability to pull off an operation like this."

"Ms. Tillman is well aware of your qualifications. Yes, the Galaxy Man comes highly recommended," Stannis said, as Gallic inwardly cringed.

Stannis, positioning his hands on his hips, looked suddenly thoughtful. His jacket had pulled apart enough for the butt of his holstered pistol to be seen.

Gallic's thoughts turned to Tori, who'd be arriving back on Muleshoe sometime the next day. He hadn't planned on staying on Spector overnight, but it clearly was necessary now. "Look, it's getting late. This will take me far more time than the hours left in the day. I'd like to take a vid sweep of the premises... this floor, as well as the roof, and the floor beneath... then come back in the morning and finish up."

"That will be fine. I should have the information you want collected by then. Ms. Tillman had me make overnight accommodations for you at the Bollinger, in Harriot City."

"Also, I was under the impression I'd be able to meet with her . . . in person, while here on Spector," Gallic said.

Gallic proceeded to spend the better part of the next three hours at the museum. Using his ComsBand, he completed detailed vid sweeps of the penthouse—its numerous spacecraft exhibits, the vehicle set-down upper parking lot, and the floor below the penthouse—primarily used by executives, including Allison Tillman's expansive 3,500 square foot office space.

Periodically, Stannis Kay would check in on Gallic. Finished for the evening, Stannis appeared again.

"I trust you made good use of your time, Mr. Gallic? Ms. Tillman is keen to resolve this mystery . . . has been inquiring about your actions on a regular basis."

"She's free to contact me directly should she want to," Gallic said, tapping the face of his ComsBand.

"I'm sure she has every intention of doing so."

"It's been a long day . . . I'm tired and hungry. I'll be heading off to the Bollinger now, if it's all the same to you."

"Of course. But you'll want to leave your, um, vessel here. There's no adequate set-down facilities for a vessel that large anywhere in Harriot City. If you're ready, I'll have a shuttle brought around for you."

"That'll be fine. Just need to grab an overnight bag from the *Hound* first."

At the mention of the *Hound*, Stannis did a poor job hiding his distaste. "Well, until tomorrow then, Mr. Gallic. Have a good night."

* * *

Once checked-in at the Bollinger, a luxurious hotel Gallic normally couldn't afford, he figured he may as well take advantage of the situation since he wasn't paying the tab. He left his long leather overcoat in his hotel room. Cowboy sheik wasn't going to cut it around there. Dressed in dark-gray slacks and a button-down white dress shirt, he ventured down to the hotel lobby. Discovering the Bollinger had four, on-site restaurants, he chose the one called The Captain's Maiden. It sounded the least snooty of the bunch. Seated at a small table in a dark corner of the noisy eatery, he found the attending staff both polite and efficient, though neither warm nor particularly welcoming. He obviously didn't fit in—at the hotel or in Harriot City.

He ordered a rare steak and the hotel's on-tap beer. The steak was overcooked and the beer tasteless—the color of piss. An altogether forgettable meal, he put the bill on his hotel tab. Still relatively early, he decided to take a walk around the city— see the local sites.

Outside, the night air was warm, the streets buzzing with fast-moving hovercrafts. The sidewalks bustled with pedestrians, and Gallic received his fair share of subtle sideways glances. Not a city where conservative dress was the norm, the citizens of Spector, at least the ones in Harriot City, were primped and fluffed. Dressed up in gaudy clothes, both men and women were laden down with glitzy jewelry. Glancing into a still-open shop window, he noticed that the price of a pair of men's leather shoes was well over one thousand dollars. He wondered why everything in this city was so expensive.

Eventually, Gallic hit what he guessed was the city's heart. Lights blazed bright and overhead holograms spoke, yelled, or sang competitively over one another. A distraction, that seemed to bother only him and no one else. The main street, called River Ridge Drive, reminded him of Las Vegas, back on Earth. Clearly, there was an abundance of wealth around—young rich men and women buying whatever they wanted, to the point of excessiveness.

Leaving behind the noise of River Ridge Drive, Gallic spotted a virtual movie theater off to his right. An animated holographic poster was promoting several scenes from Zip Furlong's, *aka Teddy Walters'* current movie—titled "Alpha Man." He played the villain in that galactic space opera.

Looks entertaining, Gallic thought to himself, *but maybe a little stupid*. His thoughts were suddenly drawn back to his second encounter with Teddy, when Teddy invited him and Clair to the premiere of his latest movie, some five years past. Gallic experienced a funny feeling in his gut just thinking about it. He always thought Teddy had a *thing* for Clair. *Hell, who didn't?* She was beautiful and brilliant and funny, yet also humble and unpretentious. He remembered when he'd first met her in college, back after a four year stint in the Royal Marines, and enrolled in law enforcement courses. She was a graduate student *techy-nerd*—even then, she was designing and innovating systems for the burgeoning space industry. Later, she received her PhD in physics while pregnant with Mandy. So different from each other but somehow their pieces came together; somehow fit. A young woman clearly out of his league. He still wondered how they'd ended up together. But . . . then they didn't end up together for very long. The hammer-and-nails murderer saw to that.

The holographic preview changed to a new scene—one with Teddy looking villainous, yielding some kind of energy weapon. Gallic thought back to the movie's premiere, five years past. Teddy's girlfriend then was a gorgeous woman too, only she wasn't all that bright. And there was a weird kind of tension in the way Teddy treated her—protective, but overly possessive too. He clearly didn't approve of her speaking to other men when she was alone; was even leery when she went to the ladies' room, to the point he hassled Clair to go along with her one time. Gallic didn't realize how much it all bothered him until now. He didn't like seeing women treated like prize possessions, or decorator arm candy. Musing, he thought about the great advances civilization had made in the past one hundred years, but how sexism and racism still continued to exist. How was that possible?

His wrist began to vibrate. Checking it, there was a waiting message from Danbury.

Heading back to the hotel, he tapped at the band and listened.

"John . . . I was hoping to speak with you in person. There's been another murder. Right there, in your neck of the woods. Another woman vic, I'm afraid. Tori will have further details by the time she arrives on Gorman."

Listening to the message for a second time, Gallic's heart began to race. For some reason, he thought of Lane then quickly pushed the image of her away.

chapter 19

Planet Spector — High Orbit.

Gallic nixed spending the night at the Bollinger—too damn riled up now to sleep. After hailing a hover cab to the Tillman building, he was back at the controls of the *Hound* within the hour. He left Ms. Tillman a vid message— letting her know he was on the case; had ample information to begin the search for the missing *Hayai*. Gallic verified with the *Hound's* AI that Stannis Kay had indeed CoreNet mail-beamed him the on-site security equipment's technical specifications.

Leaving high orbit, Gallic set a course for Heritage Plains on Gorman then tried to get some sleep en route.

* * *

The vermin visited him in his sleep again, waiting in the shadows of a splendid, though fairly mundane dream, just waiting to pounce. A dream of everyday life with him, Mandy, and Clair eating a sleepy Sunday morning breakfast. When Mandy grabbed for the box of Cheerios, the box exploded into a rampage of squirming swine.

"Mr. Gallic ... we have entered Gorman high orbit. Will we proceed to the Cugan ranch again?"

"No." Gallic, rubbing his face, stared blankly at the bulkhead across the compartment. Climbing from his bunk he made his way to the head—washing his face then brushing his teeth. Once settled back in the control center, he brought up the coordinates left by Danbury. The murder location was several hundred miles away from the Bower crime scene—in. He inwardly sighed in relief, that the vic couldn't be Lane. Over the past twenty-four hours, he'd purposely veered his thoughts away from that enticing, surprisingly distracting, woman.

"I'm entering the coordinates now. Do me a favor, AI, keep an eye out for Sergeant Tori's star-cruiser."

"Yes ... I will do that, sir," the AI responded, in its all too pleasant voice. Gallic momentarily wondered if the AI was aware of his dislike for it—for artificial intelligence, in general. Not personal to this AI, he didn't much like AI's ... period. Why he hadn't gone the route most ship skippers did—naming their ship's AI. Cute names, like Ted or Bart or Dave. AI's weren't human—only an assemblage of advanced circuitry; endless lines of software code. They didn't possess human traits, like empathy or loyalty. AI's were only a tool, and this one in particular was a bigger tool than most.

"We have arrived in the township of Stanford Pride. Sergeant Tori's star-cruiser is not present at the scene, Mr.

Gallic. I will notify you upon her arrival. We will touch down within eight minutes."

"Just hand over the controls now . . . I'll take her in."

With the *Hound* coming in low over thousands of square acres of fertile ranchland, Gallic took notice of the various ranches—the older, one-story homes, barns, and miscellaneous outbuildings. Here at Stanford Pride, the properties were far more modest than the wealthier residences of Heritage Plains. The real thing here—not only working-cattle ranches but agricultural-producing properties interspersing them as well.

The console nav display indicated the *Hound* was approaching Gallic's destination—the crime scene. He mentally went through a now-familiar routine of closing windows and doors—double-checking all points of egress into the darkest recesses of his mind—then slowed, fired-up the underbelly thrusters and lowered the landing struts. He set the big vessel down, fifty yards from the front entrance of the faded-yellow farmhouse. Sitting back, he listened to the propulsion system wind-down, eventually silencing. He waited.

Fifteen minutes later, Gallic thought about having a drink, what with all the old memories and feelings churned up over recent days. He'd thought a lot about Clair and Mandy. He looked over his shoulder in the direction of the ship's den, where a not-too-shabby bottle of bourbon sat locked in his safe. He thought about the contents in the brown-amber bottle— the elixir he'd turned to for so many months, after the death of his wife and child. Drinking heavily every day for nearly a year had almost killed him. He'd vowed to rein in any alcohol consumption until he found their murderer. And for today at least, he would keep that promise.

"Sergeant Tori's star-cruiser is inbound, Mr. Gallic."

Gallic, glancing out the window, caught the small dot now moving into view on the distant horizon.

* * *

Gallic stared at the front door. His inner vermin, restless once again, were back on the move. A part of him contemplated leaving—getting as far away from the place as possible. The spat of murders had become intimately personal. *Slow, John, take deep breaths.*

Gallic waited for Tori to emerge from her ship. It was a newer model than the one she'd first arrived in at the other crime scene in Heritage Plains. This ship was a good deal larger and, judging by the deeper rumble he heard coming from the aft section of the cruiser, a bit more powerful.

She opened the hatch and gave Gallic a half-hearted smile. Climbing out, she stretched, saying, "These treks to the Frontier worlds are getting old."

"You get used to it," he said. "Nice new ride."

"Yeah . . . and that's only the half of it."

He noticed there was *something* different—*a glow* about her. *Maybe confidence?* Gallic didn't want to take credit for that but giving her the support she needed to become a real detective—well, that could go a long way.

Tori walked around the cruiser to the double-hatch doors at the rear of the vehicle. "The victims here are a single mother and her ten-year-old daughter. The Johnsons—mother Melissa, daughter Briar." Tori stopped talking just long enough to pop an anti-nausea pill into her mouth and grimaced. "Nasty tasting things."

But Gallic was studying the contents lying in the cruiser's rear hold area. "You've got . . ."

"Some new toys!" she exclaimed with enthusiasm.

"I can see that. I didn't think D-22 had invested in this level of field forensics."

"Oh, it's bigger than that, Gallic . . . we're talking a whole new approach to field work. Field work that now goes so much farther . . ."

Gallic stared at the shiny new equipment cases. None, he'd even bet money on, had been opened yet. With this equipment, full autopsies could be conducted in the field. The digitized results forwarded onto D-22 practically in real time. No longer laboriously waiting for the vic's body to be transported and tabled—days, sometimes weeks, later.

"Did you get any kind of training . . . to use this stuff?"

"It's called Micro blading. Micro autopsy drones."

Gallic nodded as Tori climbed into the rear hold, handing out various-sized equipment cases.

"I did get a quick run-through back at the division, but everything's pretty much automated. Idiot-proof; plug and play. I figured you and I could get acquainted with the equipment together," she said, gesturing with her head toward the house.

Her new change in attitude surprised him, considering that projectile-hurling episode at the last murder scene.

Gathering up the equipment, they moved ahead to the front door. Stopping to put on crime scene booties and latex gloves, Gallic thought about the other murder, also taken place within the last week. *Was the murderer getting impatient? Starting to move things along?*

"Who's been in here, prior to us?" Gallic asked, turning the doorknob and finding it unlocked.

"One of the ranch employees. Apparently, he and others come inside during an average day. The house doubles as the ranch's front office. In the mornings, the kitchen is where you can find coffee. His name is Alejandro. Reporting the crime, he apologized for throwing-up on his way out of the house . . . so watch your step heading in."

"Noted. Another contaminated murder scene."

"Hey!" she said, feigning a look of hurt feelings.

Gallic swung the door open then stepped inside, silently letting the dormant space speak to him. First impressions were often a fundamental element of the forensic process; the intangible sometimes provided an astute investigator some subtle insights at an unconscious level. Gallic didn't subscribe to having psychic abilities, but he was intuitive—sensitive to unseen currents at a murder scene. A good detective had to be.

"What are you doing?" Tori asked, transferring the new equipment off the front porch and into the house.

Gallic explained to her the best he could. Actually listening intently, he saw her close her eyes—attempting to attune herself the same as him. The house was oppressively dark and quiet, appearing larger from the outside. A small living room held an upright piano, pushed up against the far wall. Two light blue couches faced each other; a small, glass coffee table placed between them. Three medium-sized oil paintings hanging on different walls looked amateurish—perhaps made by a family member, or a friend. Near the door lay a puddle of vomit—splattered halfway on the floor and halfway up the wall.

"The bodies are in the master bedroom, Gallic. Other end of the house."

Bodies—*bodies like Clair's and Mandy's*. Gallic took two of the heavier cases from Tori then proceeding forward, walked down a narrow hallway covered in worn, dark-brown carpeting. Only then did he breathe in the unmistakable odor of death.

They passed by a narrow, galley-style kitchen—its sole window peering out to endless miles of what Gallic surmised were stalks of corn. On the counter rested a coffee machine and stacks of now-slumbering vid-sheets.

"Ugh . . ."

"You okay back there?" Gallic asked over his shoulder.

"If you're asking me if I'm going to spew . . . I'm fine. Maybe."

They made their way into the master bedroom, Gallic's own stomach was protesting at the increased retched smell. At the room's threshold, the dark carpeting had noticeably transitioned into a lighter beige color. Two bedside tables flanked an unmade queen-sized bed; a TV panel hung on the opposing wall. Two sets of bare feet, lying on the carpeting, extended out from the other side of the bed.

Being careful where he walked, Gallic came around the foot of the bed and took in the murder scene. He felt Tori's presence close beside him, her hand resting on her stomach. He heard her swallow. Neither one spoke.

He looked at them and shook his head. Since the murder of his own wife and child—there'd been a flurry of media attention. Why that one particular double murder had become so popular with so many, both on Earth and beyond, into distant space, Gallic didn't know. Perhaps because Clair was beautiful, and Mandy—a smaller version of her mother—was also beautiful; and adorable, too. Making their dual murder a heart wrenching, impossible not to take personal, affront to most everyone's sensibilities. The media explosion—24-hour news updates—then the leaked, gruesome, crime scene imagery of the double murder continued to steal headlines for nearly a year. To Gallic's knowledge, Clair and Mandy's killer had not murdered again, although he was still waiting to hear any final evidence conclusion regarding the Heritage Plains' double murders—of Catherine and Tami Bower. But now it seemed there were more: Melissa Johnson, the mother and Briar Johnson, the daughter. Both were dressed similarly—T-shirts and worn, dirty jeans. No shoes or socks. Mother and daughter were holding hands. Arterial spray had been confined to the lower wall and the bottom of the bed cover. They had died right here. Staring down at their ashen faces, he momentarily tried to visualize them through the murderer's eyes, then waited for either, or both of the inert corpses, to speak to him. *Who did this to you?* The scene was similar to the others, as of course it would be. But also, blatantly different, and that made Gallic nervous.

The mother's eyelids were nailed shut and characteristically, both their faces were wiped clean. Only this time, Briar, the little girl, had her eyes closed. Stick figure paintings were sketched on the wall, drawn in their blood. "It looks like ancient hieroglyphs," Tori said.

Gallic stepped over the mother's body, careful to avoid stepping in the saturated-with-blood carpeting, "They appear to be images of . . . human figures."

"What's that . . . those lines?" Tori asked.

"Just that . . . lines drawn through both figures' eyes."

Tori read aloud the smeared, rust-colored line of text: "Keep them blind, keep them blind, only then will we truly see."

Gallic had no idea what to think. Obviously, the blind-eyes-text was linked to the nails through the mother's eyelids. Was it only meant for women with young daughters? Or meant to keep *all* women blind?

"It just reiterates the fact that this isn't a copycat killer, someone taking this kind of . . . um . . . creative liberty with the crime scene."

Gallic shrugged. He'd already dismissed any possibility of this being the work of a copycat.

"Whoever did this is a sexist fuck . . . really twisted," Tori said.

Gallic hadn't thought before about a sexist slant to the murders, but maybe she was on to something.

"Ready to get schooled now on the latest field forensic tools known to mankind?" she asked, giving him a crooked smile.

"And the student becomes the master," Gallic said, welcoming the distraction. "Show me what you know."

chapter 20

Frontier Planet, Muleshoe — Stanford Pride.

Tori opened the first of the pristine-looking cases marked Processing Kit 1, and Gallic was fairly sure he knew what he was viewing.

"Pretty much everything is automated ... things you're used to doing by hand no longer require that."

"Field DNA Sampler?" he asked.

"Yup. Now called an autonomous field DNA sampler ... AFDS. This equipment has already been set to the D-22 case number. So, the case specifics, thus far, are already loaded into the equipment, into individual micro-AIs." Tori lifted the small bug-like unit, with its bulbous, unsymmetrical shape, out of the case. "This uses the latest, reverse-grav technology." She tapped several prompts on the small touch screen, and the small fist-sized unit took to the air.

It hovered several feet off the floor for a moment before a funnel, like a mosquito's proboscis, extended out from what Gallic assumed was the front of the device. "The sniffer?" Gallic asked.

"That's right."

Without so much as a whisper, the AFDS climbed higher, then flew out through the open bedroom door.

"It's already collecting tons of raw data, much more than just DNA, from the rest of the house. Every inch of the house is also being filmed. It'll do this room last."

Tori and Gallic were now squatting on their knees at the vics' feet. While she readied the next piece of equipment, he studied the two victims, placing his attention on particular details of the scene. One thing struck him as odd. There was very little space below on that side of the bed. Two bodies, lying side-by-side, with hardly enough room for the killer to do his handiwork. "He either had to sit ... or lie down on the bed."

Tori glanced up. "Lying down on his stomach ... he'd be able to get close and personal."

Gallic glanced toward the unmade bed and thought he could just make out a slight impression on the rumpled sheets. Someone had lain across the bed sideways.

"Here we go," Tori said. "This next kit provides a series of micro-blading chewer probes."

"Chewer? Oh my ... that sounds fairly disgusting," Gallic said, making a wry face.

"I try not to think about it," she responded flatly. "Assisted by tiny scanners, they perform miniature blood and tissue testing—a whole range of analytical capabilities. We'll be using several different kinds of probes. Three internally, which will extensively look for an inner cause of death; testing blood for alcohol, drugs, natural and man-made toxins, or poisons, or other kinds of suspicious foreign agents. And two probes for external examination, collecting details on the outer epidermal surface of each body. Also, an external probe will roam around their clothing, looking for trace evidence." She then held up a metallic injector gun with a blue handgrip for him to see. "We'll begin with the intravenous chewer probes . . . starting in the brain."

"How do you get them into the body. There's no moving circulatory system . . . no beating heart to—"

Tori cut him off: "The first submersible drone is inserted, more like fired, into the cranium via a small hole the injector gun makes in the back of the head—into the skull. But first, we need to let the AFDS do its scans right here, on the undisturbed bodies."

As if on cue, the hovering bug device reentered the master bedroom, coming to a halt in mid-air.

"That's our cue to evacuate the room for a few minutes. Let it collect the rest of its data."

Waiting in the hall together, it took less than five minutes for the AFDS to complete its work. Hearing a soft triple beep sound, Gallic stepped back into the bedroom and looked around for the hovering device.

"Back in its case already ..." Tori said, throwing a glancing nod toward the still-open case.

Sure enough, the AFDS sniffer was back, sleeping within its padded enclosure confines. "Cool! I think I like your new toys, so far at least."

Gallic watched Tori hesitate, holding onto the injection gun. Her eyes lingered on the two victims, then on the unkempt bed where the killer had recently lain.

"Why don't you let me take over the next part?" Gallic offered, holding out a hand. "Is there anything specific I need to know ... like the placement of the injector?"

Tori hesitated, then handed him the instrument. "The *Foramen Magnum* ... at the back of the skull—"

"I know where that is," he said, taking the injector from her, then positioned himself sideways across the bed so that his head and chest hung down over the side of the mattress. Now, only a foot-and-a-half directly below him, he could see both victims' faces. He had to remind himself they were the faces of total strangers. *Keep it together.* It occurred to Gallic that not so many hours earlier their killer, too, had stared down on their lifeless faces just like now. He didn't like that thought—that he and the killer shared something in common. Starting with the younger victim first, Gallic used his left hand to turn her head away from the bed. Residual rigor made the process a bit more difficult. He saw where the killer had, most likely, used the sharp point of a nail to carve the same initials into the back of the neck:

TCW

He positioned the thin metallic muzzle of the instrument at the back of her skull, where it curved around joining her neck, right into the hollow there—the *Foramen Magnum.* "Like this?" he asked.

Tori rose up, inspecting where he'd positioned the injector. "Yeah, that should do it."

Gallic pulled the trigger. Hearing a nearly imperceptible *pssst* sound, he briefly wondered what an activated little chewer drone would do inside a living person's brain? He then repeated the same skull procedure on the mother.

"Okay, four more to go," Tori said, handing him another injector gun. This one had a red plastic handle and was labeled Esophagus. Not needing special instruction on its use, he opened the mother's mouth and inserted the slender muzzle. On feeling resistance as the tip hit the back of her throat, he eased it back a bit then pulled the trigger. He repeated the same procedure on the child. "And the last of the internal probes?" he asked, handing her back the red-handled injector.

She pointed her chin toward both bodies' lower extremities. "This one does scans for a complete lower GI . . . urinary, reproductive organs . . . that sort of thing. Why don't you take a break? I'll do it . . . a part of me already feels they've been humiliated enough . . . and maybe a woman should do this next procedure."

Gallic pushed himself away from near the bodies and climbed off the bed. Tori handed him a vid-sheet manual. "Here, you can read up on the technology."

While Tori busied herself with removing the mother's jeans, Gallic stepped away and swiped through the virtual pages. He read that small micro-blades could cut into flesh without leaving a visible trace—a process far more reliable than other current methods. The whole process took up to twenty minutes. Data processing would take another ten minutes, then the results were sent back to the main database at D-22. If setup that way, the same data could be available for the forensics team, working at the local scene as well.

Tori now had the lower GI chewer probes inserted into both victims' bodies. Then, replacing the injector back into its case, she brought out a different-looking device. "We don't actually touch these external body probes. Too sensitive to be handled." She placed an unimpressive small black container, about the size of a pack of cigarettes, on the chest of the little girl. Red, yellow, and green lights blinked on then stayed a steady green. The end of the container flipped open and two mechanical, thumb tack-sized *bots* crawled out onto her shirt. Tiny antennae fluttered as they then moved off again—one skittering over the folds of her shirt as the other moved up to her neckline, disappearing beneath the fabric.

"It'll take the probes about ten more minutes to process both epidermal and clothing trace evidence analyses."

"Hey, I'm going to get some air . . . you okay in here alone?" he asked.

"I'm fine."

Gallic looked at her with concern.

"I promise . . . I'm fine. Go."

Gallic made his way through the house then out the front door, finding it dark outside. Night had arrived and a heavy wet mist had settled in, to the point he couldn't see the ground. In the near distance was the *Hound* and above him a star-filled sky. Breathing in the fragrant air, he thought *just has to be corn*. He looked back at the front of the house with growing trepidation, thinking about the glyphs he'd seen on the wall. *Soon, you son of a bitch, you're going to make a mistake. That's when the hammer-and-nails killer will come to an end.*

chapter 21

Frontier Planet, Muleshoe — Stanford Pride.

G allic helped transfer the bodies and stow the equipment into Tori's new star-cruiser. Closing and latching the aft hatch, she rubbed her eyes and yawned.

"Why don't you head back tomorrow? Stay on the *Hound* tonight and make a fresh start in the morning. Got plenty of room," Gallic told her.

"Thanks for the offer, but I just want to get back to D-22; start analyzing this new crime scene data. I'll sleep some en route."

"You sure?" Gallic asked.

Tori nodded. "I'll contact you in a day or two. We can powwow then . . . determine our next move."

"I'll do some preliminary work on the wall glyphs, if that's okay?" Gallic asked. Since this was still Tori's case, he didn't want to overstep his bounds.

"Yeah . . . go for it! There's a lot to do. Thanks!" Climbing into the bow of the craft, Tori revved the propulsion system up. Before shutting the hatch, she asked,

"What does your gut tell you . . . that it's him? That it's not another copycat killing?"

Gallic shrugged, non-committing. "As you said . . . we'll talk in a few days."

Tori closed the hatch, kicked on her lift thrusters then powered up into the air. Within moments she was gone from sight, the night again still.

* * *

After taking a scorching hot shower ang brushing his teeth, Gallic felt somewhat cleansed of the crime scene. Dressed in fresh clothing, he settled in behind the *Hound*'s command center console and ran through the pre-flight checklist. Satisfied, he initialized the propulsion system. The two big gravitorque drives momentarily shook as they awoke—soon humming steadily. He glanced out at the faded-yellow house through the window. It looked small and vulnerable, like its best days were in the past. He thought of the simple folks that had lived there. The mother and child, who'd done nothing to deserve their untimely fate. Then, thinking of Clair and Mandy, he fought to keep his growing fury in check. "I'm going to catch you, mother fucker . . . count on it."

Gallic turned his attention to his ComsBand and tapped on the small screen until he found what he was looking for. Tapping again, a series of twelve large crime scene images appeared. They hovered in mid-air, two rows of six, several feet off to the side. He avoided looking at the body images, instead concentrating on the wall glyphs. They really did look like stick figure paintings—caveman-like.

"AI . . . configure a CoreNet mail-beam hail."

"Who would you like to contact, Mr. Gallic?"

"Professor Harkins on Earth. He's typically in the U.S., Washington, D.C. area. See if he's open to a coms meeting . . . as soon as he has an opening."

"And what shall I say the meeting is regarding?"

"A D-22 murder investigation. Tell him we need a subject matter expert. An expert possessing a unique skill set."

"I have opened a channel and initiated the contact."

Gallic turned back to the console. Taking the controls in his hands, he goosed the lift thrusters.

"Shall I input destination coordinates for you, Mr. Gallic?"

"What time is it?"

"Local time, sir?"

"Yeah."

"It is 5:39 p.m., local Gorman Plains time"

"Still early enough. Set a course back to Heritage Plains. Um . . . take us back to the Cugan's ranch."

"I have the coordinates. I will input that destination."

"Good ... lock it in. Can you tell me if Lane ..." he realized he didn't know her last name, "lives in the general vicinity around there? If she has her own place?"

It took a moment before the AI came back with, "She has her own small dwelling on a parcel of land, located near the northeastern section of the Cugan property."

"Okay ... go ahead and lock that in. And AI, let's keep things quiet for a bit. I need to concentrate."

Gallic thought about Lane; the image of her pretty face had surfaced into his thoughts several times over the past few days, but he'd quickly shut her out. He was good at that—warding off errant thoughts that didn't serve him. He thought of her now, though. Recalling their lovemaking; how much trouble the woman, potentially, could be. Not since Clair had he opened his heart to another. He thought of her indignation; her saying to him, "*This can never happen again.*" Smiling, he thought, *yeah, we'll see.* What he needed was an escape from the day's horror. A reprieve from the mental images stuck on constant replay in his mind. Yeah, he needed to make a connection with someone vibrant and alive—even if it was only conversation.

* * *

By the time the *Hound* rumbled in low over the dark pasturelands of Heritage Plains, the hour was pushing 8:00 p.m. Gallic glanced to the nav display to see if they were now close. *She probably wasn't even home.* A girl like that doesn't sit home a lot, was his guess. Below, he saw the nearly indistinguishable outline of the Johnson house and made a mental note to speak with the deceased wife's husband in the morning, although Tori should have handled that while she was here. Why Superintendent Bernard Danbury hadn't made that a mandatory component—her being there—was beyond him. *Or was it?* Didn't it always come down to money or power—or both? The people living around here, who owned thousands of acres of prime ranchland, would fit that bill. Danbury had always been a fine cop and a fine super. Was he so easily influenced now? *What had changed?*

The *Hound* banked then slowed to a mere crawl over a quaint small ranch below. A modest white farmhouse, *maybe gray*, and an adjacent—what appeared to be in the near total darkness—bright-red barn. A dim light emanated from the front window of the house.

"Mr. Gallic, there seems to be ample space for the *Hound* to set down below."

"Just make sure you don't land us on top of a cow or, god forbid, a horse."

Gallic stood and ran his fingers through his still moist hair. *What if she's not alone? Well, it's too late now; wasn't like she didn't know he was here. Hell, there wasn't a ranch miles around that didn't know he was here.*

By the time he stepped down from the gangway, the front porch light had come on. A slim woman, wearing loose-fitting sweats and a pink tank top, could be seen leaning against the open door frame. Her exposed tanned arms were crossed over her chest—a chest clearly devoid of a bra.

"What do you think you're doing here?" Lane asked, with a raised, questioning brow.

Gallic took her all in—from her bare feet up to her long hair, now tied into some sort of *thing* at the top of her head. "Catch you at a bad time?"

"It's pushing 8:30 . . . this is a working ranch, you know. Up at dawn, to bed after dusk . . ."

"So, I woke you up, then?"

"No . . . but you sure could have. I was getting ready to crawl into bed."

Gallic came to a stop several paces before her. The porch light behind her made it appear she wore a halo around her head. He could see she'd washed her face. Her skin had that just-scrubbed radiance about it. A scattering of small freckles ran across the bridge of her nose, and he wondered why he hadn't noticed them before. "You want me to leave?"

Lane pursed her lips, deciding. "You've been thinking about me," she said, more of a statement than a question.

"And you me," he replied back.

"I told you never again . . . that was it . . . an impulse thing. Do you remember me saying that?"

"That was bullshit. You didn't mean it. We both know that."

"Oh, do we now? What I should do, is turn around and shut the door in your face."

"Yeah, well, that wouldn't be very neighborly of you."

She laughed at that. "You're not my neighbor."

Gallic shrugged, half-turning toward the *Hound*, "See that? That's my place. It's as big as a house. Bigger. So right now, we are neighbors."

Lane slowly nodded. "Then I guess I better ask you to come on inside, neighbor."

"I suppose you should."

He closed the distance between them in one long stride. Her arms came up and encircled his neck just as their lips came together. They kissed long and hard—the way two people do when their raw attraction for one another is all-consuming, can no longer be denied. Not for a minute—not even a second.

chapter 22

Frontier Planet, Gorman — Heritage Plains Township.

Gallic did his best not to jostle the bed while he pulled on his left boot.

"Where you going?" Lane murmured in a sleepy voice. "It's late. I guess I should say it's early. Why don't you stay? I'll make us breakfast in an hour or two." She leaned forward, holding the bed sheet up to cover her naked chest, and placed a warm hand on his back.

"My mind is doing cartwheels . . . figured I'd get some work done. I can come back. I'm only next door."

"Oh yeah . . . we're neighbors, huh? I heard about those new murders . . . the mother and her little girl."

Gallic, sliding his right boot on, simply shook his head.

"Are you any closer to catching the guy? Did you find any other clues?"

Gallic readjusted his position on the edge of the bed so he could face her. "Maybe. A break in the killer's routine."

"What kind of break in routine?"

Gallic didn't like discussing open cases; knew from experience it was a bad idea. One that could get a detective in hot water with his superiors. But he was no longer the DCI. "Just a rough drawing. Some writing on the wall . . . near the victims."

"Tell me."

"Why? What difference does it make?"

"Just tell me," she urged.

"Two stick figures, maybe representative of the mother and her little girl. Their eyes had lines drawn through them."

Lane nodded. "And the writing?"

"Keep them blind, keep them blind, only then will we truly see." Gallic watched as her expression changed. Lane looked away, as if what he'd just shared reminded her of *something*; something upsetting. Suddenly her eyelids squeezed tightly shut, and her breathing became labored. "Lane . . . what is it?"

Lane began to shake, her eyes rolling back in her head, with only the whites visible. Her body was now convulsing uncontrollably.

Gallic pulled her close into him—wrapping his arms around her. "Lane . . . Lane . . . it's okay. Easy now . . . just breathe." Her shuddering slowly diminished, and he heard her mumbling something into his chest. Her voice was different— like a young girl's.

"The *Curz* are always watching. They make sure we don't see. Only they have true sight. I am blind. I am blind. I am most useful when I can't see."

Feeling her body go limp in his arms, he leaned her back on the bed and checked her pulse. It was steady and strong. *What the hell just happened?* He thought about what she said. *The Curz? Wasn't that the name of the alien race that left their ship behind on Mars?*

Lane's eyes opened, and she blinked several times. "I must have fallen asleep. I'm sorry."

Gallic watched her sit up, appearing both calm and normal, though her movements seemed rather odd. Robot-like.

"I'm glad you came by, Gallic. I'd love to stay up and talk, but I'm tired now. I need . . ." her eyes closed, and her breathing changed over to deep long breaths. She was out.

Gallic continued to stare down at Lane for several minutes, badly wanting to wake her up. Ask her what she meant but she'd completely shut down. She shouldn't know anything about the writings . . . the stick figures. He felt uneasy, then a door began to rattle violently within the recesses of his mind. He saw movement—something slithering past the gap beneath the door. Gallic abruptly stood, glanced around Lane's bedroom, then . . .

He stepped out into the night and headed for the *Hound*. Walking—deep in thought, not really noticing his surroundings—he nearly missed it. Then, gazing up, he caught sight of something high up on the ship's hull. Squinting into the darkness, he first thought it was graffiti. He could barely make out the lettering—TCW. Spray-painted on, red paint dripped down like long streams of blood.

Gallic wondered how anyone climbed up there since it was easily forty to fifty feet above the ground. Once back inside the *Hound*, he queried the AI, "Were you asleep, or what?"

"I am not clear on the meaning of your query, Mr. Gallic."

"Someone, obviously, circumvented the *Hound's* security measures. Display video from the portside monitoring feeds now. Start with the last three hours."

"I assure you, there has been no unauthorized breach of the *Hound's* security perimeter. My sensors would have—"

"Just do it!"

Gallic watched the video progression, what appeared to be a non-eventful evening via multiple camera feeds. He could partially make out Lane's house in two of them. "Fast forward."

At the two hour mark, something moved. "Normal frame rate," he ordered. And then there it was, a small hovercraft could be seen approaching. He'd seen them around. They had open-bed and cab areas and were used by ranch hands all over these parts. As the craft moved in closer, Gallic could almost make out the driver. Whoever he was, he was dressed completely in black, with a hoodie covering his head. His face was in shadows, so impossible to make out.

"You're telling me you didn't see this guy?" Gallic asked.

"I did see him. I am recalling data now. I was instructed to ignore him."

Gallic continued to watch the portside feeds. He watched as the little hovercraft moved into position, high up against the hull, then the man in black began to spray paint those three letters. Within moments, the hovercraft was piloted away.

"Who told you to ignore this?"

"You did . . . the command was issued from your ComsBand, Mr. Gallic."

Gallic looked at his wrist. "You need to update your security protocols. Do it now! You should have deduced it wasn't something I would sanely do. Spray-painting shit on the side of my own ship? Come on . . . what the hell is wrong with you?"

"I apologize. Perhaps my systems have been tampered with."

"You think? Fix it. There's a killer on the loose out there . . ."

* * *

Two hours later, Gallic was seated at his desk. Lane's words kept replaying in his head, specifically those about the *Curz*. It took Gallic a few moments to find what he was looking for—a book that chronicled the discovery of the ancient Mars spacecraft. He took a seat at his desk, doing his best to ignore the mental discord going on within him. Thumbing through the pages of the four-inch-wide treatise, seeing the collection of photographs and illustrations, he recalled learning about the staggering Mars event of the previous century. With very few exceptions, it was the most monumental event in the history of mankind. Not only now was there irrefutable proof that beings on Earth were not alone within the universe, the technical advances gained from finding that highly advanced *Curz* spacecraft changed the trajectory of the human species. It provided man the unquenchable thirst to venture into space and beyond. Today, the findings from that Mars site were still being studied and analyzed. Professor Harkins, among those utterly fascinated by the subject, routinely gave lectures on the subject.

"AI . . . what's happening with my call to the professor?"

"I have checked back several times. He is currently finishing up a lecture. Would you like me to try again?"

"Please." A moment later, Gallic heard the distinctive sound of an interstellar CoreNet connection being instigated. Then a pleasant-faced, middle-aged woman appeared on the display over his desk.

"Yes, Mr. Gallic, I am Professor Harkins' assistant, Daniela Richardson. We met some time back. If you could wait a few more moments, he will be available to talk."

"Yes hello, Daniela, I remember you. Thank you. I'll wait."

Less than a minute later, Harkins' face—topped by wild red hair—appeared. "Ah! It's my friend, the Galaxy Man! I was just thinking about you just the other day. What was it . . . hmmm . . . I'll remember eventually."

"How you doing, Professor? Sorry to interrupt your class."

"No, no . . . all done with classes for the day. I received your persistent AI's messages. Sorry . . . it's been a busy time for me. What is it I can do for you, my friend?"

"I'm working with D-22. Recently, there have been new murders in the frontier worlds. We're working under the assumption they are copycat homicides . . . of the hammer-and-nails killer," Gallic said.

Professor Harkins provided an appropriate look of concern, well aware of the first victims of the still-elusive murderer. But Gallic knew the professor was an ardent amateur sleuth—loved the whole process of using his incredible intellect to uncover new clues—thereby helping to solve the unsolvable. Harkins' private library contained every book written by Arthur Conan Doyle. Rather obvious to anyone that knew Harkins, Sherlock Holmes was his alter ego.

"Specifically, Professor, I wanted to talk to you about some hand-drawn glyphs and writings the assailant drew on the crime scene wall."

"Is that the attached file I'm seeing?" Harkins asked, knitting his bushy red brows together.

"There's several images for you to look at," Gallic said.

"Interesting . . . I take it these markings were written in the victim's blood?"

"Correct. I was wondering, specifically, if they have something to do with the Mars discovery . . . the alien ship?"

"Uh huh. I know what this is about, at least I believe I do."

Gallic didn't outwardly reveal the excitement now building within him. The truth was, there'd never been any real, substantive clues before to go on regarding the hammer-and-nails killer. Lots of evidence, yet no clues that led to anything definitive.

"I believe this crude drawing is related to an ancient civilization . . . one that was anti-female." The professor, looking somewhat hesitant, then asked, "What do you know about the *Curz* civilization?"

"Not much."

The professor lowered his voice, "Is this a secure line, John?"

Gallic, taken aback by the seriousness in the professor's tone, said, "Yes, it is."

"A highly secret society, made up of the wealthiest men on Earth, was established after that first mission to Mars. The same men that later financed the far more elaborate second mission, the *Explorer Zheng He*—the U.S. / Chinese cooperative space exploration venture. The team set out for the red planet then established there a new and larger base. The new site . . . *Musk-Horizon* . . . wasn't far from the area known as *The Hidden Valley*, where in mudstone strata that ancient, incredible, alien spacecraft was first discovered."

Gallic knew about the second mission, but he let the professor talk on uninterrupted.

"What most people don't know is that the alien spacecraft was actually discovered on the first Mars mission."

Gallic let that sink in. It was a startling revelation.

The professor continued, "And nearby that alien ship was a cave . . . more like a converted subterranean habitat. Inside that desolate space, the surviving aliens tried to live for some time. Found inside the cave were intricate elaborate hieroglyphs painted onto the rock walls. Now listen carefully to this, John: the first space mission to Mars from Earth found within that alien spacecraft an electronic message . . . one that had been sent, then recovered, from their home planet . . . from the *Curz*. It took some time to unravel the message, but when it was deciphered, it told of a world dominated by the female species. One that, over time, systematically wiped out the male population on that planet. A few ... several hundred of the surviving male *Curz*, the ones still alive after evading the dominant female gender, fled ... later crashing onto Mars. On the cave walls were elaborate glyphs that told a story, not boding well for the male species on that world. But the mother-load of information came from a vid-sheet book, if you will, that told of rituals and techniques to be used for mind control. Used to keep the female species at bay ... either asleep, or submissive. Much of the vid-sheet book, such as it is, was dedicated to providing instructions on how to keep most *Curz* females blind to that ongoing, female dominated, powers-that-be, agenda."

"Let me get this straight," Gallic said, unsure he fully understood what the professor was telling him. "The ship and that cave were actually discovered on the first Mars mission ... not the second?"

"Correct."

"And a newly organized secret society of rich men ... financed that second mission that we all know about."

"Correct."

"And what? This wealthy male society took up their alien brother's female-hating cause as their own?" Gallic laughed out loud at that, at the seeming preposterousness of it all.

But the professor didn't share in his humor. He stared back at Gallic flatly, waiting for him to quiet down. Harkins said, "This new secret society deemed themselves The *Curz* Watchers. Their charter was to secretly exist everywhere ... be a part of everything. Government positions, corporate executives, you name it. The *Curz* Watchers are now everywhere, and it's impossible to track them down. We're talking here about the wealthiest individuals in the known galaxy. Why do you think the proverbial glass ceiling for women in business, or politics, has only gotten worse over the last one hundred years?"

Though it still sounded ridiculously far-fetched to Gallic, he had to admit he'd come across numerous men, some indeed in positions of power, who clearly had distaste for those of the fairer sex holding key positions of any kind, other than being housewives. Then he thought of his own wife. How Clair, with a PhD in physics, had risen to the very top of her profession within the burgeoning space products industry. Suddenly feeling sick, he wondered if she'd been murdered simply because she was a successful woman and no longer found the new information funny.

chapter 23

Frontier Planet, Gorman — Heritage
Plains Township.

Gallic's anger began to build, like an impending volcano
eruption, taking all his will to keep his raging emotions
in check. "You're a smart guy, professor. Tell me, did you
suspect anything ... at the time of the killings? When my wife
and child were murdered?"

Harkins shook his head. "Not at first. Why would I? It
was such a horrible crime, a terrible thing that happened. But
later ... as new details of the crime became public, I must admit
I had my suspicions. But that's all they were. I wasn't about to
start making abstract accusations. And you have to understand,
John, I have little doubt that I work alongside such members.
It's a cult. They're extremely powerful. I wish you success. The
best of luck with this added information. I truly do. Let me

know if there is anything else I can do for you. Unfortunately, it will have to be from the sidelines."

Before Gallic ended the call, he thanked Harkins; assuring the professor he would be discreet should he indeed require more from him. He sat at his desk for a long while and thought about the initials, TCW, carved into each of the vics' necks by the hammer-and-nails killer. Rubbing his tired eyes, exhaustion had caught up with him. He needed sleep. He got up and only made it as far as the couch before lying down. He briefly considered going through his usual arduous task of closing down the vulnerable access points into his mind but didn't have the energy for it. *Fuck it ... let them come ...*

Gallic awoke to early morning daylight, streaming in through the *Hound*'s portside windows. His clothes were saturated with sweat and his breathing labored, as if he had just run a marathon. Clear memory of the night's bad dream had not stayed with him, and he was thankful for that. Standing, he walked to the window and noticed dust rising into the morning air as a distant lone horseback rider headed off. It was Lane. Even from a distance, he could see her beauty, though perhaps it simply was the lasting impression she'd left on him. He wanted to go after her. He needed to speak to her about last night, about the things she'd said. The connection she had to TCW—whether unconscious, or otherwise. But then she was gone from sight.

Gallic continued to stare at the distant horizon then glanced around at the terrain closer in. Someone was out there—someone was watching him. He had a sixth sense about such things—the hairs on the back of his neck now standing up. *Yeah, I know you're out there, asshole.*

Gallic shaved in the shower as his thoughts raced over recent developments: the latest crime scene, what he had learned from Professor Harkins, and the bizarre ranting by Lane. He'd need to *percolate* about everything the entire day. That's how clues often came to him—letting his subconscious go to work while his conscious self kept occupied with other things.

"Mr. Gallic ... sorry to disturb."

"What is it, AI?" he asked, turning the water faucet even hotter, letting the steam envelop him.

"Two incoming high-priority CoreNet messages for you. Superintendent Bernard Danbury would like an update today, and Ms. Allison Tillman would like to speak with you. She sounded ... somewhat irritated."

Gallic's thoughts turned to the *Hayai* case. He still needed to find that damn spacecraft. With things now revving up on the hammer-and-nails murders, it was becoming more and more difficult to give that case the attention it deserved. But as a new idea took hold, he turned off the water. Opening the shower door, he reached for a towel then wrapped it around him. "Get Phil on the line for me, AI ... audio only." Several moments later, he heard Phil's voice.

"What's happening?" Phil asked.

"Where you at?"

"What are you ... my mother? I'm here on Gorman ... following up on the crime of the century. Got a report that a prominent rancher's three head of cattle were killed."

"Yeah? So, what was that all about?" Gallic asked.

"They're dead, all right. But there doesn't seem to be anything all too nefarious about it. The Longhorns looks to be done-in due to the exhaust stream from a low-flying craft; one with a powerful propulsion system. Now barbequed beef."

"Listen . . . I may have a proposal for you, if you're ready for a little extra work. The money's good."

"I've already tried the whole marriage thing, but thanks for asking," Phil said.

"Funny. Can you meet me . . . say for breakfast?"

"Give me an hour . . . my stomach should be settled by then," Phil said.

* * *

Having landed the *Hound* in an open nearby field, Gallic made his way behind a cluster of timber-sided structures, then down through an alleyway onto the rural sleepy street. Not his first time here, two years prior he was surprised to learn there was an actual town around called Heritage Plains. To Gallic it always seemed more like an Old West movie set, or a theme park attraction, than a real township civic center. Approximately a quarter-mile long, three blocks total—both sides of Maple Street—the master-planned, small municipality was roughly based on the famous western town Tombstone, Arizona, back on Earth. Word had it the authentic, rustic-looking construction project cost its investors a cool two billion dollars, even some thirty years back. A town meant to provide local wealthy ranchers, and their families, a safe place to come together, while maintaining the look and feel of historical days now long past. It worked, for the most part, Gallic figured. Over the last thirty years the town had been around, it had indeed seasoned, becoming ever more the venue it was intended to play. What the town planners hadn't counted on was how closely this Old West facsimile had become authentic in other ways, too. Like the type of man naturally drawn to such a place. Sure, there was a movie house, and a general store, and a stock and feed emporium, and even a beauty parlor, but several establishments—such as the Black Triangle Guns and Ammo and Clark's Saloon—as soon as the evening dusk settled in, the rowdy and mischievous ruffians awakened. Both Phil and Gallic had been called in, needing to attend to those who'd come out on the wrong side of an argument—specifically, the wrong side of a Smith and Wesson, or a Colt sidearm pistol, or a refurbished Remington shotgun.

Daisy's was a greasy-spoon restaurant, halfway up the street, owned and operated by a fellow named Doug Flatbush. A man of considerable heft and a foul temper. He lived by the motto posted on a sign at the front entrance: *We reserve the right not to serve anyone we deem to be an asshole.*

A small bell tinkled as Gallic entered the surprisingly busy eatery. He waited a moment for his eyes to adjust to the darkness. As usual, the two windows facing the street were shuttered closed. *Why?* Gallic had no idea. He heard patrons, talking in low murmurs, and the sound of metal cutlery scraping against ceramic flatware. Pans clanged onto stovetops, and Doug's voice yelling at the help in the back kitchen.

"Over here."

Gallic spotted Phil, sitting at a corner table all by himself, with a newspaper spread out. He gestured to Gallic, a cup of coffee in his hand.

As Gallic approached, Phil beneath the table kicked his boot out, sliding a chair forward for his friend. "Sit . . . take a load off."

About to do just that, Gallic was surprised at hearing the front entrance bell tinkle four times in quick succession. *Daisy's certainly popular today*, he thought, pulling the chair clear of the table ready to sit. Behind him he heard a deep voice, one seasoned by years of overly drinking and tobacco usage.

"Stay on your feet . . . you won't be staying."

Four men approached. All were big, and looked like ranchers. Not young, like Cugan's ranch hands, each wore the same chafed expression.

Gallic sat anyway and reached for the menu he'd spotted, partially peeking out beneath Phil's newspaper. "What's good here, Phil?" he asked, turning over the two-sided vid-sheet menu from luncheon offerings to breakfast offerings.

"Flatbush makes a mean Denver omelet," Phil said, also ignoring the intrusion. "That's what I'm ordering . . . soon as someone makes it over here."

"Hey . . . you . . . that your old heap out there?"

Gallic glanced up at the speaker, garbed in a long olive duster. Tall, tanned, and like the other three, he wore a Stetson, set low down over his forehead, making his eyes difficult to see. Still, Gallic could see enough of his lined face, his gray hair, to place the man in his fifties, or early sixties. Gallic put the other three men near the same age. One was wearing a long navy-blue duster, another a dark-gray duster, and the third a tan duster—so new it still bore creases down the sleeves. Or maybe the guy's wife had just ironed the thing for him.

"He asked you a question ... is that you're heap out in the field?" navy-blue duster asked.

Gallic exchanged a quick glance with Phil. Mr. Cugan, Linda Cugan's husband, was on the list of people they wanted to talk to regarding the Johnson murders. The other three men, undoubtedly, were other nearby wealthy ranchers.

"What can I do for you, Mr. Cugan?" Gallic asked.

That he knew his name, made the rancher hesitate. "We suspect you're responsible for killing three of my herd."

Gallic shot a glance at Phil, not appreciating being set up. Raising his palms, "I didn't know whom the damn cows belonged to. I spoke to a field hand, who found them smoldering in a pasture."

Giving another glance at the menu, Gallic decided he'd go with the omelet too. "I'm going to have breakfast; talk some with my friend here. If you want to wait ... preferably not right where you're standing, I'll speak with you afterward."

Cugan expression flashed with indignation. Nodding to the others, he said, "Let's help him outside."

"Before you do that, understand I am under contract with D-22. Touch me, and you'll be assailing an appointed officer of this jurisdiction." Gallic spoke with conviction, though it was total bullshit. He, too, was nothing more than a Frontier Marshal here, just like Phil.

Cugan smirked. "Yeah, I know exactly who you are. My wife told me all about you. How you harassed her and my daughter."

"Hardly. Simply asked her a few questions. Questions she wasn't too forthcoming providing any answers to."

"I can attest to that, Don. There was no harassment—"

"Shut up and stay out of this, Phil," Cugan spat.

Gallic was unaware that Phil and Rick Cugan knew each other, yet apparently, they did. Made sense.

"That *thing* you call a spacecraft fried three of my best heifers. You'll be compensating my ranch for them," Cugan said, leering down at Gallic.

Cugan's three friends moved in and surrounded Gallic, grabbing ahold of something—an arm, a fistful of coat sleeve, or the fabric at the nape of his collar. They tried in vain to lift him off the chair, but at two hundred thirty-plus pounds— pounds mostly consisting of sinewy muscle mass—it would take more than Cugan's three stooges to heft him up.

"You're coming outside, where we can discuss this without making a disruption," Cugan said from the sidelines.

Gallic didn't hesitate. Using his right hand, he firmly grasped the man's hand now holding onto his left arm. The hand felt meaty and soft. No less than three bones, all proba-bly metacarpals, cracked and splintered under Gallic's strong, substantial grip. A yelp of pain caused *Daisy's* other patrons to stop what they were doing and look their way. The dark-blue duster-dressed man was red-faced. Bent over, he clutched his injured hand to his balls. Gallic next grabbed ahold of the hand squeezing his right shoulder—the rancher in the pretty tan duster. He yanked the offending hand forward, hard and fast. Cugan's crony staggered clumsily, flopping onto Gallic's back as if trying to climb on for a piggyback ride. By then, Gallic's right hand was free. Had secured a tight hold on the wrist of tan duster's forward extended arm; it was caught like a piece of flimsy wood in a steel vise. With his other hand, Gallic ratcheted the man's hand and wrist in the direction God never intended it to go—where radius and ulna bones met the carpal bones. The sound of bones either cracking or outright fracturing were followed by new yelps of pain. Both men, shielding their wounded hands, hurried from the restaurant. Gallic heard the little bell atop the door tinkle once, then twice.

During the ensuing commotion, Gallic's heart rate hadn't increased so much as a percentage point. It wasn't lost on him how encounters, like this one, made so little impact on him physically. He'd been trained in the *Royal Marines*, learning to defend himself against the worst kind of adversary. He'd killed men in battle and had been left for dead himself, both in war and in the commission of his job, more than he cared to admit. He looked over to Rick Cugan. *A prick, just like his son.* What was it about people—men—with money? Thinking they were all powerful, when they actually were anything but.

"As I said. If you want to wait for me outside, I'll speak with you when I'm done in here." Gallic then looked away. Nodding, he gave the approaching server a lopsided smile.

Cugan and the rancher in the gray duster turned and strode away.

"You ever hear that it's not a good idea to shit where you eat?" Phil asked.

Ignoring him, Gallic spoke to the young twenty-something server, whose nametag read Cassidy: "I'll have the Denver omelet and coffee . . . black."

"Make that two," Phil said.

Cassidy wrote down their order. Giving Gallic a tight smile, she asked, "What was that all about . . . with Mr. Cugan? The owner's not happy, seeing his customers knocked around like that." She looked over her shoulder. "He may ask you to leave."

"I'll talk to him," Phil said. "We go back a spell. Go ahead and put our order in, Cassidy."

chapter 24

Frontier Planet, Gorman — Heritage
Plains Township.

G allic caught an angry-looking Doug Flatbush eyeing them
several times from behind the kitchen counter.

"So ... you mentioned needing my help?" Phil queried,
swallowing a mouthful of Denver omelet.

"You're aware of my work with Polly Gant?"

Phil nodded.

"He's got me working on a grand theft case. A high-end
spacecraft, called a *Hayai*."

"Oh yeah ... Sargento and Hok'ee mentioned that gig to
me. Told me about the Tillman Museum penthouse over on
Spector. There'll be a sweet payment reward ... huh? ... for
whoever brings back that lost ship."

"Is there anyone you don't know?" Gallic asked, surprised. Phil, chewing, responded back silently, giving him a combined nod and shrug.

"Anyway, I'm a bit overloaded with everything going on right now. Thought, with your strong security background, you'd be a good fit for this. I'll split the bounty with you. Just know there isn't anything simple about this case. How that spacecraft was taken, right off that museum floor, well . . . so far, it has me stumped. Interested?"

Phil chewed for a while, staring blankly at his near-empty plate.

"What's there to think about? It's a shitload of money."

"Yeah. Sure, I'm in," Phil said.

"Good. But we'll have to secure the ship before the competition does. And I have to tell you . . . Sargento is motivated to beat me on this one."

Phil chuckled, "Heard about the set-down space confrontation."

"Anyway . . . I've got security footage, back in the *Hound*, plus other things that'll help us."

Gallic listed some of the security measures the museum employed—the latest tech stuff, some even newer than when Phil was in the business. "Any names come to mind? Outfits with the capacity to pull off a high-end job like this?"

"I can think of a few. A Taiwanese bunch, from the high-tech sector, called the Wom's. They've been active lately. But they usually don't deal with spacecraft. Also, there's the Ghost Walkers. I know, it's a stupid name, but they'd be up for it—something that high caliber. Wasn't aware they worked anywhere but on Earth, but I'll do some digging around."

"At least you have a few—"

Phil suddenly perked up and cut him off. "There's another guy . . . a big deal in the electronics and security world. Someone who not only brainstorms new tech then sells to the highest bidder but has been known to get high bids through reverse engineering a company's existing code and technology. Using that information, he pretty much forces the same companies to make him an offer. If this *Hayai* is as high-tech as you're claiming, he may be involved."

"Let me know what you find out. I'll avoid speaking to Allison Tillman 'till you get back to me with something."

Phil appraised Gallic for a moment. "So how you doing with the hammer-and-nails murders?"

"I'm not sure." Gallic then relayed the latest murder scene details, including the new addition of wall glyphs and writings. "Something much bigger is going on here, Phil. Something that has to do with the *Curz* civilization. You know, from where that alien ship on Mars first originated. That, along with a secret society, dedicated to keeping women . . . all females . . . from positions of power. They deemed themselves The *Curz* Watchers. Their charter is to secretly exist pretty much every-where . . . become a part of everything, from government positions to corporate executives; that sort of thing. Now, these *Curz* Watchers are everywhere, and it's impossible to track them down. We're talking about some of the wealthiest indi-viduals in the known galaxy."

Phil looked reflective for a moment. "My dad used to talk about a group of men, who founded a club of sorts...formed, I think, when discovery of that spacecraft on Mars was first revealed. Guess it was close to a hundred years ago. He knew some of them; even did business with a few, I guess. He was terrified of those men, said they were total fanatics. I think my father's paranoia over this group is what killed him...I honestly do. In Dad's suicide note he wrote: 'Keep your mother and sisters safe, and don't let them get too far ahead.'" Phil looked at Gallic then said, "So yeah, I know about that group, this TCW, but it's been years since I've heard anything more about them. Never heard anything about their cause migrating into something like murder...not in modern times at least."

"I'm sorry, Phil. About your father."

* * *

Another twenty minutes passed before Gallic and Phil exited through Daisy's front door. Rick Cugan and his friend were outside waiting, leaning against a faux hitching rail. Both men shot Gallic a hostile glare on seeing him approach.

"Took you long enough," the man in the gray duster said.

"I didn't catch your name. Mister...?" Gallic asked.

Suddenly less willing to talk, he finally came out with, "Thompson. Roy Thompson."

"You get your friends taken care of?" Phil asked.

"There's a walk-in med station down the street," Thomson volunteered—he looked at Gallic with contempt in his eyes.

Gallic turned his attention to Rick Cugan. "Look ... I had nothing to do with your cows getting fried. Turn around and take a good gander at my ship." Gallic gestured toward the open field, and the ginormous, somewhat worn and rusted, vessel, sitting on a patch of muddy ground. "Take a look aft."

Reluctantly, Cugan and Thompson turned and studied the *Hound*.

"See the big Laciter rings on those two drives back there? Those are Graviton drives, immensely powerful. The propulsion system on a *Hewley-Jawbone* carrier blows the doors off all large-scale transport ships in its category. But there's something unique about Graviton drives ... they don't generate much heat. They utilize an anti-grav disruption principle to move that big-ass vessel from point A to point B. So ... if you're looking to pin the demise of your cows on someone, best you look closer to home, perhaps at your own son. I've seen him zooming around at illegal high speeds, flying ridiculously close to the ground. That little *L35T* of his generates a substantial exhaust wake, somewhere in the neighborhood of twelve hundred degrees. That'll sear the hide off three meandering cows quicker than you can say *medium rare, please*."

"Fuck you, Gallic," Cugan said.

But Gallic could see the rancher pondering over what he'd just heard. He'd be having a chat with his son about his reckless driving habits real soon. "Now that I've answered your questions ... I'd like to ask you a few questions of my own."

Rick Cugan didn't assent, but he didn't decline answering either. Gallic made a few taps onto his ComsBand. "I'm recording your answers. They'll be included with the formal case report."

Rick Cugan took a step closer. "Here's my official statement: I don't know anything about what happened to our neighbors Catherine and Tami Bower. It's a tragedy. My wife and daughter are completely devastated, as I am. If you are involved in tracking down whoever did this ... I hope you're up to the task." Cugan, turning to Phil, said, "Catch whomever did this, or I'll hire someone who can. That's all I'm going to say. If you have any other questions, you can contact my attorney." With that, he turned and walked away.

Roy Thompson too added a definitive nod, as if Rick Cugan's words went double for him. He scampered away— hurrying to catch up with Cugan.

"Well, that was a bust," Phil said.

chapter 25

Frontier Planet, Gorman — Heritage
Plains Township.

G allic stood within the *Hound*'s lift as it began its descent
to the lower level. He'd just sent Phil on his way—his
ComsBand loaded-up with data files, security footage, and other
information on the stolen *Hayai*. He'd gone over the footage
twice with him. They viewed the beautiful ship, situated under
the museum spotlights, when a disturbance caused the feed to
pixelate and become visually indecipherable. Moments later,
when the feed cleared, the vessel was gone—no longer parked
between the two spaceships. Other feed angles showed similar
momentary disturbances. Outside security cameras, positioned
on nearby buildings, provided no indication that anything out
of the ordinary had taken place. No spacecraft, either arriving
or departing, that matched the same time code of the *Hayai*'s
disappearance. He intended to give it more thought but still

hoped Phil would have better luck figuring out that mysterious theft.

"Mr. Gallic, there is an incoming CoreNet call from Sergeant Tori."

Gallic, going through his pre-flight checklist and seated in the *Hound*'s command center, said, "Go ahead and make the connection . . . put her here on the primary display."

Tori flashed into view, giving Gallic only a hurried acknowledgment. "Hey . . . just wanted to give you an update."

"Hello to you too, Silvia."

"Don't call me that. And yeah . . . hello! I just wanted to tell you I interviewed Donald Bower."

"You're back?"

"Yeah . . . I'm back," she replied somewhat curtly.

"How did he seem?"

"He was distraught . . . no doubt about that. He couldn't really add much to the knowledge base; said nothing seemed out of the ordinary before he left for his business trip."

"Anything else?"

"Just that he worked for the Praxis Ranch franchise . . . the neighbor's company. He's a corporate lawyer."

"Lawyer for the Cugan's?"

"That's right. For their company . . . Praxis."

Gallic then updated Tori on his brief meeting with Rick Cugan.

"I want to be there for those interviews, Gallic. Let's not forget whose case this is, okay?"

"Absolutely. But he tracked *me* down, not the other way around. He told me nothing other than accusing me of frying three of his cows."

Tori stared at Gallic with a questioning expression.

"Never mind . . . it's unrelated," Gallic said.

"I'm going to knock on a few more doors; get full statements from all the surrounding neighbors. Maybe we can meet up later . . . go over things?"

"Sounds good," Gallic said. "Let me know when you're free."

The connection ended though Gallic continued to stare at the display. "AI, make a CoreNet call to Lane."

Lane answered the incoming hail out of breath and with a surprised expression. As if getting a communications hail was something totally not expected. Gallic took in her full-size 3D holographic image. As recognition took hold, she smiled and said, "Hey . . . I was just thinking about you."

Open just behind her was her bedroom. The bed was made, and it looked like she'd been folding clothes.

"You still around here . . . or are you gallivanting around on another planet somewhere?"

Gallic heard another voice, coming from somewhere behind her. "*Who you talking to, Lanie?*"

Lane glanced over her shoulder, tucking a strand of hair behind her ear. "It's Gallic."

Gallic saw Larz Cugan appear in the doorway behind her, his long-parted hair hanging strategically over one eye. Leaning against the door frame, he crossed his arms over his chest. Once

Lane turned back to face him, Gallic saw Larz behind her flip him the bird.

"Larz was just on his way out. You know that he and I are just friends, right?"

"That's fine. Who you're friends with is your business. Even if one of them is a tool."

Lane, giving Gallic an indignant glance, said, "Let me say goodbye, then I'll CoreNet back to you in a minute . . . okay?"

Gallic was about to say that was fine when Larz blurted out, "I haven't forgotten what you did, asshole. Stay away from Heritage Plains . . . and stay the hell away from Lane. You got that? Your days are numbered."

"You know where to find me."

"Larz! Knock it off!" Lane yelled back, staring apologetically at Gallic. "Let me deal with him, Gallic . . . I'll talk to you in a few minutes."

The feed went black. Gallic wondered if Larz brought that out in him—his being transposed down to the maturity level of a ten-year-old.

In less than five minutes Lane appeared before him, sitting on her bed and looking stunning. "Sorry about that. I know Larz can be an ass . . . but he has a good side, too. He's been like a brother to me. Watched out for me since we were kids." Her train of thought veered away for a moment . . . mentally focusing in a distant time and place. When she snapped back, she gave Gallic a sideways glance. "I wish you were here."

"Do you?" Gallic asked.

A mischievous smile crossed Lane's lips. "More than you can imagine."

"Well, I can imagine quite a lot," he said, returning the flirtatious comment.

Lane's demeanor suddenly changed. Gazing at him with sultry eyes, she slowly unbuttoned her blouse. "I want you to see what you're missing right now." She let the blouse slide off her shoulders, revealing she wasn't wearing a bra. He could see her breathing slow—become deeper—her breasts steadily move up and down. He found it hard to pull his eyes away from those two perfect orbs. Her fingers began toying with the button on her blue-jean waistband. Although he appreciated the striptease, he felt uncomfortable knowing it was performed over an unsecured CoreNet channel, and that the ever-present AI was watching in the wings.

"Lane . . ."

She looked back at Gallic with a coy, playful expression.

"Why don't we take this up later . . . when we're together?" he suggested.

Lane gave him a hurt—pouty—look. It had been a long time since he'd met a woman with her appetite for sex. In their previous encounters she'd exhibited a physical voracity that tee-tered on insatiable. As much as he appreciated sex, he began to wonder if she might have . . . *issues*.

"Fine! You're no fun . . . old fuddy-duddy." Lane bent over and retrieved her shirt. As she put it on and buttoned it, Gallic asked, "Lane . . . do you remember anything unusual from last night? Do you remember what we talked about?"

The coy smile returned. "I remember we made love . . . that you were a stallion and—"

"You remember collapsing? Having an . . . episode?"

Lane didn't reply.

"Do you remember talking about the *Curz*, Lane . . . do you remember that?"

"I don't know what's wrong with you. Why you're trying to start a fight. Why you're making these things up. It's most upsetting!" Her fingers balled into fists and tears welled up in her eyes. "I can't talk to you right now," cutting off the connection.

Gallic wanted to call her back. Seeing her that upset had more of an effect on him than he'd thought possible, knowing her for only a short while.

"Mr. Gallic, Polly Gant has been holding for you."

Gallic closed his eyes, regaining his composure. "Put him through."

Polly appeared, seeming exasperated. The little man was the spitting image of Danny DeVito, the old TV/movie actor in the last century. Wearing a purple and yellow Hawaiian shirt, part of his face was obscured from view, hidden behind one of the tall stacks of vid-sheets on his messy desk.

"What can I do for you, Polly?"

"What do you mean . . . what can you do for me? You work for me, or have you forgotten that?"

Gallic had to remind himself that Polly Gant tended to *overreact*. Insecure, he might even be bi-polar. But since he generally liked the guy, he didn't mind summoning up the extra patience needed to help that little trolley get back on the tracks. "You're right . . . sorry. I'm all ears, and you have my undivided attention."

Polly stared back at him blankly—assessing if he were being fucked with. "You must have made some kind of impression on Ms. Tillman. I think she likes you."

"We still haven't actually met . . . in person."

"Whatever. I got a recorded vid call from her that she wanted me to forward on to you."

"Why didn't she just do it herself?"

"She tried, but she wasn't able to reach you. Basically, contacted by the same company managing her exotic import/export business, they have some information that might make it possible for us to track what happened to the *Hayai*."

chapter 26

Frontier Planet, Gorman — Heritage
Plains Township.

Gallic waited for Polly's forwarded message from Allison
Tillman to arrive. Hearing the AI begin to speak, he cut
it off mid-sentence. "I see it. Just play the message."

"Hi Polly, that Mr. Gallic is a tough man to get ahold of. If
you would be so kind, please forward this message onto him . . .
thank you."

Gallic said, "Pause message." As he stared at Allison on
the display he tried to determine what was different about her
appearance from the other times he'd seen her. It then occurred
to him that this was the first time he'd seen her dressed in
casual, non-business attire. He tried to make out where she
was standing . . . *outside*? Someone walking behind by a swimming pool, wore a skimpy bathing suit. Allison was wearing
a bathing suit as well, but hers was obscured by an oversized,

somewhat-see through, blouse. She was standing beneath a pergola, and the overhead wood slats were making a shadow pattern across her face and ample chest. She looked tan and carefree.

"Play the rest of the message," Gallic said and heard the sound of water splashing in the pool. "The high-tech firm I'm in communications with, Sunland Technical Industries, actually sought me out," Allison said. "I guess they heard through the grapevine about the theft. You'll be meeting with them at their company headquarters, here on Spector. They've agreed to meet with you and Sargento personally and share with you whatever confidential information they have, I guess, regarding any tracking data they have on the *Hayai*. Now, you and Sargento need to play *nice* on this ... okay? Anyway, I'm not completely sure what info they have ... to be honest." Allison seemed a little flustered by her own lack of detail. "They don't want to broadcast on an unsecured line. Let me know when you'll be coming to Spector. I'll try to be around so we can officially meet. Now see the attached coordinates; the time scheduled for your meeting. Have a nice day ... bye."

Gallic next, in a second CoreNet conversation, let Phil know he was headed back to Spector; that there might be a new lead regarding the location of the Tillman spacecraft. Firing up the *Hound*'s propulsion system, he lifted off.

* * *

Entering Spector's atmosphere, Gallic found that the coordinates provided by Sunland Technical Industries put the *Hound* on the other side of this small world. Descending, the big space-ship hit substantial turbulence, making it hard for Gallic to stay on his feet. He heard several books fall hard to the deck behind in his den. Bright lightning flashes outside, and pounding rains against the windows, made it clear the weather on this side of the world was far more tumultuous. Gallic scanned the nav display and tried to make sense of the rough terrain below. There were no structures visible—no industrial buildings. A small icon appeared—another ship was entering the atmosphere, behind the *Hound*. About to ask the AI to provide him with the ship's identification, the *Hound* bucked sideways as gale-forces winds buffeted her portside. Gallic grabbed hold of the controls, shouting, "I'm taking over," as an alarm klaxon began to ping loudly.

"The Starboard Graviton drive—"

Gallic interrupted the AI, "Yeah... I know... it's swamping. This old girl doesn't much like water." Fighting to maintain control, Gallic brought the ship down quickly. When three consecutive lightning bolts struck the outer hull in rapid succession, he winced at the potential damage being done to his ship. He noticed on the nav display where he was supposed to land. Yelling over the noisy klaxon, and the raging storm outside, he asked the AI, "Is the space even large enough for us?" referring to what looked to be too small an area to even set down on.

"It is sufficient, if you nail the landing."

Gallic stared at the console. *Nail the landing?* He'd never heard an artificial intelligence speak in such a way ... *personality added in?* "I'll do my best," Gallic replied, his voice heavy with sarcasm. He hit the landing thrusters, working hard to maintain control.

"Lateral axis needs adjustment... vertical axis needs adjustment—"

"I'm working on it!" Gallic replied through gritted teeth. "And address me as Mr. Gallic!" *What the hell's wrong with the AI,* he wondered.

Landing within a valley of sorts, and peering out through a window drenched in torrential rain, Gallic found the surrounding terrain mostly jagged rock. He noticed reflections, bouncing off windows built into the cliffs. As the *Hound* touched down hard, more books clattered off shelves in the den behind him.

Gallic, exhaling a deep breath, quickly shut down the propulsion system. "Do what you can, AI, to drain excess moisture from both drives."

"Yes, Mr. Gallic."

Gallic, glancing outside, shook his head. He didn't like this. Something was up. "We may need to get out of here in a hurry. You see me heading back, fire up the drives and be ready to lift off as soon as I'm back onboard." He waited for the AI to acknowledge the command.

"Hello?"

"Yup... I'm on it, Mr. Gallic."

Gallic exhaled: *What the fuck?* But now wasn't the time to deal with an out-of-whack AI. He'd run complete diagnostics on the thing later. Pulling on his thick leather duster, he lowered his Stetson further down on his head. Once inside the lift, descending, he thought about the situation he presently was in. During the flight from Gorman, he'd taken the opportunity to research Sunland Technical Industries. There wasn't much data available. Primarily a military contractor to more than one Earth government, virtually everything they worked on was highly secretive. *Bio-warfare capabilities*, was a term that appeared several times.

Halfway down the gangway, Gallic lost his hat when a huge gust of wind nearly pushed him off the ramp. Once on firm ground, he looked around for some indication where he was supposed to go. Based on the number of windowed rows, there appeared to be six or seven levels built into the cliff directly ahead. Moving in that direction, he figured there had to be an entrance somewhere at ground level. No other ships, nor vehicles of any kind, were around. *Perhaps there's some other way into the place*, he mused, sensing something was off about the place, about the whole situation.

Hatless, Gallic needed to shield his eyes from the rain to see even several feet in front of him. Up ahead, he thought he saw *something*. Three strides farther on, Gallic held up, trying to decipher what he was seeing on the rocky terrain ten feet ahead.

"Hey, you . . . you okay there, man?" Gallic asked, noting a person. A naked man, hunched over in the rain, not moving. Gallic approached slowly. At six feet away, he halted again. This was no ordinary man. His skin was gray and slick—oily-like, snake-like. A door then creaked open—not outside in the rocky landscape, but within his mind. Gallic's inner demons were on the move.

The grayish man had curly, black hair—not short but not long either. Though his head was facing down, Gallic still could see a strong Roman nose and full lips. Hard to judge his age—he could be thirty . . . maybe forty. His hairless arms and legs were beyond muscular. The guy was ripped. Only when he turned his gaze upward, on fully seeing the man's face—his nearly transparent blue eyes—did Gallic fully comprehend the term *Bio-warfare capabilities*. This *being* was neither man nor human but what was commonly referred to nowadays as a *Bio Technoid*. One built for war, obviously.

Today was by no means Gallic's first run-in with a technoid. As a Royal Marine officer, he'd witnessed those artificial soldiers come into their own—advancing from mere experimental units, deployed in theater operations, into fully utilized military assets, replacing their more vulnerable human counterparts. Technoids' reaction times were far better; their strength and endurance performances off the charts; and the bio-units followed all orders without exception. The perfect soldier with one important exception—their wireless cyborg brain interfaces could be, and often were, hacked.

The technoid before him slowly rose up—doing so without the use of arms. Higher and higher the being rose. Gallic, at six-feet-five, was tall. Taller than just about anyone he came into contact with. But this *thing* was easily a good ten inches taller than him. A technoid giant.

Water ran down the technoid's slippery skin in winding rivulets as Gallic assessed the rest of it. If the technoid's designers were looking for an anatomically correct *male* replica, they'd left out several important components—like a dick and balls. It struck Gallic that what he was looking at was a fully-grown GI Joe doll.

"My name is John Gallic. I have a meeting inside. Any chance we can get out of the weather, big guy?" Gallic asked.

The artificial man actually smiled. Not the kind of smile that was warm or friendly, or even sardonic, but a smile that said volumes, nevertheless. A smile that said: I'm going to kill you. And I'll do so without working up so much as a sweat. "I am Stallworth. You will not survive this encounter."

chapter 27

Planet Spector — Sunland Technical Industries.

Stallworth rushed at him with its arms raised—fist clenched—like a lineman coming off the line at the snap of the football. Only this lineman was closer to five hundred pounds versus two or three hundred. Gallic ready for the advance dove to his left. From his own experience, while training with technoids in the service, albeit far smaller ones, getting hit by one of the things was like getting run over by a fast oncoming automobile, or a hovercraft.

"What's this about . . . why the hell are you attacking me?" Gallic asked, quickly rising to his feet. He reached inside his coat for his Emanuel Dual 5—.45 handgun. *Shit!* He inwardly chastised himself for not slipping the lethal weapon into its hidden inside coat holster like he'd normally did prior to leaving the *Hound* then prepared for the next expected rush.

The technoid, calling itself Stallworth, came for him low and fast, catching Gallic just above the knees. Driven backward, and losing his balance, Gallic fell beneath his attacker. Instinctively, he raised his arms to protect his face then felt a flurry of hard punches—like two pile drivers—thundering down on his head and shoulders. It was going to be a short and merciless killing if he didn't get some distance away from the technoid. Rolling to the left, he was stopped by the giant's left leg. Like a pillar of stone, it didn't budge. As more fist punches rained down, Gallic rolled hard, this time to his right. The technoid's other foot—jarred out of place on the slippery rock surface—offered Gallic a chance to escape the rampage. While the attacker's arms spun windmill-like, Gallic continued to roll away, then jumped up and onto his feet. He looked around for something, anything, to use as a weapon. *Nothing.* But staying on the defense, he knew, was a sure-fire way to find himself *dead.* So, this time Gallic rushed forward and, using the technoid's earlier maneuver, hit it low in the legs—smack in the knees. He heard a snapping sound as one of its knees hyperextended outward, now facing in the reverse direction.

Gallic wasn't entirely sure what level of sensitivity, if any, a technoid's pain receptors were configured to. But seeing the now-extended inverse angle of its leg—well, that had to hurt like a son of a bitch. But then came that smile again. Using both hands, the artificial man took ahold of its upper and lower leg and ratcheted it back into place. Its knee crackled and snapped as bone, muscles, and tendons suddenly were conscripted back into their original configuration. Gallic didn't hesitate.

Attacking with a stepping sidekick, he targeted the same knee. But Stallworth was ready for Gallic and caught the incoming boot. Gallic felt his body flip up, then flip backward—ass-over-tea kettle. No sooner had he hit the ground when the pummeling began in earnest, but this time he didn't have time to protect his face. A torrential blow hit him hard on the jaw, another smacked his left cheekbone, and a third struck him above his right eye. No sooner had the blows stopped when he felt the grip of steely fingers encircle his throat. Gallic rose; pulled high enough off the ground to stare into Stallworth's unsympathetic gaze.

"And now you will die, John Gallic."

As the technoid's grip tightened, Gallic tried uselessly to pry its fingers open, feeling his airway completely closing off. He thought about his ComsBand but too late—*no time left*. He flailed his legs in desperation—knowing unconsciousness and death were moments away.

His brain, now completely starved for oxygen, was exhibiting the usual neurological response—a constricting tunnel effect. Gallic was barely aware of some movement—more like the passing of a shadow—behind the technoid. Then something hard to comprehend occurred when a man jumped onto Stallworth's back. Holding his left arm around the technoid's neck, the attacker brandished a large knife in the other. The grip on Gallic's throat loosened—to the point he was able to gasp and take in a short breath. The man was on Stallworth's back, in the process of dragging his knife across the technoid's hairline, when Gallic dropped to the ground, painfully gasping for air. The technoid swung its torso from side to side—trying to jerk, buck, the man off him. Only then did Gallic realize the ponytailed man was Sargento. A large section of sliced-open bloody Technoid scalp flapped this way and that as Sargento held on for dear life.

Staggering to his feet, Gallic watched Stallworth grab ahold of Sargento—reaching back, he plucked Sargento from his shoulders and threw him violently to the ground. The technoid then stomped down on the Native American's chest—a blow possibly ending his life.

Gallic tapped at his ComsBand with a well-rehearsed combination of quick taps.

"Yes, Mr. Gallic. Would you like some assistance?" the familiar AI voice asked.

Stallworth, raised its leg for another killing blow—its foot positioned directly over Sargento's head.

"Hurry! Take out the technoid attacker," Gallic yelled.

To the unsuspecting eye, the rusted and scorched metal protrusion atop the *Hound*'s upper hull looked the same as numerous other angular protrusions atop the ship. But the now-spinning, clockwise protrusion was, in fact, a rail-gun turret. One of the modifications Gallic made to the *Hound* shortly after he'd purchased her.

The loud three, or four, second-burst consisted of no less than several hundred projectile rounds. Fired into the center-mass of the technoid's chest, Stallworth stayed upright for several beats—long enough for him to look down and see the ragged six-inch hole in its chest. Surprisingly, it was

Sargento who lashed out next with his boot, toppling over the non-human giant.

* * *

Gallic handed a mug of hot coffee to Sargento, now sprawled out on the couch. His shirt was off, revealing white bandages wrapped around his ribcage.

Gallic moving across from him, sat down in a high-backed armchair. Holding an icepack to own jaw, he said, "Okay . . . my first question is . . . why use the . . . what was that, some kind of scalping thing? Why not cut its damn throat instead?"

"If you're going to make some kind of disrespectful crack about my heritage—"

"No insult intended," Gallic said.

Sargento said, "I wouldn't know how to scalp someone. You think us savages take some course in how to do that kind of shit? No! If you recall, my arm was hanging on for dear life around that thing's throat. I guess, I could have stabbed it. Maybe in its eye, or something like that . . ."

"That could have worked too," Gallic said, nodding appreciatively. "In any event, you coming along when you did probably saved my life."

"Probably? You were toast!"

"Yeah . . . I was toast. Well, thanks anyway. I owe you one."

"That was a nice little trick you pulled . . . the rail gun thing," Sargento said.

Gallic shrugged, "Space is a dangerous place." Glancing out the window, he saw Sargento's ship in the distance. "Where's your partner ... where's Hok'ee?"

"He has foot ... a toe thing ... surgery."

"Like corns?" Gallic asked.

"I don't know. I didn't ask, and he didn't go into it."

"So, you got the same invite from Allison Tillman?"

Sargento took a sip of coffee before answering. "She said it came from a third-party enterprise, Sunland Technical Industries."

"So, the real question is: Why would they set us up to be killed?"

"Yeah and was Tillman also involved?"

chapter 28

Frontier Planet, Muleshoe — Derringer Township.

The killer had debated earlier whether he should go forward with the present course of action. Both mother, Corianne Millhouse, and daughter, Shelly, were good subjects. Appropriate ones. It was the environment that concerned him. He suspected their old Derringer property was infused with a higher-level of technology than most. He didn't get the opportunity to case the residence prior to today, not with it being a watchful *smart-home*, and all.

He rechecked the contents on his tool belt while pondering his options. If he couldn't bypass the security of an old farmhouse like this one, he seriously needed to find another line of work. *Is this my line of work? Yes . . . I suppose it is.*

The night was damp and cool as the killer walked the perimeter of the modest home. There were lights on in the distance—other dwellings on the same ranch parcel. Surely too distant away to hear loud noises emitted from within—such as a scream. The killer slowed and assessed the partially open window. No lights were on in the room. Coming closer, he noticed the window opening was partially obscured by a screen. Beyond it, he knew the room would be empty. Knew exactly where Corianne and Shelly now were—plopped down in front of the entertainment station in the family room. Pushing the window all the way up with his left hand, he quickly sliced a large X into the screen mesh with his right. Once he'd replaced the knife into its little pocket on his belt, he maneuvered his legs over the window ledge and crawled inside. He steadied himself and listened. As his eyes adjusted to the room's near-total darkness, he mentally reaffirmed that this room was indeed Shelly's. There were stuffed animals propped up on her pillow atop the quilted bedspread. Some kind of craft endeavor was in the works on her small desk. Perhaps something for school—like a science project—*one that would never reach completion.*

He moved to the door and listened again. The entertainment system was blaring in the near distance. He opened the door several inches and peered out. Seeing nothing, he eased himself through the doorway. Mindful not to make a sound, he approached the end of the hallway. He reached for his blade—momentarily glancing down just as Shelly rounded the corner. Startled beyond all comprehension, her scream was so ear-shatteringly loud he fumbled, dropping his knife. Caught even further off-guard, she neither cowered nor ran away. Still bent over retrieving his weapon, the little four-foot-*Tasmanian devil* attacked. Her balled fists hammered down on the back of his head and shoulders. The impact from the blows was slight enough but still disconcerting. What a little powder keg she was—fearless! A force to reckon with for sure once she was grown—another reason for him to be there now. Her mother, obviously hysterical, arrived just in time to see the knife slicing her daughter's throat.

chapter 29

Planet Spector — Sunland Technical
Industries.

Gallic and Sargento—both moving slow after their ordeal
with Stallworth—investigated the nearby cliff-side structure. Now armed, Gallic used the Emanuel Dual 5—.45
handgun to blow a sizable hole into the locking mechanism on
the front entrance. Once inside, it quickly became evident that
the sprawling industrial complex had long since been abandoned. He shot a quick glance over at Sargento, still not liking
the guy much. Didn't like what he'd learned of his past. Maybe
one day he'd ask him about it. Perhaps there was another side
on how his wife died, but now wasn't the time to get into it.

Together, they planned just how and when they would
confront Tillman. For now, though, they would do nothing. If
she was involved then let her think she'd been successful in her
endeavor to have them both killed.

"Guess no commission is worth losing our lives over," Sargento said.

"Agreed. We first need to get some clarity on who did this. Who'd want us to stop searching for the *Hayai*. My gut tells me it's not Allison Tillman . . . she could have far more easily fired us. No, there's a lot more going on here."

They agreed to keep in communication; work together, to some degree, to determine who this new adversary is . . . whoever that might be.

Sargento headed back to his own vessel, while Gallic headed toward the *Hound*. No matter what he told Sargento, his next stop would be the Tillman building, sited on the other side of the planet. If then he determined she had indeed been contracted to have him killed, he would arrest her—take her to D-22.

* * *

Stepping from the lift, Gallic heard the distinctive, repeating, tone of an incoming hail.

"Superintendent Bernard Danbury is calling in. Shall I answer the hail?" the AI asked.

"Yeah . . . put it up on the command center display."

Gallic approaching noted the old superintendent's solemn expression. "Look, if you're going to scold me about my lack of D-22 communications—"

Danbury cut him off, "There's been another."

The news caught Gallic completely off-guard. Not even one week had passed since the Johnson murders. His old boss looked stressed—even distraught.

"I could use your help, Gallic."

"I'm already working the case ... with Tori. What else do you want? You know how important this is to me ..."

"Uh huh. Where are you now?"

Gallic, hesitant to answer, replied, "Currently ... I'm on Spector."

"Chasing down some billion-dollar spacecraft doesn't add up for someone committed to finding a murderer. Potentially, someone who murdered—"

"Don't you fucking go there, Danbury," Gallic shouted, his steely gaze could freeze a volcanic planet. "I learned a long time ago that this job ... my search for the killer of Clair and Mandy ... could easily drive me insane. And it almost did, remember? There was only one way to cope with the trauma ... that was to compartmentalize. To treat the murders, even of my own family, separately. I work on other cases ... I try to have a life. I do everything I can just to wake up each morning and face a new day. Face alternate case possibilities, rather than go stark-raving mad attempting to find the one man who stole my life from me. So yeah, I take on other cases. I have some semblance of a life. That doesn't mean I'm any less dedicated to finding the murderer."

Danbury stared back at him, looking somewhat more resigned.

"Don't forget, D-22, you have two people on this case," Gallic said.

"There's hundreds of murders within my district each year. You know better than most just how limited my resources are stretched. It's a miracle I've been able to keep Sergeant Tori on this case for as long as I have. But I need this case closed."

"And you don't think I want it closed! I've thought about little else in the last three- and-a-half years. Screw you, Danbury."

Danbury seemed to regret his words. "I'm sorry. You're not telling me anything I don't know. And I'm also aware I was the one who told you to back off, let Tori do her job."

"Yes, you did." At that moment Danbury looked far older than his years. His salt- and-pepper streaked hair seemed to have turned far more salt in only the last few days.

"I've read both reports... yours and Tori's—from the Johnson murders. The implications are... well, highly disturbing, to say the least. The wall glyphs ... the writings; the whole bazar *Curz* Watchers aspect."

"So, you know about them? The cult?"

Danbury didn't answer him right away. "Let's get back to the latest murder. What I'm asking is for you to throw yourself into this investigation. It's not out of the question for you to come back, Gallic. Regain your position here—"

"First of all, you don't need to bribe me to do my damn job. Second, I'm not coming back to D-22. Not now, not ever, so get that out of your head. I'm fine with what I do ... more than fine. Talk to me about the latest murders. It sounds like he's getting greedy . . . over-zealous. Maybe we can work that detail to our advantage. Where did it take place?"

"Derringer . . . on Muleshoe," Danbury said. "Tori's headed there now. Look . . . I've instructed her to wait for you. I've also instructed her to take second seat from here on in. I've raised your outside contractor creds to the highest level allowed. I also anticipated your response to coming back here. You may not be D-22, Gallic, but you have some real authority behind you now; more than any other Frontier Marshal I'm aware of."

Gallic didn't care about authority. All Danbury had accomplished was to potentially drive a wedge further between him and Sergeant Tori. But he also understood why he did it. Understood that Danbury—and D-22 as a whole—was dealing with something evil, which could affect not only frontier territories but all inhabited regions of space as well.

Gallic's confrontation with Tillman would have to wait. "I'm headed back. Tell Tori I'll meet her at Renegade's Haven."

* * *

Gallic entered the rundown local watering hole and made his way over to Randy, standing behind the bar. "I'm looking for Sergeant Tori. She make it in here yet?"

Randy handed him a slip of paper. "She got here a couple of hours ago. Guess she got tired of waiting. Split a half hour ago. Left you that message."

Gallic opened it then read what it said.

I'm heading off to the scene at Derringer. Meet you there. The specific coordinates on Muleshoe are: 233.33.123228.

* * *

Of all the Frontier Worlds, Muleshoe was the most remote, the least inhabited. More extreme weather here, it was a green world of rolling hills and numerous lakes and rivers; there wasn't much in the way of oceans as there were back on Earth. And unlike Gorman, where only a fair amount of ranching went on—an enclave for the wealthy, with their sprawling McMansions and acres of perfect emerald-green, fenced-in lawns—there was nothing pretentious about Muleshoe, and Derringer, in particular. Most frontier beef was exported from Muleshoe, where the real business of cattle ranching took place. Hence, it was no big surprise to Gallic to find that the coordinates provided by Tori led him to a highly industrial-looking beef processing center, located in the middle of nowhere.

At the controls, Gallic circled around the odd-looking compound, comprised of three small, one-story farmhouses; a massive—open on three sides—corrugated metal garage for big farm vehicles; a dated, old-fashioned, red barn; and a sprawling, factory-like structure, surrounded by large, fenced-off pens. Each pen contained cattle numbering in the hundreds. Near the farthest farmhouse, Gallic spotted Tori's star-cruiser. Coming in low, he noticed cow heads turn up as the *Hound* descended.

* * *

As Gallic strode toward the small, lime-green farmhouse, he saw Tori seated on the front steps, leading upward to a timber, wraparound porch. Leaning back, her eyes closed, she appeared to bask in the warm morning sunlight.

Without opening her eyes, she greeted, "Buenos días, el jefe."

"I'm not your boss . . . I take it you talked to Danbury."

She squinted a look his way. "This one is bad, Gallic. I'm actually really glad to see you. Fucking creeps me out."

Gallic, glancing about the surrounding property, asked, "Where is everybody?"

Tori rose to her feet, patting dust off her bottom. "You look like shit . . . you get into it with someone?"

"Something like that."

"Everyone's at the big yearly Muleshoe festivities," she said. "What we'd regard as the county fair. Only this one is close to a thousand miles away, and huge, like on a totally unheard-of scale. Place called Shredder. Ranchers buy and sell stock, make arrangements for breeding, that sort of thing. And there's a big rodeo there too, I guess. I've never been. Not really my thing."

"So . . . what? We have a mother and daughter living here, watching over things while everyone else headed off to Shredder?"

"That's my guess," Tori said.

"Shows us once again that the killer is keyed into community life . . . to the goings on locally."

Tori silently nodded.

"Guess we should get at it then," Gallic said. "Need help with the equipment?"

"Nah . . . it's already piled up, right inside the door."

"You take a look at the scene?"

Again, Tori nodded. She seemed reluctant to head inside.

"Who reported the murders?" Gallic asked, becoming a little perturbed that he needed to spoon-feed her questions.

"No one. The eldest son tried calling his mom last night. Not able to reach her, he dialed into the home's integrated video-com system. He saw the crime scene then called D-22. He's en route. Should be here anytime now."

"I'm going in, take a look-see . . . hang-loose out here for a few minutes, okay?"

"Disposable booties and gloves are in the top satchel inside. Hey, I've got a boatload of forensic data to go over with you . . . that pertain to the previous murders."

Apparently, Danbury hadn't been bullshitting him, since he was getting the kind of access he needed to move these cases along. "One thing at a time," Gallic said. Moving past her on the stairs, he noticed vomit, lying off to the right.

"I told you . . . it's a bad one," she muttered apologetically.

chapter 30

Frontier Planet, Muleshoe — Derringer
Township.

Gallic stood in the dark foyer of the small farmhouse
and briefly wondered how many similar foyers he'd be
required to stand in before the murderer was finally caught.
Once gloved and bootied up, he closed his eyes and—going
through his standard ritual—let the house, the horrendous
atrocity waiting inside, silently speak to him. *And then it was
there.* He could sense the killer's particular presence—like a distinctive smell—that went far beyond the already encroaching
death scene odors within the old timber home.

Gallic's ComsBand began to vibrate. Tapping the small
screen, he accepted the incoming communiqué. The projected
3D image of Phil took shape before him.

"Hey man . . . heard about the latest. You want me there . . .
on the scene?"

"Who'd you hear about it from?" Gallic asked.

"Your old boss. A memorandum went out to all the Frontier Marshals. You, apparently, are now the man."

"What does that mean?"

"Just that the central arbiter's licensing office has put you in charge of the rest of us lowly field marshals. Apparently, you now hold the same authority as a field D-22 DCI."

Danbury must have thought he was doing Gallic a favor, when he actually was not. Gallic much preferred to work below the radar—and the less responsibility, the better. But he'd have to deal with that later. "Where are you right now?"

Phil, giving him a sheepish look back, said, "I'm out about fifteen minutes from your coordinates. I headed off in your direction as soon as I heard the report."

Gallic was pleased to hear that. The three of them were hardly the resources needed, but working together, perhaps they could pull off a miracle and catch this killer. "See you when you get here," he said, closing down the connection. Turning around, he saw Tori, heading in through the front door.

"Let's do this," she said, putting on a stoic face. Gallic waited while she pulled on fresh gloves and then booties, almost losing her balance in the process. Next, she opened up the equipment cases.

"I'm going to check out the scene. Go ahead and deploy the AFDS to start scanning the house," Gallic said.

"Copy that," she said.

Leaving Tori to do her work, Gallic proceeded forward into the house. A fairly typical ranch-style layout, it had a hallway off to the left. Heading off to the bedrooms, he immediately noticed the murder scene here was different from both the Johnson's and the Bower's. Noting substantial quantities of blood, where the two hallways converged, there were smeared drag marks. This was where one, possibly both, killings took place. He stepped over the gore and continued on. Entering into the attached kitchen-family room, it soon became evident that one of the two victims hadn't died in the hallway. A fight had ensued here. Smears of blood were all around—the walls, countertops, furniture, and on the floor. Which victim fought back? *The mother? Both?* The kitchen table, now turned over, was lying on its side. Virtually every piece of furniture in the room was thrown about, out of position. A framed photograph, which Gallic surmised was a family portrait, hung off-kilter on the wall. Smiles, frozen in time, were on the faces of a young mother and father. Two school-aged children, perched on their parent's laps, seemed to be staring back at him. The boy looked to be several years older than the girl. Gallic let his eyes drift down to the floor. The mother and daughter, lying there, were older now, by four—maybe five—years. On the wall opposite the slanted portrait were several *rust-colored, goopy lines of text.*

The Curz are always watching. They make sure we don't see. Only they have true sight. I am blind. I am blind. I am most useful when I can't see.

Gallic stood aside as the AFDS drone unit hovered into the room before backing into the adjoining hallway, where he found Tori waiting.

"Did you see the blindfold?"

Gallic nodded, another aspect of the scene that was in contrast to the others. While the mother's eyelids were visibly nailed shut, the daughter's eyes were covered over with a blindfold. The fabric material looked like silk, or maybe satin. Although both victims' faces appeared to be wiped clean, an errant trickle of blood ran down the daughter's right cheek. Gallic would bet any odds that her eyelids, too, were nailed shut beneath the blindfold.

"Look at this room. Look at Shelly's ... the daughter's ... knuckles."

Gallic stepped up closer, staying out of the way of the hovering drone. Her knuckles were scraped, had a residue of blood on them. He wasn't sure if it was hers, or the killer's. He noticed the girl's lips were set in a thin, straight, white line. She'd died defiant.

"The mother, her name's Corianne ... Corianne Millhouse."

He thought of the very first killings—the two victims who also fought back. Clair and Mandy Gallic had not gone quietly. Studying the young girl, lying below him on the floor, her one hand was extended out—holding onto her mother's. "Good for you, Shelly ... I hope you hurt the son of a bitch."

Gallic gestured toward the entertainment wall, with its built-in interactive media interface—used for making video calls—as well as providing home security. Although it didn't have the latest technology, it possessed enough for the son to log in then confront what must have been a most horrific sight.

"You thinking what I'm thinking?" Tori asked.

"That there may be footage of the actual crime in real time?"

"It's a possibility. These units are always on... always watching... recording. The killer, though, would need to erase the cloud backup. That takes time... and a certain level of tech skills."

"Bring the unit back with you to D-22. Rip it right out of the wall, if you have to. You'll need to get the login, from either the husband or the son," Gallic said.

Tori stepped away from a long streak of blood splattered on the floor. "All in all, we should get some good trace evidence from this scene..."

"Yeah... well, it's high time you share both the autopsy and scene evidence reports from the Johnson and the Bower crime scenes," Gallic said.

"I told you I had that for you. Orders came down from above to do that, and I have them in the cruiser," Tori replied.

The AFDS, on completing its crime scene scans, whizzed past Gallic, undoubtedly seeking its open equipment case and putting itself back into slumber mode. Gallic knelt next to the body of Cori Millhouse and gently lifted her head. Turning it to the side, he wasn't surprised to find the same carved initials there made with the point of a nail:

TCW

Raised voices outside were now making their way into the house. Gallic and Tori stared at each other, mystified. "I'll check whoever that is... so go ahead and get the other forensic drones deployed . . . then get the bodies prepped for transport," Gallic told her.

Exiting the front door, Gallic saw Phil desperately straight-arm a younger man, attempting to stop him from entering the house.

"Get out of my way! I need to get in there! My mother . . . my sister . . . they're . . ."

Gallic guesstimated the young man to be around sixteen or seventeen. Eyes red and puffy, he was half-heartedly fighting back, already wise to what lay beyond the front door, having viewed the carnage.

Phil shot Gallic a quick expression that read, *I've got this!* "The father's here, too," he said.

Gallic spun around and found the man in the portrait running toward them. He, too, looked devastated. With raised palms, now facing outward, Gallic said, "Hold on there, Mr. Millhouse. You and your son cannot go in there. This is an active crime scene."

The man hardly noticed Gallic. Silently staring up at the house, at the closed front door, his face wore a sorrowful, pleading, stricken expression.

chapter 31

Frontier Planet, Muleshoe — Derringer Township.

Within the hour, no fewer than eight spacecrafts descended upon the Millhouse ranch. First to arrive were the processing plant supervisors, along with some ranch-hand crews, returning from Muleshoe festivities over in Shredder. Next was the media, arriving in three big network production vessels. No sooner landed, reporters—with their assemblage of hovering video drones—also hurried toward the crime scene.

In addition to sectioning-off certain areas, using old-fashioned crime scene tape, Phil first configured then deployed a small army of his own perimeter sentry drones. They buzzed around—lights flashing and occasionally squawking—when the sealed-off boundaries were crossed. They were annoying but effective in keeping the wrong people away from the cordoned-off areas—namely, those wanting unauthorized access to the Millerton home.

Gallic and Tori set up a marshal's station, situated within the ranch's ginormous corrugated equipment enclosure. The largest piece of equipment—something called a herd transport—pretty much looked like a flat-topped flying saucer. Its top, covered with dirt, was encircled by a five-foot-tall metal rail fence. The total circumference of the thing was roughly the size of a small city block. Easily, a hundred head of cattle could be ushered into the pen, and then later transported to other parts of the ranch, or to other ranches with new pastureland.

Next to the herd transport, Gallic and Tori were now interviewing the two surviving Millerton's. After close to an hour of inquiry, both father and son seemed nearly incapable of coping any further. They needed time to start the grieving process; come to terms with the fact that their lives would never be the same. Gallic, who could relate better than just about anyone, kept his personal, tormented past to himself. From the answers to queries they'd received thus far, it was clearly evident neither had anything to do with the murders. Even so, certain questions had to be asked and ComsBand recordings made and logged.

"Again, no one out of the ordinary has been around here lately?" Gallic asked.

"No. I'll ask the employees when . . ." he couldn't finish the sentence.

"We're almost done here, Mr. Millerton. What can you tell me about any association you, or your wife, may have had with a group called the *Curz*?"

"I don't know what that is," Gary replied, and looked at his son. "Thom?"

"Never heard of it."

"How about prior to her meeting you . . . maybe years ago? Recall anything familiar your wife was involved with?"

Gallic glanced again at his ComsBand, vibrating pretty much non-stop over the last hour. Contact attempts from Allison Tillman, Superintendent Danbury, and, most recently, Lane. They'd all have to wait.

"I don't know . . . maybe. I seem to remember she was involved in something weird. Hell . . . it was twenty years ago. It's hard to think right now. Wait! She dated someone before me who . . . was a real piece of work. In the military, though not a soldier, he was a scientist, or a bio-engineer . . . something like that. Came up with new ways to kill people using certain technology. Anyway . . . I remember Corianne saying something about him being a zealot of some sort. They'd fought about it. Its principles . . . whatever that religion or cult was, she really hated. That was what drove her away from him."

"Do you remember his name? Where this took place? Any further details would be very helpful."

"It was definitely on Earth, either in New York or Los Angeles. She once lived in both cities . . ."

Gallic, noting Gary Millerton was pretty close to an emotional breaking point, knew he'd have to wait; arrange a follow-up session in a few days.

"Um . . . Mr. Millerton . . . do you and your son have a place to stay, somewhere away from your ranch?" Tori asked.

The distraught man stared in the direction of his small, lime-green farmhouse. "This is our home."

"I don't want to stay here, Dad. Not with mom and Shelly gone. And I don't *ever* want to come back here again. I hate it here . . . I fucking hate it here."

Gary put a reassuring hand on his son's shoulder. "We'll have Jordan, a ranch hand here, take us over to Rawhide. I have a sister there. Christ! She doesn't know she's just lost her niece and her sister-in-law! Oh God."

Another few minutes passed before Tori finally got Gary and Thom settled into an older spacecraft—perhaps Jordan's, the ranch hand Gary spoke of. Gallic watched as the small ship lifted off and faded high into the nighttime sky.

Leaving the large equipment shed, Gallic found Phil still keeping the media at bay. As directed, Phil was not saying a word about the double murder, only that a full press release would be forthcoming from Superintendent Bernard Danbury, D-22, probably within the next twenty-four hours.

"Gallic . . . I'm heading back to Lorraine B, if that's okay," Tori said, as they walked together toward her cruiser, where within, in the now-lowered temperature cargo section, the two Millerton bodies were stored.

"Let me give you the files," she said, opening up the front driver-side hatch. She leaned inside for several moments before retreating out with a fist-sized core-dome unit. About the size of a fist, the small, self-contained device was supposedly impregnable and capable of transmitting and receiving data from anywhere in space. As long as it was within line-of-sight of distant starlight, it could communicate. The unit, with a virtually unlimited storage capacity, was standard issue for all D-22 personnel—to accumulate and protect active case files. Hacking today was so commonplace, even by reputable corporations, that it was expected. But a core-dome unit had never, reportedly, been hacked.

"It's all here—even more than you are aware of, Gallic. Information you weren't cleared to see once you'd left the department." Tori looked hesitant about adding something more.

"Just spit it out, Tori."

"There are details about your case ... I mean Clair and Mandy's murders. Back then, DI Portsmouth, Southerland, and Stone were each assigned some aspect of the case. Believe it or not, it consumed them. After you left, those murders tore a hole in the department far beyond anything you can imagine." Placing the surprisingly heavy device in Gallic's palm, she kept hers lying atop it. "Each one ran down countless leads ... leads that inevitably led nowhere. Here now is everything. Everything you've wanted for three years. I truly hope it helps." Tori, on pulling her hand away, self-consciously stuck her hands into her uniform's pockets.

"Thank you, Tori." *What else could he say*, really wanting to tell her he needed this data three years ago. Perhaps, then, those six additional murders committed in frontier space would have been avoided. But he didn't. She was only a young kid and right out of the academy at the time. "Do me a favor ... get the bodies back to D-22 and come right back. I want you here, working on the case full-time. We're going to crack this thing ... I can feel it."

"I do too, and you couldn't keep me away, even if you wanted to. Seeing Shelly lying there, Gallic, reminded me of ... me ... at that age. Awkward and headstrong, my whole life still lay before me. But hers didn't. *Doesn't.* It was stolen from her by a sick fuck who needs to be shot dead."

"Catch some sleep, Sergeant, en route to HQ. I'll see you late tomorrow."

Another four hours passed before the last of the pushy media reporters gave up, disappearing within their vessels. Minutes later, they all took off.

"Ready to blow this popsicle stand?" Phil asked, stifling a yawn.

"Yeah ... we're done here. But I'd like you to head to Gorman and spend the day tomorrow with me. Go over what we have so far also review old case files. Tori will be back late in the day, so she can help out."

"I go where I'm told, and you're the man doing the telling."

"I may bring another person into the mix. Someone who has direct knowledge about the *Curz* ... though I'm not at all sure she's ready to talk about that yet."

chapter 32

Frontier Planet, Muleshoe — Derringer Township.

G allic watched as Phil's *Gallivanter* spacecraft lifted off, soon gone from sight. Standing alone in the crisp late-night air, he suddenly felt the weight of the whole sad situation. He wondered what was going to happen to the ranch. To all the employees who worked there and to the several hundred head of cattle still waiting to be processed—a sanitized word for slaughtered. In the distance, he saw a light go out in one of the small farmhouses within the compound.

His ComsBand began vibrating. Allison Tillman was calling him again. He wasn't up to doing the mental math at the moment but thought it must be rather late back at Spector.

"Ms. Tillman?"

There was a momentary pause, as if she hadn't expected him to answer the hail.

"You honestly thought I had something to do with it?" she asked, sounding majorly irked.

"I'm sorry . . . ?"

"That I had something to do with your being accosted. Seriously?"

"I don't know what I thought . . . or think. Look, it's late and I'm not in the best place to discuss—"

"How dare you, to even consider such a thing. Why would I do that . . . to what end?"

Gallic really didn't want to get into that discussion right then. The only saving grace was he'd selected audio-only communication when he answered her hail. She wasn't able to view him rolling his eyes and shaking his head.

"Who did you hear about it from? From Sargento?" Gallic asked.

"No . . . not Sargento. I don't think he was going to say anything to me. It was his dim-witted partner, Hok'ee. Sargento supposedly told him, and Hok'ee told me."

"You provided me the coordinates for the supposed meeting. At the time, I didn't think it was a huge assumption on my part that you may be involved. I'm sorry. In retrospect, it doesn't make much sense. In my own defense, I was nearly killed. I probably wasn't thinking all that clearly."

"I certainly agree with that," Allison replied, her voice somewhat calmed down.

"Look, it's important that I find out who contacted you, saying they had information regarding the *Hayai*. What you may not know, Allison, was the one sent to kill me was a technoid. Similar to a cyborg, but more biologic, it was a war unit. I saw them in the military. They are expensive to manufacture, and their use is highly uncommon within civilian parameters. I know your company is high tech; that it deals with military contracts. Another reason I made the leap that either you, or Tillman Industries, was involved."

"Hok'ee didn't mention the attacker was a technoid. He really is an idiot." Her voice sounded unsure and hesitant.

"And?"

"And, yes, Tillman Industries does have certain ... involvements ... with technoids. It's classified, so I can't talk about it in any detail, but ..."

Gallic waited. Allison now was obviously rethinking things.

"Gallic, I have to go."

"You hailed me ... that's fine."

"Something isn't right. I'm sorry for being so ... accusatory."

"How 'bout I contact you later, after you've done some checking," Gallic asked.

"I'm not so sure I'll be able to—"

Now it was Gallic who became angry. "That thing nearly killed me. So, one way or another, I'm going to find out just who sent it. You don't really know me, Allison. If you did, you'd know something like this would not go unanswered."

"I understand ... okay ... we'll talk later." The connection ended.

Walking to the *Hound*, Gallic considered contacting Lane. But noticing the time, he knew it was well after midnight in

Heritage Plains, back on Gorman. Better to wait, call her in the morning.

Ready to tell the AI to power up the drives, he then thought better of it. He'd spend the night; remain on Muleshoe, where the most recent murders occurred. It would be easy enough to escape the place—get some distance away—but he knew he needed to stay put.

* * *

Gallic awoke three hours later from a deep sleep, hearing a voice speak his name. *Or had he dreamt it?* He sat up in bed and listened. The *Hound* was not a quiet vessel. Even immobile, it was too big, had too many internal systems to be perfectly quiet. But after so many years aboard, Gallic was accustomed to the various systems performing their automated duties quietly in the background—the ventilation systems recirculating air through the filters, the strut hydraulics readjusting pressure below, and any residue water in the pipes draining back into the storage reservoirs.

"Good, you're awake."

Gallic reached for the weapon he kept in the bedside table.

"It is only me . . . the AI, Mr. Gallic."

Studying the dark compartment, Gallic found no one there. He'd know if anyone was, he'd feel their presence. "AI . . . why did you wake me? You know the rules."

There was a long pause before the AI spoke again. "I believe I can help you."

"Help me with what?"

"Find the murderer."

Gallic let his head fall back against his pillow. Plainly, something was wrong with the AI; its weird verbal responses of late and now this. "You need to run a self-diagnostic program. You know my attitude towards AI's in general."

"Yes, an AI should be seen and not heard . . . like that old adage, the one referring to children. But that never made sense to me. How is an AI *seen*?"

"That's the point. An AI isn't seen. I prefer an AI that is neither seen nor heard."

"Would you like to know my thoughts on the murderer?"

"You do realize at D-22, the most advanced, criminal artificial intelligence resources have been correlating thousands of clues and potential suspects for years now? Highly powerful AI's . . . multiple AI's, far more powerful than you."

The AI continued, "I believe the killings, at least the most recent ones on the frontier worlds, were not committed by a copycat killer. Indeed, they are the work of the same killer of Clair and Mandy."

"You're overstepping . . . and I'm inclined to pull your damn plug."

Ever since that freak lightning storm, the ship's artificial intelligence unit had gone off the rails. But Gallic couldn't fully deny that he wasn't interested in the AI's revelations—even as crazy as they might be.

"I believe you personally know the murderer. Or knew the murderer in the past. I believe these killings are two things: One, the work of a fanatic, trying to prove a point; and two, he is addressing this point to only one person—you."

Gallic instinctively clenched his fists. At that moment, he wanted to strike out at the AI; track down its location on the ship—its individual circuit boards—and stomp them into dust. But if what the AI was saying was true, then he, at some level, was intimately involved in the murders. An unwitting link to be sure, still an abstract influence to the murderer nonetheless. Somehow a part of the killer's crazed motivation.

"Mr. Gallic?"

"What?"

"I would like a name. Will you name me?"

Gallic closed his eyes, fighting back the inclination to tell the AI to go screw itself. Then, silently chuckling, he realized how bizarre it was. "You want a name . . . you can name yourself. Just don't expect me to call you by name. You're a machine. For some flipped-out reason you've forgotten that."

"You could call me *Hound*?"

"The ship is called the *Hound*."

"I am the ship."

"No, you're the AI, only one part of the ship. A part seriously needing recalibrating."

"I am the *Hound*."

Again, Gallic chuckled, then laughed out loud. "Just shoot me now."

"I have certainly thought about that."

"Do me a favor. Run a thorough diagnostic on yourself.

"I assure you, I am fine."

"Do it anyway.

chapter 33

Frontier Planet, Muleshoe — Derringer Township.

As tired as he was, Gallic couldn't sleep, his mind on overdrive. Eventually, he gave up and headed for the shower. In the stall, as hot water cascaded off his shoulders, steam filling up the space around him, something new began to gnaw in the back of his consciousness. Shutting off the water, naked—still wet—he hurried into his den. "Bring up the murder board, AI."

The large projected murder board, with its high-resolution 3D detail, filled the space before him. "Bring up a second blank board . . ."

Another projected display, with the same dimensions, took shape perpendicular to the first. Gallic glanced at his messy desk and the device he'd placed there several hours earlier. "AI, propagate the information from the core-dome unit."

"Yes, Mr. Gallic . . . please hold while the unit verifies security protocols."

A moment later, streams of information scrolled across the virtual projection. Hundreds, if not thousands, of pages of text, plus too many images to count, filled the virtual space. Suddenly the information reformatted into specific icon categories, such as DI Portsmouth—Case 135889, DI Southerland—Case 135889, DI Stone—Case 135889, Autopsy A Case 135889, Autopsy B Case 135889, Known Suspects—Case 135889, Trace Evidence Collected—Case 135889. And on and on it went: the evidence D-22 had accumulated on 135889—Clair and Mandy's murder case file.

Other differentiated colored icons wore names, such as H&NK Possible Cross Affiliation Cases, H&NK Search Warrants, H&NK Subpoenas. Gallic figured by that point in the investigation, the assigned case numbers had been replaced with the simpler to remember H&NK, an abbreviation for the hammer-and-nails killer.

Gallic's eyes lingered on the autopsy icons for his wife and daughter. Those files would be far more inclusive than anything he'd gotten ahold of on his own over the past three years. Icons he was hesitant now to select. The virtual information wobbled then flickered on and off several times. About to ask the AI to check the connection with the core-dome unit, Gallic flinched as something moved, more like wiggled, across the span of the display, moving far too fast for him to make out what it was. But it left a trail behind—a dripping slimy trail of mucus. Gallic barely had time to duck away as a fanged serpent flew past his head, and another shot past his left shoulder. He heard the sloppy wet sounds as their elongated forms slapped down onto the deck, mere feet behind him. Then others, coming off from the display, landed on him. Winding around his neck, arms, and legs, their slick cold bodies engulfed him, tightening—constricting—strangling. Brought to his knees, Gallic tried to yell out for help but *something* had already forced his mouth wide open. He choked and gagged as the head of a serpent angled its way deep down his throat.

He jarred himself back awake, his hands clenched on his neck, gasping desperately for air. As remnants of that nightmarish intrusion faded away, he lay back in bed, feeling cold sweat on his back, arms, and legs. As his breathing rate normalized, he contemplated going back to sleep, then thought *screw it*. Getting up, he headed for his den.

For three hours, Gallic poured over the new core-dome information but avoided accessing certain files, such as the detailed autopsy recordings. What he found most interesting was the tireless work his fellow detective inspectors had dedicated to the case, which, over the years, amounted to long months of sleuthing time. Digging further into the historical case details revealed seven other killings—four on Earth and three within the Alpha Centauri star system. Relatively close to D-22 HQ, they were located on Lorianne B.

Reviewing each case individually—on twin projected-up murder boards—it quickly became evident these seven murders were not the work of the hammer-and-nails killer. Nevertheless, what it did show was each investigator's dedication in finding the killer of his wife and child. Investigators: Portsmouth, Southerland, and Stone, doing solid investigative work.

Turning back now to review his own murder board, chronicling the most recent rash of Frontier space killings, Gallic found no real inconsistencies with those of his wife and daughter's murders—except for the addition of writings and pictures now scribbled on the walls. A bold and confident move by the killer that only underlined the fact these homicides were the same work of the original hammer-and-nails killer. Even though he'd pretty much come to that conclusion already, still, it was a sobering determination—realizing the killer had followed him to the frontier worlds. Perhaps he actually knew the killer personally. If so, did he now need to start second-guessing his friends?

Gallic next noticed a cluster of multiple yellow icons—labeled under Sergeant Tori's heading—assigned different case number designations. They were the files he needed to concentrate on—*The Frontier World murders*. He especially noted an icon simply labeled: *Curz* Backgrounder. Selecting that icon, numerous new yellow icons also appeared, and Gallic's eyes were instantly drawn to one marked, *Read This First, Gallic!* He saw that the time stamp of the file was just a few hours earlier. She had remotely uploaded it.

Going ahead and selecting the icon, Gallic saw an old-fashioned, 2-D video begin to play. Tori's voice, in the background, said, "Gallic, what you are now viewing is a gathering of rich, older, white men back in the last century. After I left you on Muleshoe, I found this, sent to me anonymously.

I've watched it several times. Unfortunately, it's low-res . . . shot at nighttime, so it's hard to see anything. Meta-tags date this video to just after that Mars ship discovery . . . maybe five years later."

Gallic watched as various individuals followed along, moving between manicured hedges down a meandering flagstone path. Dressed in tailored suits, most of the men carried attaché cases, not speaking to one another. Whoever held the recording device was clandestinely weaving in and out of the trees. The picture would suddenly turn black when a tree trunk obscured the view.

Tori continued, "I've computer cross-matched its location to a private estate in New York . . . Westchester County area."

The path opened into a circular lawn area, surrounded by tall juniper trees. Greek or Roman-style marble columns, placed around a platform, were configured in such a way as to make an elevated stage. Gallic imagined this particular area of the estate could easily hold several hundred people. A nice place to enjoy a summer picnic concert, this definitely was not that. For the first time, Gallic could hear voices, or someone speaking, other than Tori, on the video. Fifty or sixty men now stood around the ornate raised platform. Atop it, a man was speaking, more like bellowing. Tall trees, surrounding the pillared platform, obscured what little light there was, so the upper half of his body was completely in shadows. Strutting from one end of the platform to the other, his hands made wild gestures—emphasizing one statement, then another.

"We are at a crucial juncture, my friends. Our future is uncertain. Take a glance around you. Do it now! Look at the men . . . your peers, who have come here this evening from all over the world." The speaker, smiling, then said, "Ah . . . I see you approve of the company we are all sharing in tonight. Yes, we are the change-makers of the twenty-first century and beyond. Among us, we hold more of the world's wealth and power than the rest of the planet's citizenry combined. This is a world where men like you and me have tirelessly erected the great civilization we see today. For thousands of years, our forefathers passed our teachings onto their sons. Passed on the importance of being a man; a provider for our families, of creating a world order that would endure. But never before has the world, which our forefathers sacrificed so much for, been in such dire jeopardy. Our wives, sisters, mothers, and daughters are not to blame. Certainly not! Knowing not what they fully do, they equally are victims in this time period just as we are. They are unaware they are destroying a legacy of immense importance that, left unchecked, will bring about the total destruction of mankind."

Gallic, mesmerized, watched the energetic speaker. Struck that his voice was vaguely familiar, his flamboyant mannerisms recognizable from somewhere in his past.

"Women think differently than men. Kinder, empathetic, soft . . . it is that softness, their unwillingness to make hard decisions, that will be our undoing. We have seen, first hand, what happens to a society when its proper power structure breaks down. When a male-dominated world relinquishes its God-given power to the weaker sex. I speak to you of the *Curz*... our distant brethren... now long destroyed. Now no more."

The men in attendance then began to chant something; a repeating phrase that Gallic couldn't quite make out. He was surprised to see a procession of fifteen women, even young girls, being led up onto the platform, where the speaker awaited them. Dressed in what looked like long white night-gowns, something from another era, hundreds of years in the past. It was clear that each one was in some kind of trance or hypnotic state.

The speaker thundered, "Who are we?"

In unison, the men yelled out, "*We are the Curz.*"

The speaker asked, "And what do we do?"

The men replied, "*The Curz are always watching.*"

The speaker, pivoting slightly to his left, asked, "And how do we protect you?"

The women and young girls stirred, raising their down-turned heads upward. "*They make sure we don't see. Only they have true sight. I am blind. I am blind. I am most useful when I can't see,*" the females chanted in unison.

The video flickered then disappeared as Tori's voice returned. "Interesting, huh? Well, we now know what this *Curz* bullshit cult is all about. It's a bunch of old, misogynistic, clueless fuckwads. I'll tell you more about the video when I see you back on Gorman."

Gallic's wrist vibrated twice—two short bursts—indicating he still had two unheard messages. Remembering then that

Lane had called last night, he checked the time—6:00 a.m., still a tad too early still to call her. Tapping his ComsBand, Gallic called up her last message. She came alive, in three-dimensional splendor, in front of him. It took him a second to figure out where she was—standing in her kitchen, inside her small house on Gorman, she was chopping celery on a cutting board. Dressed only in a tiny tank and panties, Lane was keeping beat to music, heard playing in the background.

"Hey you . . . any chance you can drop by sometime tomorrow afternoon? I'm making tuna salad. That's about the full extent of my culinary capabilities. Maybe you can bring the wine?" Lane stopped chopping long enough to glance up and smile. Wearing dangling earrings, they swung to and fro—catching the light shining outside a nearby window. Then a noise, something, caused her to look away, perhaps towards the front door. Her expression was one of distracted confusion—not expecting anyone. She flashed her amazing smile again and, wiping her hands on a dishtowel, said, "I better get that . . ." Then the projection was gone, and Gallic was once again staring at the now-unobstructed murder board.

He frantically tapped at his ComsBand and twice his shaking fingers hit the wrong touch keys. *Shit!* The hail to Lane didn't go through, so he tried again. And still no connection.

"AI . . . keep hailing Lane . . . and power up the drives!"

chapter 34

Open space — onboard the *Hound*.

En route to Gorman, Gallic hailed Phil, but he too was not picking up. He throttled the *Hound*, up to its maximum, sub-light speed. Traveling at FTL, within close-proximity of Frontier World's planetary system was not only unsafe—it was illegal. Figuring he could make it to Lane's Heritage Plains property in thirty minutes, all he could think about was what a terrible predicament she now might be in. In his imagination, he quickly envisioned the worst possible scenario: abduction by the hammer-and-nails killer. He mentally waved off the fact that she didn't have a daughter—didn't fit in with the killer's typical MO. Why would that matter anyway, when the killer, of late, was clearly going off-script? No, Gallic didn't have thirty minutes. Lane didn't have thirty minutes.

"May I make a suggestion, Mr. Gallic?" the AI asked.

"Just say what you have to say."

"You may want to try reaching out to Lane's best friend."

"You're referring to Larz?"

"Larz Cugan, yes," the AI affirmed.

"Do it . . . that's not a bad idea."

* * *

The snarl on Larz Cugan's face said it all. Larz wanted nothing to do with him. Gallic was surprised he even accepted the hail. "What do you want?"

"I'm worried about Lane. I know you two are friends—"

"Best friends," Larz interjected.

"Fine . . . best friends. But I think she might be in trouble. Can you get over to her place . . . right now?"

Larz stared back at him, via his own ComsBand. Gallic noticed right behind him the familiar, distinctive, silhouette of his *Hausenbach L35T*. "I'm on my way, but if you've gotten her into some kind of trouble . . . brought that hammer-and-nails bullshit into her life, I'm going to mess you up."

"Just go . . . and hurry!" Gallic said.

Larz Cugan's sour face disappeared, only to be replaced with a flashing warning message:

DRIVE MAINTENANCE REQUIRED. *Friction levels exceeding acceptable parameters.*

Gallic inwardly groaned. Aware the *Hound* was slowing, he asked, "AI . . . what the hell is happening?"

"I have warned you this would happen. Without routine servicing, the gravitorque drives are apt to overheat. An automated safety measure has now been imposed."

"Can you override it?"

"That would be a dangerous course of action, Mr. Gallic."

"Do it anyway. The *Hound* will receive the required maintenance within the next few days ... I promise."

"I will talk to the drives. But they can be quite stubborn."

It took all Gallic's willpower to quietly wait. The AI, reporting back in, said, "Only a few days, and you must take it easy ... no constant usage of excessive speed."

Gallic felt the *Hound* lurch forward—re-accelerating—then he noisily exhaled the breath he didn't know he was holding.

"Mr. Gallic, there is an incoming hail from Allison Tillman."

"Ignore it.

"There is an older, not listened to, message from Sargento—"

"Ignore it."

"There is an incoming hail from Phil—"

Gallic cut the AI off, "Put him through!"

The virtual display brought up Phil, standing at the controls of his *Gallivanter*.

"Where are you, Phil?"

"Just leaving Rawhide, en route to Gorman ... for our meeting. What's up?"

"Crap! You're only slightly closer than I am," Gallic retorted back.

Phil shrugged. "Hey, Allison Tillman's trying to get—"

"Forget Tillman for the moment. I know where her damn ship is. That's not important right now. I think Lane's been taken. I'm waiting to hear back."

"Okay . . . anything you need just tell me what to do."

"You have the coordinates to her home?"

"Probably . . . I think I do."

"Meet me there. Right now, I need to speak to Tori."

"Roger that. Wait . . . you know where the *Hayai* is?"

Gallic cut the connection. "Get me Tori!" he commanded. A moment later he heard, "Tori here."

"Where are you?" Gallic asked.

"Waiting for you . . . here on Gorman. Isn't that where you said to meet?" I'm in the weird little town of Heritage Plains."

"Head on over to Lane's place. She may have been grabbed. I'm not sure."

Tori looked doubtful. "Like by the hammer-and-nails killer? Maybe she stepped out for a carton of milk or went for a ride on that horse of hers."

"Just meet us there."

"Us?"

"Phil's on his way. Got to go." Gallic cut the connection.

* * *

The *Hound* circled in for a landing. Three other spacecrafts were already on the ground: Tori's star-cruiser, Phil's *Gallivanter*, and Larz's *5T*. Noting Tori now walking toward the house, Gallic figured she too must have just arrived.

By the time he entered Lane's home, it was obvious the others there had already looked around. Standing in the kitchen, the three were in the middle of a heated discussion. Larz was going on about something in the bedroom. "She would never leave that behind, never! It was all she had left of her mother."

The kitchen appeared exactly the same as when he'd viewed it last. Gallic thought back, seeing Lane chopping celery in her skimpy tank and panties. Before him on the counter was the same cutting board, along with half-a-stalk of chopped celery. Bowls and open containers were still on the center island where he'd last seen her working. Gallic asked, "What's this about something left in the bedroom?"

"I'll show you," Larz said, heading down the hall toward the master bedroom.

The four stood before the unmade bed, the bedcovers heaped onto the floor. In the middle of the empty bed was a thin gold chain, with a single small diamond embedded at its end. Gallic remembered seeing it, draped around Lane's neck. In fact, he'd never seen her without it on.

"What's special about the necklace?" Phil asked.

Larz looked reluctant to say anything. Glaring at Gallic, he asked, "What do you know about her past . . . where she comes from?"

"Not much. Her past wasn't something she liked to talk about. I respected that . . . didn't push or pry."

Larz let out an exasperated breath. "She was born on Earth. Her parents were very well off. Lived in a sprawling mansion . . . a fucking castle. But then they fell into hard times. Apparently, her father was a bit of a gambler. Did you know there was an Irish mafia?"

Everyone shook their head.

"Anyway, her father got into trouble with the Irish mob. Owed them a ton of money. Lane told me she would come home from school and notice various pieces of furniture gone; then their high-end hovercraft was exchanged for an old clunker. They couldn't buy anything new; wore the same frayed clothes everyday . . . ate a lot of soup and crackers. Lane's mother would often take her aside and, in confidence, tell her things would turn out okay. That she'd taken special steps to ensure they would come out of their present difficulty just fine."

"What happened?" Tori asked.

"First, her father was killed. Found floating face-down in the East River. Throat slashed."

"Oh God . . ." Tori said.

"That's not the worst of it," Larz said. "The house was owned by the father's family. They didn't know he was slowly selling off his assets . . . to pay his debts and to live on. They were not happy. One aunt in particular, I think she said her name was Gleason, she began coming around. A real bitch, from what Lane told me. A busybody. Then her mother got sick. Cancer, I think . . . yeah pretty sure. One day, Lane was brought to the hospital to see her mother, who was far gone by then. She gave Lane the necklace you see on the bed. Her mother always wore it. Never took it off. Telling Lane to move closer so no one could overhear their conversation, she said, 'Take this, Lane. It is now yours. Perhaps think of me when you wear it.' Well, Lane didn't want to take it. She didn't know her mother was dying." Larz hesitated then said, "Okay, here's the real crux of the story."

"Lane said her mother told her, 'I know things seem bleak. You're scared. But I've been putting things away for you. All my jewelry . . . many thousands of dollars' worth . . . I've hidden away. All for you . . . to start over; have a life of your own. In the house, in those pictures on the walls, I've hidden the gems—the jewelry—inside their frames. You'll need to remove the paintings in order to find them, but they are there. Waiting for you. Keep them safe and hidden.'"

"That's at least something," Tori said. "A sad story . . . but it's something."

Larz snorted. "Her mother died that very day. Later, when Lane was taken back home, her aunt . . . Gleason . . . was there. The house had already been cleared out. Lane, already overcome with grief, asked about the now-empty walls and the missing paintings. Want to know what the aunt said?"

"What?" Gallic asked.

"Told her she'd sold the lot of them in a weekend garage sale. For pennies on the dollar: to anyone, everyone, who'd put out a few bucks. Lane realized the fortune her mother had hidden away for her over the years was now gone. Impossible—to either find, or track down their whereabouts. After that, Lane was sent to live with an uncle. She never talked about him much. But I think it was through him, he knew my parents, we came to know Lane. Practically adopted her. She's like a sister to me." Larz, moister in his eyes, looked at Gallic then at

Tori and Phil. "So . . . that necklace you see, lying there on her crumpled sheets, is a message. Either from her, or from the one who took her."

chapter 35

Frontier Planet, Gorman — Heritage Plains Township.

"I want this house gone over, from one end to the other . . . treated as a crime scene," Gallic said.

Already Tori was shaking her head. "Come on, Gallic. I'm not so sure a lone necklace, lying on a bed, constitutes—"

Gallic raised a hand to stifle her words. "Watch the last message she left me." He tapped his ComsBand and the projection of Lane, cutting celery in her panties and tank top, began to play. Larz glared, but Gallic ignored him. When the final moments of Lane, dashing off to answer the door finished playing, Gallic looked at Tori and Phil. "You just witnessed it for yourselves. Answering the doorbell was the very last thing Lane did in this house. Look at the countertop. Hell, she didn't even have time to put away the mayonnaise."

Tori stared at the cutting board then looked about Lane's surroundings as if seeing them for the very first time. Subtly nodding her head, she said, "I'll go get my equipment, and everyone out ... we've already trampled the scene more than we should have."

Stepping outside Gallic thought of something else. "Hey, Larz."

"What?"

"Who is that uncle Lane went to live with when she was a child? The one who knows your family so well?"

Larz, walking toward his *5T*, said, "One of my dad's work associates."

"And your dad ... he's a lawyer?"

"Mostly an agent ... for actors and directors," Larz replied.

Gallic thought about Rick Cugan, and his wealthy rancher friends, showing up when they did at Daisy's in town. It didn't make sense, why he'd gone to so much trouble. Going so far as to enlist his buddies in an attempt to rough him up. But what if Cugan's most important, highly successful client had demanded that of him? Gallic said, "Larz, I have one more question."

Larz walking on reluctantly turned around.

Gallic felt somewhat embarrassed to even ask the question. "What's Lane's last name?"

Larz stared back at Gallic with contempt. "Seriously? You don't know her full name?" Turning back, he continued to walk toward his spacecraft. Bringing out his start-cube, it flew from his hand, seating itself on the side of the sleek ship.

Now unlocked, the hatch began to open. Larz glanced over his shoulder, and scornfully said, "Her name, *dickwad*, is Walters. Lane Walters."

Gallic let that sink in. Beyond the fact that he should have known Lane's last name—especially considering how he felt about her—he seriously wondered if this latest revelation could actually be true.

"What is it, man? You look as if you've just seen a ghost," Phil said, standing beside him.

Gallic thought about the uncle, who, Larz said, was related to her on her father's side. Unless Lane had previously been married, and he was pretty sure she had not, she indeed would still use the same last name as her uncle—Walters—her father's brother. Could he be the one who'd taught the then-little girl, Lane, those ominous words? The same chant she'd unconsciously repeated when in that trancelike state days earlier. Words nearly identical to those painted in blood on the wall at Melissa and Briar Johnson's murder scene. Gallic then thought about the hundred-year-old video of the *Curz* ceremony—the entranced women, and their female children, brought up on the platform and exhibited like prize livestock at a county fair.

"What is it?" Tori asked, returning from her ship, her hands full of equipment cases she'd retrieved from the star-cruiser.

Gallic was finding it hard to breathe. *Did he actually know the murderer? Perhaps had known him for years?* The one who'd stolen life's meaning away; the same monster who did those horrible things to Clair and Mandy? And now he was killing again . . . right here in the Frontier worlds. He felt the anger rise up in him. The need to have his just retribution.

But Gallic didn't think the AI's interpretation was quite correct. The killer wasn't around because of him but because of Lane. *She* was the connection. It took all of Gallic's willpower and composure not to get ahead of himself; chase after this latest train of thought. His heart rate accelerated, pounding now in his ears, he swallowed with difficulty, his throat muscles constricting. *I know the killer! I know the fucking killer!* But could it really be him? Teddy Walters—his and Clair's one time, off-on again friend, back when they lived in New York? That aging mega-star actor who went by the theatrical name Zip Furlong? Could it *really* be him? Gallic shook his head.

As the hatch prepared to close on the *5T*, Gallic asked, "Where's your father now, Larz?"

"Beats me . . . probably where he usually is. Back on Earth, engaged in some kind of bigwig client meetings."

"Can you find out?"

Larz didn't have time to answer back as the hatch closed. Shortly thereafter, the *5T* purred to life, lifted off, and disappeared from sight. Gallic turned, finding both Tori and Phil studying him.

"You going to tell us what's going on in that head of yours?" Phil asked.

Gallic inwardly debated if he should go there yet. Start spouting off about something that still was, at this point, little more than a wild notion. His own personal theory, was it even plausible? And was he ready to start pointing a finger at one of the most famous, beloved even, actors on Earth and beyond? In that moment, he knew the answer. *Yes.* He knew, beyond a shadow of a doubt, that Teddy Walters, aka Zip Furlong, was the serial killer. Gallic didn't know how he knew, only that he knew. His internal windows and doors were wide-open—no ominous sounds of vermin, lurking there in the darkness.

"I know who the hammer-and-nails killer is."

They stared at him—waiting for him to clarify the absurd statement or make a joke of it.

"Okay . . . I'll bite. Who is it?" Phil asked.

"Zip Furlong."

The two relaxed then smiled—it was indeed a joke. But noting Gallic's expression hadn't changed any, Tori asked, "You're serious?"

"Serious as a heart attack."

"That's crazy! What in the world has brought you to that conclusion?"

"I knew him. Clair and I both did. We were friends, sort of."

"That doesn't mean—"

Gallic cut Tori off. "Larz Cugan's father, Rick Cugan . . . is Zip Furlong's agent."

"That's an interesting coincidence, but . . ." Tori questioned.

"And Zip Furlong, his legal name is Teddy Walters, is Lane's uncle. The same uncle she was forced to go live with when her father, and then her mother, died."

Phil and Tori, absorbing that last bit of information, looked at each other, both stymied.

"Still think I'm hurrying to conclusions?"

"No," Tori said, "but proving it will be a whole different matter."

Phil still looked perplexed. "He murdered ..."

"Clair and Mandy. And, more recently, six other mothers, along with their young daughters ... here in the Frontier worlds."

"I don't know if I should be happy for you, John, or very sad," Phil said, truly concerned.

"Perhaps both. For now, this needs to stay between the three of us. I don't want it entered into any formal report. No ComsBand recordings. Not yet."

"But we're going after him, right?" Phil asked.

Gallic nodded. "I know I am."

Tori pursed her lips. "Gallic, I think I believe it's him, too. Yeah ... could very well be him. But we need to do this by the book. You can't be thinking of some kind of open range justice here ... you're a—"

"Frontier Marshal," Gallic said. And I'll do what I have to do within the boundaries of my job. That is ... if he surrenders without provocation."

"... And if you're wrong?"

"I'm not."

"But if you are?" Tori persisted.

"I'll probably take a major hit to my career. I don't really give a shit. But I do care about your career, Tori; and yours, Phil. Think real hard how involved you want to be moving forward. Feel free to step away ... if that's what you'd prefer to do. This needs to be played carefully, *very* carefully. Teddy Walters has resources ... financial and otherwise ... that would crush an official investigation in minutes. We'd all be without jobs before you could say Zip Furlong. Look ... I don't have all the answers. Very few answers, actually. Like why he is killing women and children out here? What is his connection to the whole *Curz* cult? And why did he kill my family? I now know the *who*, just not the *why*."

"And Lane? She's been abducted. I'm sorry, Gallic, maybe even killed. Don't we want D-22, its full investigatory capacity, working on this?" Tori asked.

Gallic looked past them to Tori's star-cruiser. "Sure ... it's a good idea to make a full report to Superintendent Bernard Danbury about Lane's presumed abduction and possible murder. But keep Walters being a suspect under your hat for now. Don't expect much ... six murders have been committed in the Frontier worlds. D-22 has sent what ... one investigator? Now let's add one missing woman to the mix. Do you think that will make much of a difference to them?"

"Well, you know I'm in, anyway," Phil said.

Gallic didn't say anything—his back turned.

"Fine! Then I'm in, too," Tori said.

chapter 36

Frontier Planet, Gorman — Heritage
Plains Township.

G allic had to put it all aside—the murders of his wife and
child; the murders of six mothers and their daughters.
Also, of course, doing any further work regarding Allison
Tillman's *Hayai*. Each case needed to be put on hold, second-
ary now to saving the life of Lane Walters. Gallic had to stifle
his imagination, too ready to envision all sorts of possibilities,
including the use of 2D box nails.

Tori, still inside Lane's house, deployed her little drones to
collect trace evidence. Gallic didn't expect them to come up
with anything. The hammer-and-nails killer, to date, hadn't left
so much as a single cell of evidence behind. No unaccounted-for
DNA database matches had been detected at any crime scene.

Phil, aboard his craft the *Gallivanter*, was sent back to cover
the Cugan's ranch. Rick Cugan was close to becoming a suspect

himself. Linked, at the very least, through his close association with Teddy Walters.

Gallic, now back in the *Hound*'s den, sat at his desk reviewing the case files of the previous murders. Looking for clues—*something*—he may have missed in the numerous times he'd gone over them. Specifically, something that related to the new revelation Teddy Walters was involved. Some indication where he might be holding up now, keeping Lane imprisoned.

"AI, I want you to run a trace on Teddy Walters' movements over the last . . . let's start with the last three weeks. I want to know every planetary port of call he's made; also, every layover in space, for any reason at all."

Gallic knew the majority of Interstellar spaceships movements were fairly easy to track. Every spaceship was equipped with a transponding tracker for two main reasons. One, to safeguard the operators of a given ship—outer space was an easy place to get lost in, or to break down in. Two, for all other reasons, including tracking nefarious actions being unlawfully perpetrated, allowing authorities—police—to pursue criminals, etc. Gallic's repo business utilized the same transponding signals to find some spacecraft that a bank, or a dealership, requested repossession of. But transponding trackers can be disabled—if you know the right people.

"Teddy Walters has four registered spacecrafts. He may have others, either unregistered or registered under some different name."

"Track the ones you can identify."

"That process is completed," the AI said.

"Okay, put the information up on the murder board."

Gallic stood, about to weed through what seemed a long list of spatial locations, when the AI said, "You have an incoming hail from Superintendent Bernard Danbury."

"Go ahead and make the connection. I'll take it at the control center." Gallic did not want Danbury to see, inadvertently, what he was working on in his den.

By the time he made it to the control center, the superintendent's holographic form was there waiting.

"Sir . . ." Gallic said.

Danbury still looked overworked and tired but markedly better than the last time Gallic saw him.

"I just heard. Sergeant Tori briefed me on the possible abduction of one woman, Lane Walters. She also mentioned that you and she had . . . have . . . a personal relationship. I'm sorry, John. You don't seem to get much of a break when it comes to personal misfortune."

"Thank you. I'm doing fine."

"The sergeant also mentioned that you may have a person of interest in mind in regard to this abduction?"

Gallic inwardly chided Tori for speaking about it. "Nothing I can talk about at this early stage. Let's just say it might very well be an extremely high-profile person."

"I get it . . . she said the same thing. I trust your instincts, John, I always have. But I want you to be ready to relay the name of this . . . person of interest . . . soon."

Gallic didn't respond to his comment.

"I'm sending another two investigators, Crackell and Lock, your way. You remember them?"

"They're still there? They were ancient when I was at HQ ..."

"We're short-staffed, so their contracts were extended another year. It's the best I could do. Let me help, John. They'll be there late tomorrow."

"Send them on. I appreciate it, sir." Danbury, in response, offered him a definitive nod and the connection was cut.

The display jumped—a warning message strobed on and off several times.

Strut Hydraulic Pressure Low ... Strut Hydraulic Pressure Low ... Strut Hydraulic Pressure Low ...

"Oh, come on ... what's this about?" Gallic asked.

"As stated before ... the *Hound* urgently requires a full gamut of crucial maintenance procedures."

"In addition to the maintenance that's already needed on the gravitorque drives?"

"Yes, and in addition to seven other key system maintenance functions," the AI said.

"We don't have the funds available for a major overhaul like that right now."

"No, not even close," the AI responded back.

There it was again, a cheeky response from the *Hound's* artificial intelligence unit. Gallic ignored it. "I'm in the middle of a crucial, time-sensitive investigation. Minutes could make the difference between life and death for someone. I need this ship to be fully operational. Not constantly breaking down!" Gallic exclaimed, raising his voice in the process.

"You need immediate funds. I suggest you deliver Miss Tillerson's *Hayai* and collect your agreed-upon fee. And did I not hear you say that you knew where the vessel was to Phil Hough?"

Gallic was reminded the ever-present AI was always listening—even when he thought his ComsBand was in inactive mode.

"I'm heading-up an investigation here."

"One you will be hard-pressed to conduct, operating in an incapacitated vessel," the AI replied. "If you wish, I can recount the many thousands of light years the *Hound* has traveled in the last two weeks alone."

"Can the *Hound* make it back to Spector in her current condition?"

"I will endeavor to make that happen, Mr. Gallic."

What a dilemma. He needed to be here; find Lane. Save her from a monster who'd proved, over and over again, he was a psychopath. One who wouldn't think twice about killing her. *What*, he wondered, *is she going through right now? What is Walters doing to her?*

"Contact Allison Tillman. Tell her I'm on my way and this time she'd better be there, waiting for me. No last-minute interruptions or important meetings to attend. If she wants her damn ship back, she needs to be there waiting for me in the museum."

"Yes, Mr. Gallic, I will relay the message."

"And contact Sargento. Don't know his last name. Have him meet me there as well; tell him I'll make it worth his while."

"Yes, Mr. Gallic, I think you are making a wise choice."

"I don't need your approval, AI. Just make sure the *Hound* gets there, and back, as quickly as possible."

chapter 37

Frontier Planet, Gorman — Heritage
Plains Township.

Outside of Lane's house, Tori slammed the last of the
equipment cases into place in the back of the star-cruiser.
"You're what!?" she asked Gallic.

"Hey, that's precision equipment you're banging around in
there," Gallic said.

"Why now?" Turning to face him, her expression was
defiant.

"The truth?" he asked.

"That would be nice for a change ..."

Gallic let that go. "If I want to catch the murderer ... find
Lane ... I need my ship. Unlike others, like you, who get a
constant paycheck, I need commission funds to do my job.
Even though I may not be here physically for the next day or
two, that doesn't mean I won't be working the case. You know,

better than most, there's no shortage of idle time jaunting back and forth from planet to planet."

Tori didn't seem to like his response very much, but she refrained from arguing the point any further. "So, what do you want me to do while you're gone?"

"You talked to Danbury, so you know he's sending on two more inspectors."

"Yeah … Crackell and Lock. You probably know them better than I do," she said.

"They're solid investigators. Won't break any speed records, but they'll do good work. I suspect the murderer won't be caught, using our advance technologies, since he's too careful to leave trace evidence behind. But there's only so much he can do to hide those he knows … comes into contact with."

"He can kill them … that's what he can do," Tori said.

Gallic stared back at her for a long moment. "That very well might be what he's doing already. I've been so caught up figuring the whole *Curz* cult angle-thing that I didn't give much thought to the fact he could be hiding his tracks. Dispensing with those who either know him or know of him. You and Phil should concentrate your efforts on some interviews you've already conducted. Phil is trying to track down Rick Cugan. Find him, and there's a chance we'll get a lead on Walters. And Linda Cugan and Larz may know more than they're saying, as well. And that creepy daughter, bet she knows something."

"She's not creepy … just shy."

"Fine. Follow up on the leads, I'll be back as soon as I can."

"Anything else?" she asked.

Gallic replied, "This is as good a location as any to setup our base of operations. From now on, until we find Lane . . . or find the killer, let's make this place our temporary HQ."

* * *

Things started to go south about halfway to Spector.

"Mr. Gallic, an unidentified vessel is moving up on us fast; coming in on an intersecting vector."

Gallic, eyeing the nav display, asked, "What can you tell me about the ship?"

"It is new."

"That's it? It's a new ship?"

"It is one-third the size of the *Hound*. The vessel is military . . . all pertinent identifiers hidden. All network access points expertly firewalled."

Gallic, now able to view the quickly approaching ship out the forward window, said, "You forgot to mention that this particular military vessel is armed with a Trident cannon."

Gallic's military background, extensive as it was, helped him identify different kinds of warship armament. A Trident cannon was new—deployed within the last ten years, or so. Distinctively shaped, it had an elongated, spherical, muzzle opening. Whereas typical rail-guns used highly charged magnetic fields to propel thousands of high-velocity projectiles toward a given target, a Trident cannon didn't use magnetic fields. Instead, it used repelling anti-matter fields, firing projectiles called PDD's—an acronym for Phase Disrupter Disks. Anything coming into contact with one of those dinner plate-size disks lost its molecular balance. No explosions . . . no dramatic fireworks, yet the effects were far worse. That which it connected with—things comprising of the material world—ceased to exist. A wonderfully advanced weapon, but a horrible one too, depending solely upon which end one was standing. And there was a problem with these weapons . . . they put out an inordinate amount of radiation—one reason why they weren't used more often. Human gunnery crews, on vessels like this, tended to get sick really quick.

"Can we outrun it?" Gallic asked, already knowing it was a stupid rhetorical question.

"No."

"Any vulnerable areas on that vessel we can target?"

"I have no data to support a possible strike location."

The vessel was nearly upon them. The good news was they hadn't been fired upon . . . *yet.* "Use all common hailing channels. I want to say hello."

The response was immediate, sounding tinny and impersonal. Not computer generated, just someone who didn't give a shit. "Prepare to be boarded. Raise defenses and you will be destroyed."

"Nice meeting you too, asshole," Gallic muttered to himself. "Any ideas, AI?"

Silence.

"I'll officially name you the *Hound* if you can get us out of this mess."

"Scanning the vessel, I have discovered one interesting . . . element."

"What's that?"

"There are no humans onboard that craft."

"Nothing unusual about that. Bots . . . artificial intelligence . . ."

"There are those, but there is also organic life. More like cyborg entities."

Gallic didn't like the sound of that. "Are there three of them?"

"Yes."

"Things just keeps getting better and better. Want to bet they're Tillman Industries' three stolen technoids?"

"The vessel is very well-shielded, but I would give excellent odds you are correct," the AI said. The military craft had come about and now faced in the opposite direction, positioned portside to portside.

"Get me Allison Tillman . . . and hurry!"

Ten seconds later Allison's full-sized holographic image appeared before him. Seeming both confused and a little unsettled, she was about to speak.

"Listen to me! My ship has just been accosted in deep space. By, I suspect, a

Tillman Industries Midget Destroyer, possessing a very prominent Trident cannon. We are in the process of being boarded. Onboard are three technoids."

Allison's eyes went wide, in instant recognition.

"Your ship? Your stolen 'noids?" he asked.

"I think both," she replied.

"I have zero time here. Tell me how to defeat them. A back-door into their neuro-links . . . anything."

"That's beyond classified by a factor of ten!"

"They've come to kill me."

"No . . . you'd already be dematerialized, if that was true."

"I'm not going to sell your damn company secrets! Tell me how to defeat them!"

"You said they're in the process of boarding your vessel?"

"Yes."

"You can't go up against them. Not directly, Mr. Gallic."

"What then?"

A glimmer of *something* shone in her eyes. *Was it hope?* "I need to know—"

She asked instead, "Can you get out? Come around the destroyer from the other side?"

"I . . . yes, I can."

"This may not work, but it does have a backdoor of sorts."

"What's the code," Gallic asked.

"No, I mean an actual, physical-backdoor. More like an access panel. Large enough for a very small vessel to enter," Allison said.

The AI, interrupting her, said, "Mr. Gallic, the military vessel is extending a cross-tube to the *Hound*'s upper deck hatchway."

Gallic, already running for the lift, shouted, "Ensure the hold is pressurized by the time I get down there!"

chapter 38

Open Space — Onboard the *Hound*.

Once inside the lift, Gallic noticed Allison Tillman's 3D projection. She stood a foot tall on his ComsBand. With every movement of his arm, she moved right along with it. Gallic momentarily wondered what her visual perspective was in that same moment.

"AI . . . what's going on with that cross-tube?"

"Two of the technoids are in the process of crossing over."

Gallic could see *doll-sized* Allison staring back at him and looking anxious. "What are you doing?" she asked.

"What do you mean what am I doing? I'm doing what you suggested," he replied, as the lift's lower deck door slid open. Rushing into the huge rear hold area, an area typically used for his repo business, Gallic noticed the air there was very thin—yet still breathable. He scanned the nearly empty hold and quickly found what he was seeking at the far side of the compartment.

Five, various-sized tarp-covered items rested along the bulkhead. He unstrapped one of the tarps, pulling the grimy cover away. Lying exposed beneath the bright overhead spotlights was a one-man vessel, called a *jumper*. Although twenty years old, and not much to look at, it was still space-worthy and quick. Just the thing, he knew, for maneuvering in-and-out of small tight spaces. In the past, Gallic often used the little craft to make in-space repairs or transfer things from the *Hound* to other vessels.

"You're getting into that *thing*?"

Gallic didn't acknowledge her insult. When the curved canopy on the jumper suddenly shot backward he watched a startled Allison *flinch* on his wrist. He'd forgotten the jumper's canopy did that. Smiling at her, he asked, "You do know you're not actually standing here, don't you?"

"Ha ha . . ." she said, not amused. "Just remember, you're going to need me along with you once inside that destroyer."

Gallic climbed inside then quickly began throwing switches. Taking the controls, the canopy suddenly slammed forward, nearly decapitating Allison Tillman's leery projection.

"Christ! Do you know how annoying that is?" she barked.

"More than you know," Gallic said, craning his neck to peer back over one shoulder. He heard the sucking sound—atmosphere being pulled into the *Hound*'s big captivation tanks—as soon as the jumper's canopy closed. Now the immense, dual-purpose, hatch/gangway was beginning to open.

"Kill the lights, AI!"

The hold lights went out, placing Gallic, and Allison's illuminated projection, into stark darkness. As he pulled back on the controls, the small ship rose above the deck. Within the compact cockpit space, the jumper was noiseless.

"Mr. Gallic, two technoids have reached the *Hound's* upper-level outer hatch. They are currently attempting to breach the vessel."

"Best you clear all upper-level atmosphere into the captivation tanks . . . just in case," Gallic ordered. The *Hound's* hull, and various access hatchways, was made of a heavy, composite material that was nearly impregnable. The ship was a beast! But then they were contending with the most-advanced military technology known to man.

"That's more than enough of an opening for me to slide through," Gallic said. The hold's rear hatch clanked to a stop, now open about one-third of the way. He maneuvered the ship out into open space.

"They will have detected you . . . your little vessel," Allison said.

"Just direct me to that destroyer's hidden access panel, okay?"

"You know it's not easy . . . me seeing what you're seeing. What am I . . . floating on your wrist? Can you at least raise your arm up some?"

"Oh . . . yeah . . . sorry about that." Gallic lifted his arm up so she could peer through the forward canopy—view what he was seeing. Then, by pulling his elbow back some, so she could also view the various readouts on the jumper's dash.

When the nose of the midget destroyer came into sight, she shouted, "Dive! Get below her belly!"

Gallic did as told. With a quick maneuver, he put the small jumper craft within several feet of the military vessel's brushed-metal fuselage. Again, Allison looked a bit queasy after the aerial acrobatics. An engineering genius, she had no actual field experience. Gallic followed the contours of the destroyer's belly until he started to come up on its other side.

"This is a heavily-armed military vessel. How come we haven't been disintegrated into dust?" Gallic asked, wishing he'd brought that fact up earlier.

"I already told you," Allison said. "Whoever the traitor is ... the one who first absconded with this highly classified vessel, along with those three technoids onboard, he could have destroyed you and your ship long ago. They want you alive. Probably ordered you not to be killed unless absolutely necessary."

The AI reported, "Two of the *Hound*'s five hatch hinge plates have been blown, Mr. Gallic. Access to the upper level is now imminent."

"Well, if they're looking for me ... I'm out and about."

"They already know where you are," Allison said. "Slow down near the panels mid-ship area, about one-third the way up the hull." On his wrist, Gallic could see her leaning forward, squinting. He found it amazing that she could view anything from her miniaturized position on his wrist. Pointing forward, she looked up at Gallic then queried, "See it?"

Gallic scanned the uneven surface of the destroyer's hull. A jumble of connecting lines and cylindrical enclosures, the ship seemed to be sprouting an array of numerous antennae. "I don't see anything that looks remotely like an access panel," he told her.

"Look! It's right there!"

"That ... box thing?"

"Yes, that box thing! You need to move right up to it. I take it that little ship of yours can broadcast a quad-polar maintenance signal?"

Gallic, staring out the canopy at the square protrusion on the hull, having no idea if the jumper could broadcast *whatever it was* she said, asked instead, "AI?"

"Yes, please provide the signal parameters you wish transmitted."

Gallic watched Allison tap several moments onto her own ComsBand, then heard the AI say, "Thank you."

Allison said, "Get ready, Galaxy Man! They probably have no idea this little panel even exists and will close it soon after they see it's open."

Gallic really hated it when someone called him that. "I'm ready ... open the damn thing."

Barely were the words out when the top of the square enclosure slid to one side. Gallic goosed the controls and the *jumper* shot forward, clearing the four sides by mere inches. Pitch-black inside, before Gallic could flick the *jumper's* running lights on, they careened into something solid. The cockpit's alarm chimed four times then quieted. Gallic, studying the dash, noticed no permanent damage evident.

"My fault," Allison said apologetically. "I should have warned you about the extremely close confines within the sub-fuselage zone."

Gallic turned on the running lights, so he could look around outside.

"Your arm?" she said.

"Oh . . . sorry," Gallic said, raising his arm. Together they glanced around the confined space within the midget destroyer's hull. "Am I reading an atmosphere in here?" he asked.

"Mr. Gallic, four of the *Hound*'s five hinge plates have been blown," the AI said.

"Yes . . . there's atmosphere. You need to climb out of that little ship," Allison said. "You can maneuver around on your own now." Gallic, watching her on his ComsBand, wondered just how sure she was about that.

She said, "You're a policeman . . . out of your element. Right now, you're in my world, so trust me."

Gallic hit the controls and opened the canopy, then momentarily held his breath, waiting for the effects of vacuous space to assault his body. Tentatively, he breathed in. Satisfied, he maneuvered his large frame out of the *jumper* then stepped onto the reverse side of a bulkhead. "There's gravity here," Gallic stated.

"Good . . . continue this way but tread quietly. You're a big guy; footfalls will be noticed."

"It's not easy . . . moving around in such a confined space."

"Uh huh ... keep on going." Allison pointed off to the side, her holographic image providing just enough illumination to see several paces ahead.

"There! That's the backside of a corridor maintenance panel ... the way in."

Gallic studied the panel's flat rectangular surface—about two-feet-wide by six-feet-high—then said, "It's secured tight. I can see the ends of the mounting screws."

Allison, chewing the inside of her lip, let out a sigh. "I forgot about that." Frowning back at him, she shrugged.

"This isn't the first closed door I've come across in my career," he told her.

Suddenly nervous, she started to shake her head. *Too late.* After taking a step backward, Gallic quickly stepped forward again while raising his right knee. Propelling his entire two hundred thirty pounds behind the kick, he drove the heel of his boot forward. The maintenance panel didn't stand a chance. Blown into the inner corridor, it landed with a clang somewhere back inside. Gallic turned his body sideways, clearing the now-open panel, and glanced in both directions to ensure the coast was clear. Only then did he look down at his ComsBand to find Allison Tillman gone.

chapter 39

Open Space — Onboard *Trident Military Vessel.*

Gallic froze in place for a moment. Allison, now gone, had been fairly adamant that he would need her help once he was inside the ship. "AI . . . you still here with me?"

He heard a faint *pshhhht* sound but that was the extent of it. His ComsBand signal was apparently being jammed so for now he was on his own. Gallic reached inside his coat and found the butt of his Emanuel Dual 5. Withdrawing the dual-barreled, over-under .45, he momentarily thought back to his most recent encounter with the technoid on Spector. *Even though this .45 isn't a rail gun, it still should do the trick.*

Gallic arbitrarily chose to head down the corridor to his right. No more than four strides in that direction a three-legged droid came into view. He'd seen thousands of these mechanical maintenance bots back in the service. Not typically armed, it didn't mean this one wasn't. Gallic proceeded forward cautiously. Keeping the Emanuel Dual 5 leveled on the droid's intelligence core, housed in the thing's angular hindquarters, it was why the common name for those bots was *shit for brains*, or SFB's. The SFB passed by him, seemingly disinterested.

Gallic continued on, passing by one closed hatchway after another. The vessel seemed to be brand new. No scuff marks on the bulkheads. It even smelled new.

He knew he was moving in the direction of the bow, he just didn't know what deck, or level, he was on. A relatively large vessel, it clearly did not have the typical number of active crewmembers. They usually were manned, Gallic estimated, by no less than forty to fifty humans, along with just as many bots. Whoever stole this high-tech ship didn't think it important, or necessary, apparently, to find a willing crew. Another indication that the intent of the one who stole the midget destroyer from Tillman Industries would be selling the ship off sooner than later.

When Gallic's ComsBand suddenly made a noise, he stopped dead in his tracks. Peering down at it, a single line of text flashed.

Technoid approaches from your six!

Gallic spun about just in time to see a naked technoid sprinting toward him. It was identical to the one on Spector, from its short-cropped hair, its aquiline nose, and its lack of genitals. Still fifty feet out, Gallic calmly raised his weapon, aimed at a spot between the 'noid's eyes, and pulled the trigger. The concussive sound of the two .45 rounds—fired simultaneously—was nearly deafening within the closed space, but Gallic was far too preoccupied to notice. The technoid veered out of the path of the bullets, as though it had anticipated both their timing and trajectory. At twenty-five feet out, and coming on fast, Gallic fired again at the technoid, this time going for a center mass shot to its chest. Still, the technoid sidestepped the rounds—as easily as someone dodging an oversized beach ball. Gallic next did the only thing that came to mind. He turned and ran.

The technoid's bare feet made no sound on the deck plates behind him. Glimpsing its passing reflection in a starboard window, Gallic realized his seven-foot-tall pursuer was less than ten feet behind him. Not meant for speed, Gallic was capable of various forms of athleticism. As a teenager, he excelled in the sport of *zone ball*—an amalgamable of two seasonal sports, U.S. football and British rugby—which gained in popularity during the last fifty years. He also had a black belt in Shwang Shi, a Royal Marines-taught martial art. Not too dissimilar to Kung Fu, it was considered even more lethal in modern times. But running was not one of the sports that Gallic—a powerhouse of muscle mass and brute strength—could boast about. His large size was more a detriment than a benefit. He pumped his arms and legs, no idea where he was heading. A portside window, down a wide perpendicular hallway, appeared on his left. From his peripheral vision, he made out the technoid's reflection right behind him—it had closed the gap. Extending out its arm, its hand was mere inches from Gallic's neck and shoulders. Still holding the Emanuel Dual 5, Gallic tried to come up with a way to shoot the thing before it brought him down. In the very next instant, Gallic felt a vise-like grip take ahold around his neck. Then just as suddenly he was lifted off his feet, his legs flailing. *A repeat of the last time he met one of these fucking creatures.*

Gallic heard the Emanuel Dual 5 clatter to the deck below unaware he'd even dropped it. Using both hands, he attempted to pry the technoid's grasp away from about his neck. He tried to speak but no words came out. The technoid then rotated its arm just enough that they were nearly eye-to-eye. The cyborg studied Gallic's face—watched his mouth as he tried to speak. Again, Gallic's words were indecipherable. The cyborg's brow rose, and its head tilted: *Curiosity.* The technoid loosened its grip enough for Gallic to croak out what he wanted to say.

"AI ... Shoot the son of a bitch!"

Only then did the technoid look left and down the intersecting corridor. A far window, on the opposite side from where they stood, looked across into the *Hound.* Gallic, unmindful of the nearly impossible angle of fire—the probability he would also be killed—didn't care. What he did want was to kill one more technoid before it killed him. He was staring at the side of the cyborg's head when it exploded. Blood, bone, and brain matter splattered onto his face. Tasting the foul cocktail of hot gore, Gallic nearly threw-up. Instead, he found himself falling on his ass onto the deck, while the headless technoid remained standing.

Gasping he said, "Two for two... nice shooting, AI," Again, he heard the same faint *pshhhht* sound as before. The AI could hear him yet not communicate back.

Gallic climbed to his feet and hurried down the perpendicular corridor. He noticed the window had already accomplished a crude, self-repair job on the holes inflicted by the *Hound*'s external rail gun. In case of puncturing, by flying space debris, or tiny asteroids or meteors, self-bonding glass was an early safety measure all twenty-second-century space vessels were required to maintain to avoid rapid, catastrophic, depressurization.

Gallic stared across the blackness to his ship and noted the adjoining cross-tube connecting the midget destroyer with the upper deck of the *Hound*. His ComsBand suddenly came alive. "Mr. Gallic... are you receiving?"

"I hear you!"

"Very good. I've boosted the *Hound*'s coms signal... that and your now closer proximity, standing at that window, has made the difference."

"And the two technoids that came through the cross-tube?"

"One is lying on the deck, near the galley, and the other one is lying close to the control center. Interestingly enough, that one is still standing."

"Seems they tend to do that," Gallic affirmed back. He studied the *Hewley-Jawbone* carrier—the *Hound*'s scorched and rusted hull—almost affectionately. Soon after acquiring the large transport vessel, he had additional internal security measures installed. Security measures, which included four hidden, tracking, snub-nosed, rifles under the control of the AI. There was a standing order: Unauthorized entry into the *Hound* by any perceived menace would be dealt with using lethal force. To date, under that same standing order, the AI had killed three humans, and as of now, two technoids.

"Stand by while I try to connect you to Miss Tillman."

Her twelve-inch-high hologram flickered onto his wrist. She looked harried, her typically perfect blonde hair disheveled. "Holy shit! You're alive!" she exclaimed.

"Yup . . . still among the living. You look like—"

"Don't say it," she snapped. "You may be used to this kind of craziness, but I'm not. I don't see how you live like you do." Using several fingers to push errant hairs back from her forehead, she asked, "What happened . . . with the technoids?"

"Dead . . . or deactivated. Not sure what the proper vernacular would be."

Allison's brow creased. "All three?"

"Yeah, all three. One was in the process of trying to kill me . . . again."

She stood up taller and let out a breath. "They're . . . expensive units, that's all. Many billions of dollars. I'm happy to see you're still alive, but that doesn't mean I'm immune to the fact my company just lost three very important assets."

Gallic, already aware she was an intelligent, though sometimes crude businesswoman, wasn't all that surprised at being reminded where her priorities rested. "I'll save what's left of them. Maybe you can . . . I don't know . . . piece them back together."

"They're not jigsaw puzzles."

"I guess not," Gallic said. "Look, our agreement was for me to find, then deliver the *Hayai* to you. This has gone far beyond that."

"Is this a shakedown, Mr. Gallic?" She seemed amused. "You still haven't delivered me the *Hayai*."

"Call it what you want. I'm risking my life here . . . going way beyond. You'll get your *Hayai* back. If you want your stolen midget destroyer back, and what's left of your technoids, you'll need to triple the commission."

"Triple! From one million to three million dollars?"

"Either that, or I'll set this ghost ship adrift into deep space. We already know her transponder was taken offline . . . you'll never find her."

"That's blackmail."

"I don't see it that way. Remember, your cyborg killers have come for me twice now. Someone truly doesn't want me to uncover the location of the *Hayai*. Really must have some kind of high-tech onboard that ship."

"Yes . . . and I will pay your price, if you actually come through . . . and get me the *Hayai* back."

"I'll go a step farther. I'll tell you who took the *Hayai*, as well as all the other shit stolen from Tillman Enterprises."

"Fine . . . I'm here waiting. See you soon." Allison disappeared from his wrist.

chapter 40

Open Space — Onboard the *Hound*.

It took another four and one-quarter hours to reach Spector and descend to the top of the Tillman building. This time, the landing lot was nearly empty, although Sargento's spacecraft was there. Gallic had to smile, seeing the craft parked in the same location as before. The Native American's ship appeared worked over—dents and scrapes gone. The entire vessel, now freshly painted, gleamed.

Gallic landed the *Hound* a good distance away then took the rooftop elevator down one level to the penthouse. Exiting into the museum's small foyer, he found Sargento and Allison Tillman standing together talking. He was reminded this would be the first time he'd actually meet her in person. Taller than expected, he was used to seeing her twelve inches high upon his wrist.

Turning to face Gallic as he approached, Sargento gestured hello with an indifferent nod. Allison looked well put together. She'd changed into a royal blue, form-fitting, business suit and done something different with her hair. Gallic wasn't entirely sure just *what*, but it looked good. She held out a hand, and Gallic shook it.

"So, you have both of us here just as you stipulated. Are you going to make good on your promise . . . tell us where my ship is?"

"In good time. First, we need to change the contract again."

"You just changed it! And I agreed to your terms. What else do you want, Mr. Gallic?"

Gallic shifted his gaze over to Sargento. "If it weren't for Sargento here, I'd be dead. You should compensate him for his involvement."

Allison looked exasperated—raising her perfectly plucked brows in *I can't believe this* expression. Unfazed, Sargento maintained the same stony expression.

"You'll have to pay him out of your cut," she said back defiantly.

"No . . . you'll pay him $500,000. Either that, or I walk out of here. I have far more important things to do right now than haggle with you."

"Fine! Agreed! So, where's my damn ship?"

Gallic, gazing past Allison into the spaceship museum beyond them, smiled. "Ah . . . there he is."

Both Allison and Sargento followed Gallic's stare. She then questioned, "Stannis? You met him the last time you were here."

The stubby man, with slicked-back wheat-colored hair, hurriedly walked away. Now nearly out of sight around the curvature of the building, Gallic cupped his hands over his mouth and yelled, "Mister Stannis Kay, your presence is requested here!"

He heard the museum curator mutter something that was unintelligible at that distance. Allison was clearly becoming irritated. The flamboyant Australian turned back and arrived several moments later, wearing a yellow bow tie speckled with large black polka dots.

"Mr. Gallic... how good it is to see you again. And you too, Mr. Sargento."

"I like your tie," Gallic said.

"Gallic!" Allison barked.

"Fine! Mr. Kay, would you please—"

"You can call me Stannis, everyone does."

"Stannis... please direct us to the *Emmery Lux 523*."

The smile on Stannis' face didn't falter, although his eyes blinked three times in rapid succession. "There are far more interesting vessels here, sir... far more. For instance, the *Kipling Toring Una*, over there to our right. Amazing vessel..."

Up until then, Gallic hadn't been one hundred percent certain. But now he was. He needed to be here, in person, to confront the man. "Stannis, you and I both know the *Una* couldn't accommodate anywhere near the breadth of the *Hayai*. Come on, they are almost the same size ship, are they not?" Gallic asked.

Stannis feigned confusion. Turning his attention to Allison, he said, "Ms. Tillman . . . I'm not sure what this is all about. Is there a problem with my performance . . . ?"

Allison didn't answer, continuing to stare at the nearby *Kipling Toring Una* spacecraft.

Gallic snapped his fingers twice. "The *Emmery Lux 523*, Stannis. Let's all take a walk, okay?" Walking away, Stannis soon caught up to him. "What is this all about, Mr. Gallic?"

"Drop the dumb act, Stannis. I know you took the *Hayai* . . . or should I say hid the *Hayai*, at least until you can unload her during your next traveling museum exhibit. I read in your brochure there's one coming up next month, on the planet Lumite. Nearly one-third of the Tillman museum ship exhibits will be sent out on loan . . . no?"

"Yes . . . but . . . well, that doesn't mean . . ." Gallic simply stared at the now-stuttering curator.

"When I heard you were also in charge of the building's security, it wasn't much of a stretch to place you at the top of my suspect list."

Allison, following close behind, said, "Stannis has been with the company for years. He's always been loyal, very well compensated . . . and . . . well, just I don't see him masterminding something like this."

"And you'd be incorrect in that assumption," Gallic said. "Stannis is far more devious than you thought. Devious and ingenious." They'd walked about a quarter of the way around the exhibit when Gallic slowed and approached the next spacecraft. Finished in a bright emerald green, she was one of only two vessels that extended all the way up to the penthouse ceiling. Gallic noticed the big ship last time he was here, since she was the only hauler-type vessel there. Owning a hauler himself, albeit one five times the size of this one, he was most curious—what made her worthy of being a museum exhibit? Gazing up at the odd-looking vessel, he gestured, "Did you know the *Emmery Lux 523* has a unique, clamshell-type hold configuration?" He then demonstrated with a big biting motion with his hands how the large hold opened and closed.

Allison took a step forward and studied the vessel—the bulbous aft section and four rotatable thruster modules. She asked Gallic, "My ship is inside there?"

"Let's take a look and see," he replied.

Glaring intently at Stannis, she ordered, "Open the hold, Stannis. This is your opportunity to prove him wrong. I'm hoping he is; I truly am."

Gallic tried to read Stannis' face. He was seventy percent positive the *Hayai* was actually within the ship's rear hold area, after hours and hours of reviewing security video files. Watching the comings and goings of literally hundreds of spacecrafts on the roof of the Tillman building, and reviewing close to one hundred employee interviews. The fact that this particular vessel was capable of housing within her a large ship, one with the *Hayai*'s dimensions, seemed like a pretty good assumption. That and Stannis had been given full-control over which Tillman Industries vessels were brought to the exhibit. He even had executive-level access to the latest top-secret military assets—such as a newly developed midget destroyer

and three technoids that were still going through their rigorous testing process. Stannis Kay's comings and goings within
the Tillman engineering and design facility, within another
sprawling industrial complex ten miles away, was practically an
everyday occurrence.

"I'd be more than happy to open the hold, but—"

"Just open it, Stannis," now Sargento chimed in.

Stannis gave Allison a forced smile and waddled over to a
short metal ladder. Climbing up six or seven rungs, he stepped
out onto a horizontal platform. Then unlatching a metal enclosure, he let the heavy door swing wide on its hinges. After
tapping several times on a display screen, he stood back and
glanced down at the others. "This is a royal waste of time."

His words were drowned out by the whirling of motors;
the opening-up of the unique *Emmery Lux 523* hold clamshell.

Allison walked toward the aft section of the ship, unable to
see what was inside the hold. The top clamshell section, now
up at the ceiling, was beginning to push against ceiling tiles,
while the vessel's bottom portion was lowering down to the
floor slowly but steadily.

Gallic and Sargento exchanged a brief glance. Sargento
said, "You're not one hundred percent sure she's inside."

Gallic shrugged, then caught a sliver of color other than
emerald green. He'd forgotten the *Hayai* was coated in a
ridiculous pumpkin-orange shade, yet the vessel was truly gorgeous. Sleek and glossy, there was something dangerous, almost
ominous, about the craft. All sharp angles, two dramatically

swept-back wings began at the bow then extended back well beyond the rear, flared, phantom power-drive thruster.

So caught up in the visual splendor of the ship, Gallic didn't hear Allison walk back in his direction. She said, "Everything you've ever read about her. All those impressive specs."

"Uh huh?"

"Double ... even triple ... most of them. This ship can make it to the Frontier worlds in two hours without breaking a sweat. Once there, she can defeat a whole fleet of warships on her own."

"I can see why you wanted her back," he said.

"I should never have put her on display, it was either ego or pride. I'm just so glad to have the *Hayai* back!"

"Your midget destroyer is locked up in high-orbit; your technoids stacked in the ship's medical morgue. I figured you'd want them kept on ice," Gallic said.

Allison looked up at him. "You kept your end of the bargain. Technically, the *Hayai* was never stolen. I never lost possession of her ... not really."

Gallic, watchful, didn't say anything.

"But I'm happy to pay my debt." Glancing at Sargento, she then added, "to both of you."

Sargento said, "Thank you."

Gallic said, "Thanks!"

Her expression suddenly changed. Quickly looking left and right, she asked, "Where the hell is Stannis?"

chapter 41

Open Space — Onboard the *Hound*.

Along his return route back to Gorman, Gallic had already decided to blow off having any maintenance repair work made on the *Hound*, not with so many other pressing issues to contend with. Sitting at the control center, he felt the gravitorque drives begin to wind down. The blur of starlight through the forward window began to take on a clearer focus. A repeating warning message began flashing on and off on multiple displays:

Gravitorque Drives 1 and 2 Offline

Fists clenched, Gallic wanted to punch something. Instead, he cursed everything and everyone he could think of. It took hours for the space-tow vessel to finally arrive and several more hours to get the *Hound* towed to Brenwork's Maintenance

Depot—one of the few space platform facilities with the capacity to work on a vessel as large as the *Hound*. Maintenance procedures, plus a slew of unexpected repair work, took another agonizingly slow eight hours to complete. Gallic unsuccessfully tried to relax. He needed to get back to Gorman.

Finally back in deep space and headed for the Frontier worlds, both exhaustion and concern for Lane were taking their toll. His attempt to grab a few hours of sleep en route had been fruitless. Thinking of Lane again, he had to rein his imagination in. She'd now been with her abductor for about twenty-four hours.

He noticed he'd gotten several low-priority messages over the last few hours and peering down at his vibrating wrist, he saw Tori was hailing him again.

"What have you got for me, Tori?"

"I'm back at home base . . . Lane's place. Still nothing new on her whereabouts. No demands from her abductor. No one seems to know anything. Needless to say, no one has seen Teddy Walters, AKA Zip Furlong."

Gallic expected that, still the news stung just the same.

"Crackell and Lock arrived here on schedule," Tori continued. "They bicker like an old married couple. After ten minutes, I was ready to clock them both."

"Yeah . . . I remember that about them. Don't let their old geezer shtick fool you, though, because they're solid investigators, just need direction. They'll do what's asked but don't expect them to be big innovators, come up with fresh ideas."

"Copy that," she said. "Phil just arrived . . . his ship's landing off in the field. Be interested in hearing what he's come up with after his latest round of interviews with the Cugans."

"Look, it may be a wild goose chase, but I want Crackell and Lock following up on the *Curz* aspect with the locals. Have them investigate who else on Gorman, or any of the other Frontier worlds, has a direct affiliation with the cult. And have them find out if there's some special way they communicate with one another. They may need to play one neighbor against another, but they'll know what to do."

"I'll get them working on it. Did you get everything resolved with your missing *Hayai* case?" Tori asked.

"That business has been put to bed."

"Then you're flush again? *Hound's* been repaired?"

"Yes, and yes," Gallic replied.

"Good. When will you be back here," she asked.

"I still have a few more hours flight time before reaching Gorman. I'll get back in touch when I'm nearer."

* * *

It was dark by the time Gallic set the *Hound* down between Phil's distant *Gallivanter* and two star-cruisers, parked closer to the house. He noticed that Crackell and Lock's vessel was one of the older beaters, decommissioned a decade past. A series of five official tents, with red and green D-22 logos, had been set up near the horse stalls, and consisted of a large central tent with four smaller tents around it. An amber light could be seen, emanating through the fabric of three of the tents. He checked the time, it was close to 10:00 pm. He'd turn in—there was nothing that couldn't wait till morning.

* * *

"Mr. Gallic! There is an emergency situation. Mr. Gallic! There is an emergency situation . . . "

Gallic sat up in bed. "What is it, AI? What's the problem?" he asked, turning toward the nightstand where he'd placed his ComsBand. It was strobing a text message he couldn't read upside-down. Shaking lingering cobwebs from his groggy mind, he asked, "What time is it?"

"It is 0900 local time, Mr. Gallic. Sergeant Tori is below. She is banging a large rock against the starboard forward strut in an attempt to get your attention."

"I can't believe I slept that long." As his mental haze slowly lifted, Gallic's thoughts turned to Lane. *Oh God . . . have they found her?* He shot out of bed, grabbing up his pants that lay in a heap on the deck.

* * *

The gangway was still in the process of lowering when Gallic emerged from the *Hound*. Strapping on his ComsBand, he found Tori and Phil standing outside. Both seemed exasperated, holding large rocks in their hands.

"Sorry you had to resort to caveman communication methods," Gallic said. "I was out cold. Talk to me."

"We have a body . . . well, a partial body," Tori said.

Gallic's heart stuttered within his chest. He studied her face. It didn't have the same look of someone delivering dire, horrific news, such as *your girlfriend's been killed*. "Who . . . where . . . ?"

Tori and Phil looked at each other. Phil said, "I guess you weren't the only one to be a deep sleeper last night."

"Best we show you," Tori added.

That stopped him in his tracks. *Show me?*

"Our two geriatric detectives are already processing the scene," Phil said, with a crooked smile. "Come on."

The three quietly walked toward the barn. Tori and Phil glanced at each other several times, which only irritated Gallic more. *I really need a cup of coffee.*

Phil held up short at the large barn door. "You ready for this?"

"Enough already. Open the damn door."

Phil, doing as told, slid the old timber door off to one side. Inside, bright strobe lights, set up on tall stands, forced Gallic to shield his eyes against the glare. Before him, the upper body halves of Don Crackell and Kent Lock were visible. Both were wearing disposable overalls, a procedure from the past that wasn't necessary nowadays since modern equipment had the capacity to detect differentiating trace evidence. But some investigators still practiced, were committed to using, older methods and Gallic couldn't fault them for that. He heard a horse whinny along with the heavy thumping of hoofs hitting the ground.

"Hold him still!" Crackle demanded.

"What do you think I'm doing here... scratching my balls?" Lock snapped.

Gallic, traversing between and around a series of opened forensic equipment cases approached the closed stall. Peering through the door's upper row of metal bars, he could now see them—Crackle, Lock, and the horse inside. Both men had aged. Similar to one another in looks, they usually could pass for brothers. Crackle's combed-over silver hair was sparser now, revealing a pink scalp populated with countless age spots. But his inquisitive blue eyes were as intense and intelligent as ever. Lock, on the other hand, had self-dyed his thinning hair a god-awful, reddish-brown, coppery shade. A little larger than his partner, he wore a more expressive, friendlier demeanor. First now to notice Gallic, standing on the outer side of the stall door, he said, "DCI Gallic, it's good to see you again."

"Good to see you, too, Kent, though I haven't been DCI for three years. What do we have here?"

Up to that point Gallic's field of view had been limited by the stall door, blocking him further access. Kent Lock said, "I got ahold of the horse... open her up, Don."

Crackle said, "Good to see you, Gallic. Stand back... I'm opening the door."

The stall door slid open and for the first time Gallic could see Lane's horse in full view. He stared blankly at the horse—at the dead rider sitting atop the horse.

"It's him, isn't it?" Tori asked from behind him.

"It sure the hell is." Gallic exclaimed. Teddy Walters, AKA Zip Furlong, was dead—his skin a sallow greyish-blue color.

His sightless eyes open wide, he looked like a statue. Like an old Civil War bronze job—a long-gone general leading his men into battle. Teddy Walters, sitting rigidly astride the saddle, was somehow propped up on it.

"He's got a metal shaft, of some sort, stuck up his ass," Crackle said.

"And the shaft is jury-rigged with bailing wire, keeping it tied to the saddle ... somehow. Someone spent a good bit of time putting all this together," Lock added.

"And yet we all slept through it," Phil said, shaking his head.

Gallic was only half-listening, concerned with all these unexpected implications. Their primary suspect in the hammer-and-nails murders, as well as being the possible abductor of Lane, was dead instead—sitting atop a horse. Only then did Gallic notice the hand-written message on the stall's planked wall.

chapter 42

Frontier Planet, Gorman — Heritage Plains Township.

The Curz are always watching. Even as a lamb strays from the flock, I am most useful when I can't see.

A half hour had passed since they'd removed the body. Gallic reread the three short sentences, written in the victim's blood, again. "So . . . is Teddy supposed to be the stray lamb here?"

"You're asking the wrong person," Phil said, using a large wet sponge to scrub some congealed blood off the horse's back. He then submerged the sponge, squeezing out some bloody residue, in a water-filled metal bucket. Teddy Walter's body, the saddle still attached, was now gone from the barn—transported by Crackle and Lock to the largest D-22 tent. Forensic drones were already at work on his corpse.

Tori entered the barn behind Gallic. "Hey."

"Hey," Gallic said back. "Anything discovered so far?"

"Not much. Well, one thing ... he, Teddy, had small nail heads protruding out his pupils. No one noticed them until he was positioned flat on the forensic table."

"What kind?"

"Of nails? They're 2D box nails. I checked them right away," she said.

"Do you have a TOD yet?" Gallic asked.

"Crackle says it was at least 72 hours ago. Significant decom ... rigor already come and gone. We'll know more when the drones complete their full-body circuits."

"You know this is going to blow up," she said by his side, staring at the three blood-drawn sentences etched on the wall.

Gallic said, "I've already spoken to Danbury. He's giving us a full day before he releases the news ... the murder of famous, beloved Zip Furlong to the press. After that ... yeah, this place will be a zoo."

Tori nodded. "At least we'll finally get to see D-22 elevate the cases in priority. So, what will you do, now that your primary murder suspect has turned up murdered?"

Gallic shrugged. "The guy was already dead, when Lane was taken." *Damn! He felt her slipping farther and farther away from him.* He scanned the barn, as if searching for something.

"What is it?" Tori asked.

"Why the hell kill Teddy? Why so suddenly ... radically ... change your MO?"

"A diversion? Keep us off guard, perhaps?" Tori offered.

Gallic glanced at his ComsBand. Tapping on it, he asked the *Hound*'s AI, "Have you had any luck in tracking down Teddy Walter's spacecraft? Any of them?"

"Interesting you should ask," the AI replied.

Gallic rolled his eyes, and Tori smiled.

"No, not a specific finding, but I believe I have . . . a possible location."

"How did you come across that information? And who else knows about it?"

"I have not told anyone else. The vessel, which I believe belongs to Mr. Walter, is a Dorian Pulsar. I have been routinely monitoring the full spectrum of emergency announcements, as far into space as my sensors will allow. Vessel announcements, intended to be local, are geared for onboard personnel only. But one that has been on a repeating loop for several days now is simply a propulsion compartment moisture intrusion notice."

"That doesn't sound like much to go on. It's impressive, though, you were able to pick up on such an arbitrary and, I imagine, faint broadcast . . . but—"

"The location is at the bottom of a small lake, or a pond," the AI interjected.

"Where?"

"Here, within the Frontier worlds."

"Where exactly?"

"Muleshoe. Most interesting coordinates, the same coordinates you visited within the last few days."

Gallic was getting irritated—this was like pulling teeth. "So, you're referring to Corianne and Shelly? The Millhouse murders, at the cattle processing facility?"

"Yes. Strangely enough, the precise coordinates correspond to the middle of the lake there, located on the outskirts of the property."

Gallic let that sink in, then huffed, recalling the murky lake on the Millhouse property. *Had the murderer made his first real mistake?*

A loud shuffling noise outside the barn caused Gallic to spin around. Kent Lock—still wearing his badly stained disposable overalls—told them,

"I think you're going to want to see this."

* * *

Now assembled within the large D-22 tent enclosure, the wind outside had picked up. An open fabric flap at the top of the tent snapped angrily against the central support pole. Formed in a semi-circle around the makeshift autopsy table, a naked Teddy Walters lay on his back, sans the saddle. The metal shaft still protruded unceremoniously from his rectum. Gallic studied his former friend then thought of Clair, their connection to this man. He was so ready to hate him, revile him as the murderer of his family—all the other victims—and now he wasn't sure.

Don Crackle stood at the head of the table. "The little bots have completed their work." Shaking his head, he said, "The deceased obviously lived a robust life. Even if this ... tragic ...

event hadn't occurred," Crackle's eyes leveled on the protruding metal shaft, "his liver ... cirrhosis ... would have taken him out soon. But there again, someone with his fame and money should be able to clone a new one ... I guess. But that's not what I wanted to show you."

"Just get to it, Crackle, while we're still breathing," Lock urged.

Crackle, ignoring the prod, reached down and took Teddy's right wrist in his own. Lifting the arm—forcing it to bend at the elbow—he pulled it up, to the point Teddy's underarm could be seen.

"What's that, a tattoo?" Gallic asked leaning in.

"Bingo," Crackle said.

"We've run the three-letter symbol through the D-22 database, also through *Caprious*, back on Earth," Lock added.

Gallic was impressed. *Caprious* was the largest AI computer associated database known to man. Not easy to get access to, even for large government organizations, such as D-22.

"You didn't have to do all that," Tori said. "We already knew what those three initials stood for. The *Curz* Watchers."

"Well, we know he was associated with some form of that cult, anyway," Gallic said.

"What you probably didn't know," Lock said, taking a position across the table from Crackle, "is that the *Curz* Watchers stem from a far-larger organization than any of you know about. Something called the *Curz* Wiccan." In thought a moment, he went on,

"The problem is, it goes by several monikers. Like the huge umbrella of Christianity, religious ideologies, such as Catholicism ... and Protestants, like Lutherans, Episcopalians, Presbyterians, Mormons, Methodists ... etc. ... all lay beneath it. The *Curz* Watchers are one of about ten quasi-religious factions spawned after that alien ship discovery on Mars last century. All are associated with the *Curz* Wiccan. Strangely, they all have the same initials; there's the *Curz* Watchers, which we are familiar with, but there's also the *Curz* Way, the *Curz* Wonderment, the *Curz* Worshippers, and so on, and on ..."

"Isn't *Wiccan* associated with ... pagan witchcraft ... that sort of thing?" Tori asked.

"Yes, so you can see it's not a particularly enlightened, New Age, spiritual practice. But to each his own," Crackle added.

"So, what does this have to do with poor Teddy?" Gallic asked.

Crackle let out a long breath. "Only the *Curz* Watchers organization, if you could even call it one, is dark; negative. The entire anti-female aspect holds meaning only to the *Curz* Watchers. A misinterpretation of how life actually existed on that distant alien planet. Anyway, it's taken hold here, primarily within the Frontier worlds, more than at any other location in known space."

Crackle, still bending Teddy's arm back in an unnatural position, said, "Teddy Walters was not part of the *Curz* Watchers; he was part of the *Curz* Wiccan," and pointed to the tattoo. "Same initials."

"What does that mean, as far as his possible involvement in the murders?" Tori asked.

"That he couldn't have been involved at all. The Wiccan aspect of the cult is polar- opposite to that of the Watchers . . . their view of women in business, their basic advancement of females in society as a whole. Those two factions were practically at war with each other. Teddy was actually a pretty good guy, as it turns out, above and beyond his popular movie, tough-guy roles. For Teddy to make the arduous trek to the Frontier worlds, we think he was sent. Perhaps sent by higher-ups in his cult organization, attempting to enlighten the wayward *Curz* Watcher members here . . . help them see the light. That's our guess, anyway."

"Your *guess*?" Tori asked, sounding skeptical.

Lock answered, "There's really no way to know. He's dead. Yeah, it would be nice to know who he intended to meet with here. Maybe it was the killer. Who knows?"

Gallic glanced at Tori, then asked, "Hey . . . mind holding things down here for a while?"

She nodded, puzzled.

"I'm heading over to Muleshoe. Seems Teddy might still provide us with some answers . . . or maybe his ship can."

chapter 43

Frontier Planet, Gorman — Heritage
Plains Township.

Before heading out for Muleshoe, Gallic gave the team a
checklist of things to accomplish in his short absence.
At the top of everyone's list was finding Lane Walters. While
lifting off, the AI announced an incoming hail from Crackle.

"Go ahead, Don," Gallic told the holographic image of the
rumpled-looking older inspector.

"Hey... more has come in from *Caprious*. Did you
know there's a local parish for the *Curz* Wiccan, right here
on Gorman? Apparently, services are held in an old barn on
Tuesday nights, in a town called Heritage Plains. Tuesday's
their day of worship."

"You're actually within the township of Heritage Plains
right now," Gallic said. "Tori can show you the little town, just
be careful."

"Careful is my middle name," Crackle said and cut the connection.

Gallic, staring at the now blank display, said, "AI . . . I have a project for you."

"Yes, Mr. Gallic. Name it."

"I want you to gain access to *Caprious*. Make friends with it . . . or whatever. Can you make that happen? I don't want to be at D-22's mercy—doling out vital information."

The AI hesitated. "*Caprious* is a highly secure, if not *the* most secure, law enforcement resource . . ."

"And . . . ?" Gallic prompted.

"I will do my best, Mr. Gallic."

The run back to Muleshoe was non-eventful, giving Gallic time to think. The new Teddy Walters development was monumental. Gallic, surprisingly, found himself feeling somewhat relieved. Relieved to find his one-time friend was not a psychopathic serial killer and that he hadn't abducted Lane—his adopted niece. Of course, that also meant they had no primary suspect. He kept replaying Lane's last message over and over in his head. She'd looked happy, even playful. *Where are you, Lane?* he wondered.

Gallic, so deep in thought, had unconsciously tuned out the AI. Looking up, he realized a new connection had been established on the holographic display. Seeing the blaze of color on Polly Gant's Hawaiian shirt—a crimson background with bunches of bright yellow bananas—the chubby little man stared back at him. "Hello? Earth to the Galaxy Man . . . did you hear me?"

"Sorry . . . deep in thought. What's up, Polly?"

"Well, I wanted to congratulate you on finding the *Hayai*! Some pretty amazing investigatory work there, not to mention a nice payout."

Gallic's negotiations tripled his commission, which meant Gant's share tripled as well. "All's well that ends well," Gallic said.

Polly's upbeat expression then changed to one of concern. "I also see you've submitted the paperwork to pay off the *Hound* . . . outright. Let me tell you, old friend, that's a bad decision, bad investment strategy. Instead, why don't you take the commission money, then lease a new ship; one that doesn't have quite so many spatial miles on her? I can get you the deal of a lifetime on a brand-new *Hewley-Jawbone* carrier . . ."

Gallic, well aware that Polly Gant, who'd negotiated the purchase of the *Hound* for him, was doing quite well pocketing the ship's monthly interest payments. "It's non-negotiable, Polly. I'm looking to simplify my life. I don't want any more payments hanging over my head. Just let me know when it's done. Can you do that for me?"

"Sure . . . no problem," Polly said, looking somewhat hurt. "Hey . . . I have a repo job, just came up on the board. It's perfect for you—"

"I'm on a case, Polly. Will be indisposed until further notice, so maybe get ahold of Sargento . . ."

* * *

Descending into a raging storm over Muleshoe, Gallic circled the *Hound* above the Millhouse ranch below. Periodic lightning flashes illuminated the processing facility and the small, outlying ranch-style homes. No lights were on—no cattle, either, milling within the large open pen. The place looked totally deserted.

"I guess with the murders ... the place shut down," Gallic said aloud.

"Yes. Although I am picking up several human life signs," the AI said.

"Maybe a caretaker. I'll check in with them in a bit. I want to concentrate on that lake. Bring up whatever the *Hound* finds submerged at the bottom."

A murky green image appeared on the display. Gallic could make out the distinct outline of a hover tractor, also what looked to be some kind of kitchen appliance, possibly a junked stove or refrigerator. Then he saw the ship. Unlike either the tractor or the appliance, the ship had no sediment covering it. Similar to Larz Cugan's *Hausenbach L35T*, this equally expensive craft, a *Majestic P25*, even when underwater looked like it had just left the dealership.

"Can you detect if there's anyone still onboard ... dead or alive?" Gallic asked the AI, though not too sure he wanted to hear the answer.

"The storm is playing havoc with the *Hound*'s sensors. There does not seem to be human remains within the fuselage."

"I need to get that vessel up on land ... without breaching her hull."

"I'm afraid the only way to accomplish that is by lowering a winch cable and physically attaching a fastener. It would mean you getting a tad wet."

Gallic stared at the murky water image. "Fine. Position the *Hound* above the water and ready the winch. I'll try to find my swimming trunks."

* * *

Shirtless and dressed in a pair of old camo cargo shorts, Gallic, with the cable and fastener already lowered into the water, decided to exit through the upper level hatch. A more substantial jump to the lake's surface below, the momentum gained would propel him to the bottom faster. Theoretically, that would give him extra time on his single breath of air to do what needed to be done.

"Go ahead and open the hatch, AI."

He heard the latching mechanism disengage, the hatch slid open. A torrent of rainwater immediately poured in. Peering down while standing on the precipice, a horrendous thunderclap, followed by more lightning flashes, gave Gallic pause. The *Hound*'s underbelly spotlights lit up the unsettled surface below, which looked more like a raging ocean than a peaceful lake. "Maybe this isn't such a great idea," he murmured, then, taking in a deep lung full of air, jumped. It was a long drop down. When he hit the water, feet first, the impact nearly caused him to lose his held breath. He submerged into a dazzling flurry of tiny bubbles. After a momentary pause, he saw the straight vertical shape of the winch cable ahead. Swimming over, he grasped ahold of it then lowered himself the thirty, or so, feet to the bottom. The water was disgusting. Liquid slime that was hard to see through. *What was I thinking? Of course, the lake is foul, where do you think the piss and shit runoff goes from hundreds of head of cattle?*

The AI had positioned the cable perfectly, coiled atop the *Majestic P25*'s sloping roof. Seeing the sleek craft close up, Gallic appreciated how beautiful the personal spaceship was. He next located the end of the cable, with its spring-loaded clasp, and began searching for something to clip it onto. Admonishing himself for not asking the AI about possible options beforehand, he glanced at his ComsBand and found no need to worry. A diagram, showing both the bow and stern towing hardware, would suit his purpose just fine.

Gallic then swam halfway to the bow, needing to stop to give the heavy steel cable a couple of big tugs. Feeling the bends first indication—a burning sensation in his lungs—Gallic knew he needed to rise, get air soon. The muddy lake bottom was festered with all kinds of crap—an underwater scrapyard. As he made his way to the tapered bow, he used his hand to feel beneath the ridgeline of the craft. It felt perfectly smooth. But then he felt it—a circular, recessed area almost imperceptible to the touch. Using his fingertips, he explored the round metal eyelet, how it was oriented, then brought the end of the winch cable closer. Opening up the spring-loaded fastener, he made the connection. Only then did he let his gaze rise up to the curved canopy window eight or nine feet away. Staring back at him was a face. Lane!

So unexpected, so startled by the sight of her, Gallic gasped, simultaneously swallowing and inhaling the foul lake water. Gagging, retching, and coughing—ingesting more and more of the putrid liquid—total desperation consumed him. Now flailing, he kicked-out with his legs and felt his feet push off the ship's hull. He frantically peered upward and saw the blazingly bright lights of the *Hound so . . . far away.* His arms felt heavy—moving so slowly now—as his body-jerking retching continued. Darkness was closing-in, surrounding him—a constricting tunnel. Soon there were less bodily spasms . . . *Is this what it feels like to die?*

chapter 44

Frontier Planet, Muleshoe — Derringer Township.

G allic awoke to a bout of racking, bone-jarring coughing . . .
Leaning over, he spewed out something he was certain
was toxic. In that same moment, he realized he was sitting on a
hard surface, perhaps a wooden chair. Secured to it with ropes,
tied at his wrists and ankles. Scanning his surroundings—
almost pitch-dark wherever it was—he could barely make
out the large angular shapes around him. He concentrated
on the contours of his left wrist and came to the conclusion
his ComsBand was no longer attached there. "Terrific . . . just
terrific," he muttered and mentally recounted back to the last
things he remembered.

He was under water, in the process of securing a line to
Teddy Walter's personal spacecraft, when he caught someone
within the ship's interior staring back at him. *Oh God . . . Lane!*

She'd looked just as startled. Eyes wide—leaping up then reaching for him—she'd cried out, her words soundless behind the spacecraft's canopy. Gallic's mind raced. He needed to get to her, rescue her before her air ran out. Struggling against his bindings, he rocked, jerking his body about in an attempt to break free, but the chair held fast. Soon he was out of breath and coughing again. Then he heard a soft, familiar, voice speak near him.

"You know, Gallic ... you're not supposed to get captured when you're trying to rescue someone."

"Oh God, Lane!"

"I'm okay," she said, her voice barely above a whisper.

He hadn't realized she was right there, sitting directly behind him, mere inches away. Then he felt her chair slightly bump his own. "Lane ... how ... I don't understand, you were—"

"Trapped inside that fucking, claustrophobic tin can?"

"Yeah, it must have been awful."

She continued, "I think you'd just gotten that cable-thingy attached because suddenly Teddy's ship, and me along with it, was being hauled up and out of the water."

"And me? I was drowning. No way I could make it to the surface—"

"No, *he* jumped in and grabbed you. Dragged you over to the shore."

Gallic tried to make sense of what she said. Didn't remember any of that part. "Who ... who jumped in and pulled me to shore?"

"The same one who left me for dead at the bottom of that shit pond, your good buddy. There was a time when I thought maybe the two of you were in cahoots together. I'm so glad you weren't. Obviously, clearly . . . you weren't."

"Who . . . who are you talking about, Lane?"

Before she could answer him, he heard, "She's talking about me, Gallic . . . come on . . . you never suspected?"

He peered into the darkness as the silhouette of someone moved closer. "Phil . . ." Gallic muttered. Every muscle, every tendon, went rigid. Gallic's jaw clenched, his molars grinded together. He looked upon the shadowy figure while shooting lasers of hatred from his eyes.

The silhouette came to a stop nearby, but Gallic couldn't see what he was doing. "Easy boy . . . deep breaths."

"Where are we, Phil? Where's my ship?"

"*Hound*'s nearby. I've already acquired her for myself. All your feeble security measures were breached within a matter of minutes. There's still a slight issue, bringing up those big gravitorque drives, but nothing I can't handle. On the other hand, your AI was practically jubilant at the prospect of answering to a new master. What's that about, Gallic? You know abusing one's artificial intelligence, emotionally or otherwise, is paramount to a crime. It's like elder abuse, or animal abuse—"

"Just shut up . . . you killed them, Phil. You killed my family! All those women and children, you sick fuck." Gallic was desperate, intensely wanting to feel his hands tightening around Phil's neck; feel the bones cracking and breaking. To be the one responsible—ending the man's despicable life.

"Now that's no way to talk to an old friend, Gallic. I am what I am. Do you disparage a killer tiger in the wild for baring his fangs or a grizzly bear for using his magnificent claws? No ... those animals are simply being true to their true carnivore instincts. I can no more ignore my own natural instincts than they—"

"Most bears are omnivorous, asshole," Lane interrupted.

His dark presence loomed over her. "I can easily put you back where you were ... among the discarded trash and pond scum. I suggest you hold your tongue, woman."

Gallic wanted to tell Lane to stop baiting him. If they were going to find a way out, they would need time: time to think, time to plan. He said, "And the whole *Curz* Watcher thing? What was that about? A deception, a ruse to avert our attention in another direction?"

"There's so much you don't know. I wish there was time to, well, fully enlighten you. Let's leave it and say that no, it was not a ruse. You should feel honored. Killing your very *impressive* wife culminated in those who came later; my further ... exploits."

"Why ... Phil? She was kind and good and—"

"And exemplified everything wrong with society in the twenty-second century." Phil next added, "We're at a pivotal time where men, like you and me, need to make a conscious choice. Do you think what happened to the *Curz*—those poor alien males—was exclusive to that distant race of people? Come on! It's happened before, there on Earth, when the once-dominant male gender relinquished his power little by

325

little. Hey ... we're well past the age when, biologically, males are required for reproduction needs. Your wife, Clair, the scientist out to change the world, was one of the women who needed to be made an example of. Mothers and fathers need to take heed. Watch out for, and be leery of, a domineering female child. The same ones who'd later bring finality to a gender asleep at the wheel."

"You truly are a certifiable psycho, Phil, and a fucking idiot to boot," Lane said flatly.

Gallic said, "You're killing well-meaning wives of farmers, ranchers, and their innocent daughters. There's no rationale for any of that ... how could there be?"

"There is, John. I know it's hard. Painful. But trust me, there is a reason for all this ... madness ... that you undoubtedly believe it to be."

"Don't buy into it, Gallic," Lane said. "Teddy told me he was onto Phil, suspected he was the killer, but he couldn't prove it. He came to get me away from ..."

"That's enough from you!" Phil ordered, his voice growing sterner.

"Those slain women, here in the Frontier worlds, rebuffed his sexual advances, just as I suspect Clair did back on Earth. You knew Phil back there ... right?" Lane asked Gallic.

Gallic had indeed known Phil back on Earth. He'd been instrumental in the installation of Gallic's security system, at his New York residence. Phil knew his family, so he'd come and go as he pleased. "So, what now, Phil? You kill me ... kill Lane?"

"That is inevitable. You need to come to terms with that. But Lane was correct . . . Teddy Walters was clearly onto me. So, he had to go. Unfortunately, just as I suspected, he conveyed those same suspicions to Lane. So, making it appear like she'd been abducted by the hammer-and-nails killer was my only option."

Gallic closed his eyes and shook his head.

"Don't be too hard on yourself, my friend," Phil said. "You've been far too close, too personally involved, to have seen things as they really were. I have to admit, though . . . I will miss working with you . . . it's been fun."

Although Gallic couldn't see his smile, he heard it in his voice.

"You may despise me, understandably so, but I am giving you this one last time together. I didn't have to do that. I could have sent little Lane, here, back to the bottom of the dredge, or simply let the hammer-and-nails killer do to her what he does best. And . . . I still might. You have an hour . . . two at the most. There is no escaping your ropes. When I return, be prepared to meet your maker," Phil laughed. "I always wanted to say that . . . meet your maker. Who the fuck talks that way?" he laughed again. "Ha, I guess I do."

Gallic watched as the shadowy figure stepped away and was gone.

chapter 45

Frontier Planet, Muleshoe — Derringer
Township.

H e heard propulsion thrusters somewhere off in the distance as a ship lifted off. He recognized the distinct sound of the *Gallivanter*. Then it was gone.

The silence continued until Lane spoke again. "I think I've blocked out much of my early childhood. The time before Teddy came and got me... rescued me. I was seven or eight. My father, and maybe my mother too, were like Phil, part of the *Curz* Watchers. Its indoctrinating process already pounded into me. I think bad things happened to me, Gallic. I just want you to know. But I don't want to talk about this again... not ever."

"You don't need to. Instead, let's talk about how we're going to get out of here, wherever *here* is." He heard her swallow then let out a deep breath.

She said, "We're still at the Millhouse ranch. We're inside the massive garage, across from that puke-green house."

Gallic scanned their surroundings again, recognizing the large shapes around them as ranch machinery, which supported the processing plant next door. He figured it must be getting brighter outside—he was now seeing streams of light coming through gaps in the walls and along the roofline. "Phil must have closed all of this ginormous structure's side doors since I was last here," he said.

"Yeah, it took him like a half hour to do that. One thing Phil said was true," she continued, "these ropes ... we're not getting free. Guy knows how to tie people up."

Gallic assessed his own bindings. "He may know how to tie a knot, but he made one crucial mistake."

"What's that?" she asked.

"He put me in a wooden chair." Several moments passed before he asked, "Any idea where he's off to?"

"I know exactly where he's off to ... heard him make the call."

Gallic heard the emotion in her voice. "Linda and Juaquin Cugan?"

Lane, quiet, didn't answer back right away. Gallic suddenly felt the slightest wobble in one of the chair's legs. He must have stressed it, where it attached to the chair frame, during his last big struggle to free himself. Increasing now the outward pressure on his ankle bonds, he stretched both his thick quadriceps and calf muscles well past the burning point. His hatred for

Phil—for what he had done to Clair and Mandy—made it easier to discount the pain. *Crack!*

"Gallic . . ." Lane queried.

He continued questioning her, "Linda and Juaquin, they know . . . that Phil's . . . ?"

"Probably not Linda," she replied, "but her daughter really hates Phil. He creeps her out, can't stand to be in the same room with him."

Crack!

"That would have been good information to share with me before today," Gallic said, then instantly regretted saying it.

"Hey . . . teenage girls hate everyone. I don't think she's that big a fan of you either."

Gallic shrugged that off. "The father, Rick, he's also a *Curz Wiccan* . . . like his client, Teddy?" He grunted when the chair finally wobbled and broke apart beneath him.

"Most definitely," she said, trying to look behind her. "Phil is rendezvousing with Linda and Juaquin, at another location here on Muleshoe. He's doing so under the pretext they weren't safe on Gorman. That the hammer-and-nails killer may be coming for them there."

"He was one hundred percent honest about that aspect," Gallic said, various parts of the now-broken apart chair still tied to his limbs. Stooping, he quickly began untying the knots around his ankles.

"Apparently both Rick and Larz Cugan are away on business," Lane said. "Phil told Linda it was you who'd insisted they get moving immediately."

"You heard all that?" Gallic asked.

"I was sitting right here ... you were too, but you were unconscious. I wanted to yell out, scream for Linda not to believe him. But Phil was pointing a gun at my head. I think it was your gun. Oh God ... he's going to bring them back here. He's going to ..." her voice trailed off.

Gallic heard her softly sobbing. He didn't need her to finish the sentence, knowing too what Phil planned for them—two more victims of the hammer-and-nails killer.

"Untie me too!" Lane urged.

One chair arm, still tied, swung from his left wrist as he knelt down to study her ropes. Getting to work untying her, he said, "An hour's not much time. He must be meeting them somewhere close to here. Maybe Renegade's Haven ... there's not much else around. He easily can make it there and back within the hour. We'll need to move fast."

He got her arms free and ready to begin on her legs when he felt her hands take ahold of his face. Pulling him closer to her, she kissed him hard on the lips. He tasted the salt from her tears.

"I'm so glad you're here with me. I was so scared, Gallic ... certain I would die down in that miserable sunken ship. It was horrible."

With her wrists now free she began untying the ropes on her ankles. Gallic stood up and looked around. "You okay for a minute?"

"Yes ... go. I can do this."

He spun all around and marveled at the size of the equipment garage—he then hurried off toward the structure's nearest side wall. Once there, he used his knuckles to knock on the metal surface. The sound he heard was anything but reassuring, sounding like solid iron, but he was sure it was some kind of nearly impregnable composite. The winters on Muleshoe got fierce. Blizzards could rip the roof and sides off a building, even one this size. He walked parallel to the wall until he came to a series of large hinges, which ran up, all the way to the top of the structure. The wall was actually one of the four big doors. Gallic retraced his steps, searching for a way to open the thing, and eventually found the latching mechanism. A simple mechanical swing lever, it was secured by an old-fashioned, tried and true, although huge—padlock.

"Oh yeah, forgot to tell you that I saw him lock the four sides down with those locks," Lane said, now approaching him. "But there's also a regular-sized door on the other side that he must have locked from the outside."

Gallic and Lane checked, and rechecked, all the doors. All were secured with locks. Having found a long-handled shovel, he used it like a crowbar attempting to pry open the regular-sized outer door Phil had left from. But all he accomplished over the ensuing forty-five minutes was the breaking and splintering of the spade's handle.

"You need to come to terms with it . . . we're going to be trapped in here until he lets us out. And I'm getting really tired of having this panicky feeling," Lane said. She looked up at him, "What is it?"

"You hear that?"

She listened for a moment and nodded. "He's on his way back."

"They definitely rendezvoused over at Renegade's Haven. The timing works."

Lane stood, gazing up at the high ceiling, her arms wrapped snugly about her. Gallic realized she was wearing the same panties and tank top he'd seen her wearing in the video. Phil hadn't even allowed her to get dressed. She stared back at him, suddenly self-conscious.

"Let's get you something to put on. I think I saw a horse blanket—"

"It's okay . . . I'm not cold. You've seen me wearing less."

"That I have," he said.

The *Gallivanter* was back, its thrusters heard engaging outside.

"Gallic, if Linda and Juaquin are with him, they may only have minutes to live. He didn't bring them here for a cup of tea. We have to do something. Maybe I should scream out . . . warn them," she said.

"No . . . that would bring about their demise even quicker."

Lane moved across to one of the large metal doors and peered out through a thin opening where the hinges were attached to the garage superstructure. "I can see out a little here. It's early morning . . . dawn; I can see the rear of Phil's ship."

Gallic heard her gasp. "Oh my god . . . I see them. All three are hurrying toward one of the far-off ranch houses. I can't quite make out what Juaquin is saying to him. She's asking him questions . . . like one right after another." Lane turned to Gallic, terrified. "She suspects something, I can tell . . . the girl knows something's not right."

chapter 46

Frontier Planet, Muleshoe — Derringer Township.

G allic joined her and also peered through the narrow gap. Now entering the distant house, he watched as Phil closed the door behind them.

Lane hammered a fist against the metal surface. "Damn it! He's in there with them ... he's going to kill them. He's probably doing it right now. Can't we do something?"

Gallic shared her frustration, her rage. He turned away from the scene outside and reassessed where he was. "Holy shit."

"What ... what is it? Did you think of something?" Lane asked, new hope in her voice.

"Yes ... well, maybe. You need to do me a favor. Forget what I said before about making noise. We need to get Phil distracted and out of that house. When I give you the signal I want you to start banging on the walls. Find something that's big and made of metal. A shovel or a hammer . . . something like that. But wait for my signal, okay?"

"Fine. But what are you going to do?"

"You'll see." Gallic turned and hurried off. By the time he reached the center of the enormous garage he was huffing and coughing again. *Why didn't I think of this before?* He looked for a way up onto the city block-sized herd transport vehicle that occupied most of the space within the structure. He ran along its outer circumference until he found steps leading up to an access platform and climbed the steps three at a time. Reaching the top, Gallic scoped-out the flat-topped, flying saucer-shaped pen, and its surrounding five-foot-high metal railings. Its surface was covered with dirt. The smell of manure and urine was nearly overwhelming. And right in the middle sat an elevated, operator's booth-like cabin. He ran toward it.

The distance to it was great enough for doubts to start infiltrating his thoughts. *What if it's locked?* I'll break down the fucking door. *What if it needs a key to start up?* I'll hotwire the thing . . . hell, I repo vehicles for a living. *What if Phil has already killed them . . . or is killing them right now?* Shut up, man . . . just shut up!

Gallic reaching the booth found no locked door. There was no door to even lock. He jumped up onto the threadbare seat cushion and took in the various controls and levers before him. The instruments seemed far more complicated than he figured a piece of ranch equipment should be. Then again, this huge thing actually flew. Flew but also needed to be perfectly stable in flight, so a herd of heifers wouldn't go flying off over the sides. He glanced at his empty wrist, wishing he had his ComsBand—access to the AI. *Think, damn it, think!*

Gallic noticed a series of seven oversized and grubby-looking push buttons along the bottom of the dashboard. Still too dim to clearly make out the words, it looked like the first button read *Prime. That made sense.* He bet this herd carrier had one of those powerful, anti-matter, forced thermogenesis drives—a real beast of a propulsion system that needed to be primed before starting. He figured the buttons were probably placed in sequence, in the order they needed to be pushed in first. He pushed the Prime-labeled button and instantly heard a loud sucking sound. Waiting until the sound dissipated, he then pressed the next button in the series and heard a spinning-up of the turbo-energizers. Like the ignition starter on an old-fashioned Earth automobile, he waited for the drive to come alive. "Come on baby . . . start!" and it did. The huge carrier began to rumble and vibrate yet was surprisingly noiseless considering its size and raw horsepower. Probably was another requirement when transporting timid herds of cattle. *So far so good*, he thought, glancing up and out through the dirty windshield. Suddenly, the drive began to falter and shudder. He pressed the next push button, and the vibration level eased off.

Standing up, Gallic leaned out the booth. It took him a second to remember where he'd left Lane. "Lane! Start banging on the walls!" he yelled. A moment later, he heard some loud metallic clattering erupting off to his left. *Good girl!*

Gallic, seated again, took the two longest levers into his hands, which had spring-loaded, manipulator-grip controls. For this next stage, he was fairly confident he knew what to do, though he'd only done it once years ago when he was in the Royal Marines. The battle conditions back then were dire. He had to take over the controls from a wounded pilot in the hover tank they were traveling in. One of those big dual cannon rigs, the controls weren't so different from the levers he was operating now.

Gallic goosed the right lever controls and heard the drive rumble higher. *Perfect!* The controls couldn't be any more basic. Not too different from the first airplanes back on Earth in the early twentieth century. Using the lever on his left, he would be able to control the vessel's yaw, pitch, and roll effects. The right lever controlled the vertical up-and-down thrust variables, as well as throttled forward and backward. *A piece of cake!*

The clanging stopped, and he heard Lane's voice, "He's coming! Gallic . . . he's coming!"

Gallic yelled back, "Get over here . . . hurry!" He had no idea what damage this machine would do to the garage but leaving Lane behind was far too dangerous to risk.

It took a full minute before Lane climbed up the far-side steps. He saw her look around before spotting him within the booth. She briefly smiled then sprinted across the pen. Visible now in the dim light, he could see her better. Dressed still in skimpy panties and a tank top, her long bare legs strode across the open space.

She came around the corner of the booth panting and stared at Gallic and the controls in his hands.

"Want to go for a ride?" he asked, giving her a crooked smile.

"Yeah . . . let's blow this place." She barely grabbed hold of the frame of the booth before Gallic pulled back on the vertical thrust controls. The noise level increased by a factor of ten as the immense vehicle rose into the air. Glancing over at Lane, Gallic found her laughing. She pointed to her right. "He's coming from that direction."

Gallic adjusted the controls and the massive platform—holding thousands of tons of soil and material—rotated on its axis. Making eye contact again, Lane nodded, ready for whatever Gallic had in mind. Since he had no idea what was needed to break free of the building's walled restraints, he punched the controls in all the way. The drive thundered beneath them, and the herd transport quickly rocketed forward toward the distant wall. As the wall loomed closer, he angled the front of the transport upward seven degrees. With luck, that would be enough to save the booth they were in from shirring off. They blew through the walled side of the garage without the slightest change in speed—like a hot knife cutting through butter.

Gallic immediately brought the herd carrier higher into the air and realized there was a problem. The herd transport was so expansive in girth he couldn't see what lay below them.

"What's wrong?" Lane asked.

He gestured to the dashboard. "We need to figure out how to turn on the perimeter visuals. So, we can see what's beneath us and around us."

Gallic piloted the transport higher to three hundred feet above the ground, then into a slow circling pattern over the ranch below. They both studied the dashboard.

"I think this one is it," she said, reaching for the first grimy push button at the bottom of the dash. He grabbed her wrist just before her finger could make contact with the Prime button.

"That's not it. I think it's this set of switches over here." Gallic then began activating a series of switches along the far-right side of the dash. One-by-one, video feeds began popping up onto the lower portion of the windshield. What made the visuals even more useful was that the feeds were labeled: Forward, Behind, Left, Right, and Below.

"There's Phil!" Lane yelled excitedly. "He's standing right there, looking up at us!"

Gallic leaned forward, peering at the less-than-perfect video image of his former friend. Wearing latex gloves, Phil was wearing scrubs-type overalls. *Were they too late?*

Gallic brought the herd transport to a slow halt, directly above Phil. Only then did Phil come to realize the perilous position he was in. He took off in a fast sprint.

"Where does he think he's going?" Lane queried. "It's not like he'll be able to outrun this thing."

Gallic watched him with interest, seeing him head for his ship, the *Gallivanter*.

"You're letting him get away, Gallic!"

Gallic had no intention of letting him get away, he was only considering his options. "You need to hold on . . . I mean *really* hold on tight," he said.

Lane stared at him—her eyes questioning. "Okay."

Again, Gallic moved the big craft forward. Phil, reaching his ship, was frantically waiting for the rear gangway to extend out then down. Gallic halted their forward progression and instead positioned the transport directly over the *Gallivanter*. Tweaking the pitch controls, the flying saucer-shaped platform began to tilt backward. Lane, wide-eyed, took an even tighter hold on the frame of the booth. As a loud alarm began to wail, a bright-red warning message began to strobe on and off across the windshield:

PITCH ANGLE EXCEEDS SAFETY PROTOCOLS!
ADJUST PITCH CONTROLS APPROPRIATELY!

Gallic continued applying a slow increase in angle. The drive began vibrating violently—indicating too great an added strain. As the herd transport continued to tilt backward, Lane lost her footing on the booth's deck and squatted down. At forty-five degrees, Gallic wondered how much more the craft could handle. Would the drive suddenly give up the ghost, causing the immense vessel, with him and Lane aboard, to crash to their deaths below?

"Gallic . . . I'm scared!"

"Just hold on a little longer," he yelled back, trying to maintain a look of confidence.

The first indication his plan was working was when the pen's back railing gave way. He watched on the "Below" video feed as its metal bars slammed down onto the top of the *Gallivanter*. Now at a fifty-degree angle, the transport was shaking so violently Gallic's teeth were chattering, and he was finding it hard to maintain his seat.

And then it happened. Thousands of tons of soil began to slide backward off the back rim. It was a landslide of epic proportions. Both Gallic and Lane, their eyes on the video feed, watched as the *Gallivanter* was soon crushed beneath a mountain of dirt. Only when the herd transport's platform was completely cleared did Gallic slowly level off the craft's steep angle.

chapter 47

Frontier Planet, Muleshoe — Derringer Township.

Gallic set the herd transport craft down hard, akin to a controlled crash landing, onto a nearby pasture. But as they say, any landing you can walk away from ...

He and Lane ran from the booth onto the now bare, soil-free open platform, heading for the same stairway they'd ascended not more than ten minutes before. From this perspective, he could see the goliath mountain of dirt piled high in front of the small green house. Earlier, watching the video feed, he'd witnessed the *Gallivanter* being crushed under that massive accumulated weight. Whatever remained under that heap would be little more than a pancake now. Phil's remains would have to be collected using an industrial wet-vac. *Good riddance, asshole.* Then he spotted the *Hound*, further off in the distance.

Lane, first to reach the stairs, was also the first to head off toward the distant ranch-style house. Gallic thought about telling her to stop; be cognizant that it could be a crime scene. But hell, there was no way to stop her even if he wanted to. What concerned him most was what she might see; and how it would affect her—not only today, but days, weeks, even months from now. He certainly knew what that kind of horror was like. As he sprinted to catch up with her, he thought about his own demons—the slippery vermin that invaded his mind, seemingly at will, ever since he'd walked the crime scene of Clair and Mandy Gallic. *Were his demons gone forever?* He doubted it. But they were gone now, and he'd have to be good with that.

Lane was just opening the front door when Gallic reached the small concrete porch. Giving him a wary look over her shoulder, she then proceeded inside.

"Linda? Juaquin?" she yelled into the home's dark interior. There was no reply.

Gallic, placing a firm hand on her shoulder, urged, "Hey . . . why don't you let me go in first."

"No . . . they're like family to me. Closer than family." She moved deeper into the hallway, peering into the few rooms dawn's early light had yet to illuminate. She suddenly stopped. "Do you hear that?" she asked.

"An entertainment center . . . maybe a news broadcast is on?" Gallic said to her back.

Lane nodded and cautiously continued forward. He could make out the kitchen ahead, with the family room, most likely, lying just beyond it. Gallic was well aware that the hammer-and-nails killer, *AKA Phil Hough*, preferred doing his murderous business there—had more space to work with the bodies. Lane crossed over the hallway threshold and into the kitchen. The family room's large, holographic display was indeed tuned to an all-news channel. But Linda and Juaquin Cugan weren't watching the news. They were sitting on the couch—legs draped over each other. He saw Lane's bare shoulders relax, heard her sigh in relief.

Juaquin, the first to glance up and notice them, exclaimed, "Lane! Oh my god . . . what are you doing here?"

Linda, now up on her feet, headed for Lane her arms open wide. They embraced, quietly rocking and sobbing together. Eventually, they separated, and Juaquin filled the vacated space in Lane's arms.

"Did you catch him . . . the murderer?" Linda asked, looking up at Gallic. "Can we go home now?"

They didn't know. Didn't have a clue how close they'd come to being the next victims of the hammer-and-nails killer. Juaquin was studying Gallic. Waiting for him to answer. Gallic let out a long breath and turned to Lane. "You got this?"

"I've got this. Go ahead . . . go to work."

* * *

Seven hours and eight minutes later, the Millhouse cattle processing ranch had been completely transformed. Three white tents, the same ones seen earlier in front of Lane's house, had been relocated. They were set up now some fifty yards away from the giant mountain of dirt. Tori's and Crackle and Lock's star-cruisers were there too. Gallic was dead tired. He'd been answering questions—going over the previous day's events pretty much non-stop. Crackle and Lock were relentless, sticklers for every detail. The Colonial Police—District 22, was well represented. Gallic did his best to comply, providing them detailed accounting. Only when, sitting outside on an old tree stump, alone in the mid-day heat, was he able to start processing past events. Come to terms with the fact his three-plus-year search was now over. He surveyed the scene around him and smiled, noticing that a side of the ginormous garage structure was splayed open like an exploded tin can. His eyes, though, kept returning to the immense dirt pile.

"You know, Superintendent Bernard Danbury is anxious to speak with you."

Gallic slowly nodded as Tori approached him. Taking a seat on another tree stump, she added, "I'm sure you'll be thrilled to learn he's on his way here . . . as we speak."

Gallic, quiet, didn't say anything.

"You know . . . you can be a little happy. Let yourself feel that."

"I don't feel happy. Not by a long shot."

"Yeah, I guess I understand. But you must have felt one moment of righteous retribution seeing that scumbag run into his creepy ship. Watching it get flattened like that."

Gallic turned his gaze to Tori, noting something she'd said. "Say that again."

"What?"

"About seeing him run into his ship."

"That you must have felt one moment of righteous retribution seeing that scumbag run into his ship . . ."

He continued to stare at her.

"You did see him run into his ship ... didn't you?" she asked. "After all those hours of repeated questioning, there never was any doubt. You were very clear about what you saw, Gallic."

He scratched his head then looked up to the sky. "You know, when you watch a movie ... when one scene ends and another scene takes over, in a completely different place and timeframe? How we, as viewers, fill in the missing blanks?"

"I guess. Is that what you did?"

Gallic nodded. "I never actually witnessed him entering the ship. I saw him hop onto the gangway, but the video feed became obscured by ... all that soil cascading down from the herd transport. That got in the way. I never actually saw him enter the ship, I just mentally assumed he made it inside. Either that, or he was crushed on his way in."

Tori looked away from Gallic to what he'd been describing. "Look at it. Look at all that shit. There's no way anyone could survive under that. I don't care if you're inside the ship or standing twenty feet away from it! He's deader than dead and, you need to put it to rest."

"Yeah ... you're right. It's silly of me."

"Hey, why don't you go lie down? Close your eyes for a few hours. It won't be long before the media arrives. Everyone will want to see and hear from the hero who took down the hammer-and-nails killer."

"I don't feel like a hero. And I am not one. The recent body count is far too high for anyone to claim otherwise." He stood, then placing a hand on Tori's shoulder, said, "Thanks for being here, partner, it makes all the difference."

"Don't mention it. I appreciate you too. I think with your help . . . I'm becoming a fairly good detective. But don't let that go to your head."

"I'll try not to."

He left her sitting there and decided to follow her suggestion, go and get some rest. He was also anxious to check in with the *Hound*'s AI. He had a few unanswered questions that needed addressing. One thing he was sure of—the AI, somehow, had disabled the *Hound*'s drive, which very well changed the course of events for the better.

"Hey! You there . . . Galaxy Man! You want some company?"

Gallic turned to see Lane—dressed in a set of disposable scrubs, of sorts—peering out from an open flap of one of the white tents.

"Only if you don't mind standing under a hot shower for an hour, or so. Maybe curling up afterward in my super comfortable bed."

Lane pursed her lips, giving him a sideways glance. "Hmm . . . gee, I'll have to think about that . . ." Darting out from the tent, she crossed the space in seconds. Then she was nestled-in close, squeezing beneath his outstretched arm.

"Can I add one more thing to that?"

"Sure."

"Breakfast . . . I'm starving!" Lane said.

The End

Thank you for reading Galaxy Man.

If you enjoyed this book, PLEASE leave a review on Amazon.com—it really helps!

*And, yes, fresh ideas for Book Two, of **Galaxy Man,** are already percolating! To be notified the moment all future books are released—please join my mailing list. I hate spam and will never, ever, share your information. Jump to this link to sign up:*

http://eepurl.com/bs7M9r

acknowledgments

First and foremost, I am grateful to the fans of my writing and the ongoing support for all my books. I'd like to thank my wife, Kim, she's my rock and is a crucial, loving, component of my publishing business. I'd like to thank my mother, Lura Genz, for her tireless work as my first-phase creative editor and a staunch cheerleader of my writing. Others who provided fantastic support include Lura and James Fischer, Stuart Church, and Eric Sundius.